DETECTIVE ON THE MOOR

The mystery of a lockdown party murder

RIC BRADY

THE BOOK FOLKS

Published by The Book Folks

London, 2023

This book is a work of fiction. Names, characters, businesses, organizations, places and events are either the product of the author's imagination or are used fictitiously. Any resemblance to actual persons, living or dead, events or locales is entirely coincidental. The spelling is British English.

ISBN 978-1-80462-136-3

www.thebookfolks.com

DETECTIVE ON THE MOOR is the fourth standalone mystery in this series by Ric Brady. The full list of titles, in order of publication, is as follows:

MURDER ON A YORKSHIRE MOOR
BUTCHER ON THE MOOR
MISSING ON ILKLEY MOOR
DETECTIVE ON THE MOOR
COLD CASE ON THE MOOR

More details can be found at the back of this book.

Prologue

It was a fun party.

Gabriel had been a pain in the arse, but what else was new? Which made her wonder why he'd been such a pain.

Then the idea struck her.

Had he heard her and Tom in the bathroom together?

An overwhelming sense of shame dispersed fiery sensations through her body. She hoped Gabriel hadn't found out. That would make things difficult for them.

But thinking about it, she vaguely remembered seeing the door handle turn to close while she and Tom made love.

And that's what she did with Tom. Made love. Nothing like what she had with Gabriel.

Gabriel was a creep.

She should listen to everybody and get out of there. They were right, she could do better.

She could have Tom.

Her body swayed from side to side, and she tried to recall where she was. She remembered the party and having a laugh in Tom's bedroom.

Voices shouted at her from a distance, like she was deep inside a dark cave; their words echoing off the rock formations.

Once, she'd gone potholing in the Dales on a school trip. She'd hated it. At one point, the instructor made them stand in the deepest, darkest cavern and told them to turn their torches off. In the darkness, he asked them to put their hands in front of their faces. The ten sixteen-year-olds obeyed as the pitch-black dampness surrounded them.

She put her hand before her eyes, and nothing stirred in the darkness. Nothing but pure gloom. After a few seconds, she felt a grasping fear claw at her back.

She almost had the same sensation now. Looking straight ahead, she couldn't see a thing. Only blackness. Not even her hand.

Where was she? Was she still at the party? Had she gone home?

Ice-cold water suddenly splashed her, causing her to gasp. It was a shock to her system. But the blackness still remained.

Was she in a cave? Was she back on her school trip? Was she surrounded by the limestone stalactites with their long spindly alien fingers; their points as sharp as razor blades and dripping with freezing water?

She sucked in more breaths as the coldness seeped into her body. Her joints and her hands ached. She'd swear her heart had turned to ice.

The darkness in her eyes dispersed and blessed light returned to her vision. She made out a bathroom through the haze and realised she was lying in a tub and wasn't in a cave at all.

She felt some relief until she noticed the tall man kneeling at her side. Was it Gabriel? She couldn't be sure.

The man loomed over her and pressed down on her forehead. Suddenly, the cold water filled her eyes, her nose, and mouth.

She tried to fight him off, but her limbs were already numbed by the cold.

All she could do was stare upwards at the man and beg for the blackness to take her again. Because, from the look in his eyes, she knew there was no point in begging him to let her live.

Chapter One

Henry Ward walked along the gravel path that cut between the lush trees and bushes. Mayflies and bluebottles whipped past his head, and he felt the warmth of the day creep over him. He regretted layering up before he set out for his daily walk; he should have dressed for summer. Instead, he had put on a T-shirt under his red and blue shirt. He'd also brought a red fleece with him, which now hung over his shoulder.

That was the issue with May, he thought. He never knew how to dress in it.

He squinted as the sun poked through a gap in the canopy above him and shone into his eyes. He didn't want to lose track of Tessa, his wire fox terrier, as she was fast when she wanted to be. She was ahead of him, sniffing around a bunch of nettles and goosegrass. She was also short of stature and could easily get lost in the ferns and bushes within the forest.

Tessa's behaviour of late could be best described as 'playing up'. She seemed to enjoy winding Henry up by doing the opposite of what he said. Not that she understood everything he said, but he felt she got the gist of most of it.

At that moment, she'd moved past the nettles and was sniffing a pool of water, which had collected within the type of dog to 'do a Lassie' and run off to fetch help. She would no doubt hang around until she got bored and then wander off to find someone else to feed her.

Notwithstanding, the brown and white dog crept towards him, head bowed as if knowing he was in pain.

He waved her away. "It's alright, chuck. Just a bad step." He didn't know if it was a bad step or just carelessness on his part. Both, most likely.

He looked around at the trees and bushes. Ahead of him, a carpet of tired bluebells shimmered on the surface of some tall grass. The pain in his hip was dying down. It was just a sharp shock. He'd be alright, he told himself. It happened when he walked too fast or didn't pay attention when he walked downstairs. He hadn't heard the implant squeak yet. Apparently, it made a noise if one bent down too low. Thankfully, he avoided bending over at all if he could.

He listened to the birds that tweeted above him, and the insects that zipped past, but he couldn't hear anyone coming along the path.

Tessa whined a little as she glanced worriedly at him. He stood straight and put weight on his operated leg. It was alright. It didn't hurt anymore. He took a few tentative steps, and when he didn't feel another jab of pain, he continued walking along the path.

Tessa was happy with this, and she ran off ahead with her paws scraping against the gravel. Henry didn't bother to keep up. Instead, he continued at a slow pace.

He was on Otley Chevin, heading uphill. It was a large forest on a steep incline above the town of Otley, and on top of the hill was Leeds Bradford Airport. Henry was far from his stomping ground, Addingham, being nearly ten miles away, but he'd come over here to meet someone.

An old acquaintance had asked him out for lunch at a vegan bakery on the hill opposite the car park. As Henry had doctor's orders to watch his weight, he thought it would be wise to get in an hour's walk beforehand. He family of five, despite Henry living on his own. And she seemed put out when he didn't finish what she'd brought, but he didn't know anyone who could have. Besides, his consultant had told him to watch his weight from now on. "Otherwise you'll put too much stress on the other hip, and that'll need doing," he'd said.

Henry hoped not. He'd nearly spent everything on the first one. He didn't have anything left for the second.

Anyway, despite the issues around the quantity of food, Jean had helped him. Without her, the whole experience would've been worse. He had received a text or two from his son, Dean, but he hadn't come to visit.

Not that Henry could blame him completely as their relationship had been strained over the years. But he did selfishly wish Dean had popped over one afternoon with the grandkids. If major surgery wouldn't trigger a visit, he didn't know what would.

He'd heard from DI Kate Barnes, a detective inspector he'd worked with on a few of the cases he'd been involved with recently. Even she managed to call on him, stopping by for a quick cup of tea during the fourth week. She'd been busy working several investigations, all of them too depressing for her to want to talk about, and Henry suspected they were domestic murders and suspicious child deaths.

Henry hadn't wanted to ask Barnes about his application to rejoin the police, as she'd never been enthusiastic about it. However, he had sent it off nearly three months ago and still hadn't heard anything beyond the acknowledgement letter. He didn't know if that was a good sign or not.

His left foot stepped onto a large rock at an angle, and pain shot up his leg and around the new joint. He winced and let out a garbled cry. Doubling over, he tried to regain his composure as he stared at the gravel path.

There was no one around him, so if he hurt himself, he wasn't sure what he could do about it. Tessa wasn't the type of dog to 'do a Lassie' and run off to fetch help. She would no doubt hang around until she got bored and then wander off to find someone else to feed her.

Notwithstanding, the brown and white dog crept towards him, head bowed as if knowing he was in pain.

He waved her away. "It's alright, chuck. Just a bad step." He didn't know if it was a bad step or just carelessness on his part. Both, most likely.

He looked around at the trees and bushes. Ahead of him, a carpet of tired bluebells shimmered on the surface of some tall grass. The pain in his hip was dying down. It was just a sharp shock. He'd be alright, he told himself. It happened when he walked too fast or didn't pay attention when he walked downstairs. He hadn't heard the implant squeak yet. Apparently, it made a noise if one bent down too low. Thankfully, he avoided bending over at all if he could.

He listened to the birds that tweeted above him, and the insects that zipped past, but he couldn't hear anyone coming along the path.

Tessa whined a little as she glanced worriedly at him. He stood straight and put weight on his operated leg. It was alright. It didn't hurt anymore. He took a few tentative steps, and when he didn't feel another jab of pain, he continued walking along the path.

Tessa was happy with this, and she ran off ahead with her paws scraping against the gravel. Henry didn't bother to keep up. Instead, he continued at a slow pace.

He was on Otley Chevin, heading uphill. It was a large forest on a steep incline above the town of Otley, and on top of the hill was Leeds Bradford Airport. Henry was far from his stomping ground, Addingham, being nearly ten miles away, but he'd come over here to meet someone.

An old acquaintance had asked him out for lunch at a vegan bakery on the hill opposite the car park. As Henry had doctor's orders to watch his weight, he thought it would be wise to get in an hour's walk beforehand. He rethought that wisdom, however, as he hobbled along the footpath.

The acquaintance was a local landowner, Mrs Wentworth-Scott. Henry was surprised to have received her call and request for lunch, as he'd not spoken to her for well over a decade. Not since their paths had crossed briefly when he helped her with a robbery at one of her properties on the nearby moors.

She was married to a local solicitor, and both were in their late sixties. Anyone who spoke to a farmer in the area would hear of the Wentworth-Scott clan, as the family had dominated Wharfedale for over a century. Despite their heritage and wealth, they kept a low profile. Mr and Mrs weren't a flashy couple who drove around in fancy four-by-fours. But Henry had heard things about their children that suggested things had changed.

Henry had asked what it was all about when he spoke to Mrs Wentworth-Scott on the phone before the weekend. She had a clipped accent with hints of Yorkshire in the vowels, but it was fairly indistinguishable from a southern accent. Despite his request for more information, she hadn't answered. "Best we discuss this in person, Detective Chief Inspector Ward."

Henry hadn't liked the way she used his former police title as if it was the only part of him that had value. He felt she could have been talking to any old detective chief inspector. It didn't matter to her which one.

Luckily for Mrs Wentworth-Scott, Henry hadn't done much lately. Apart from the case he had worked on in February and the hip replacement in March, he'd just watched TV and taken Tessa for walks. So, he had accepted her offer for lunch without much consideration.

Besides, she had that high-pitched tone of voice which suggested to him something was wrong, and she needed help.

Chapter Two

Henry hadn't wanted to take Tessa into the bakery, as she was dirty and smelly. He'd considered leaving her on his Skoda Octavia's back seats. But with it being a hot day in May, he didn't want to risk her getting heatstroke, even if the car was shaded under a tree.

On top of that, she hated being stuck in the car on her own, and Henry didn't want to face her revenge later on that day.

He assumed the vegan bakery welcomed dogs, with it being so close to a hiking trail, and it did. There was a small chalkboard sign expressing the fact above a large bowl of water. He let Tessa drink from it and then pulled her along on her lead.

The bakery operated out of an old farmhouse and barn on the side of the road. It had a large seating area in its former farmyard. The building's old stones had grown moss over the decades, and it appeared to have been close to ruin until it was renovated.

Colourful metal tables in the courtyard faced the heather-speckled hills. They were all occupied with fellow ramblers. Some had dogs, which Tessa wanted to investigate. The majority of the human punters were dressed for high summer in T-shirts and shorts. Henry noticed all the tables were full, and a stressed waitress approached him and asked if he had a reservation.

He was in the process of saying Mrs Wentworth-Scott's name when he saw her sitting alone at an orange-coloured table in the corner. He made his way towards her.

She hadn't changed much over the years. She wore an elegant navy-blue business jacket over a light-blue shirt, and her long grey hair was brushed back over her shoulders. Her skin was tanned enough to suggest she spent most of her time abroad, and she didn't look her age, which he guessed was greater than his own.

Henry approached, feeling underdressed in the tatty jeans that he reserved for hiking in, his old hiking boots, and a red and blue shirt worn over an old T-shirt. He was grateful they were sitting outside, as he thought he'd start sweating if they weren't.

She glanced up from a laminated menu and narrowed her eyes. Her thick-rimmed glasses were modern and fashionable. "Detective Chief Inspector?"

Henry nodded at hearing his old title and pulled out the metal chair opposite her. "*Former* Detective Chief Inspector Ward." He called Tessa to him, as she'd wandered dangerously close to a Labrador at the neighbouring table.

Mrs Wentworth-Scott smiled, and Henry noticed her teeth were perfectly straight and white. A Hollywood smile, he thought. Then he wondered if they were dentures, veneers, or real.

"So glad you could come and meet me," she said, laying the menu on the table before him. "Please order what you like. I think I shall have a salad."

Henry glanced at the menu. He fancied an omelette as he thought he'd seen a waitress carrying one, but then he questioned if vegans ate eggs. Scanning the menu, he got his answer. "Yeah, I'll get a salad as well."

The waitress came over and took their orders, then headed off through an arched door into the old farmhouse.

"Nice place," Henry said, looking around the farmyard at the other tables.

"It's okay." She didn't say anything for a moment, and Henry glanced at her. She was staring at the orange tabletop, rubbing her thin tanned hands together.

"Is everything alright?" he asked.

She forced another Hollywood smile. "Yes. Let's wait for the coffees to arrive before we get down to business?"

Henry did as she said, and thankfully they didn't have to wait long, as the waitress quickly arrived with their drinks. After checking the other tables, he got the impression that they were receiving quicker service.

She sipped her black Americano and looked off into the distant hill.

Henry didn't dare touching his as it was steaming hot. "So, Mrs Wentworth-Scott–"

"Call me Agnes."

He hadn't remembered her first name, but Agnes seemed too old for her. "Right, Agnes. Can I ask what it is that brought you to contact me?"

She kept her eyes on her piping hot coffee. "You helped me in the past, I remember."

"Well, some of your stolen possessions were found during an investigation, and I had them returned to you."

"Yes. I remember. Didn't the thief later go on to kill someone?"

Henry never liked discussing his cases, but this was an old one and most of its details were made public in the trial. "Yes. Lee Briggs and his mate broke into a lot of properties around the area. And then one night, when they'd both been taking drugs, they argued over a girl, and Lee killed both his mate and the girl." He sighed at having to remember such senseless loss of life.

Agnes stared at him, and her pale blue eye lit up. "Terrible. Just…" She shook her head.

"So, this issue you're having?"

She took in a deep breath and looked back at the hills behind Henry. "I have a private matter that needs a special kind of… handling."

"Right," he said, glancing at the neighbouring diners to make sure they couldn't overhear. He then realised their table was sufficiently removed from the others, allowing them to speak without anyone eavesdropping.

"My son…" She sighed, obviously finding it a difficult subject. "He's having issues."

"What kind?"

She inhaled again. "We've given our children the very best. The best schools, best teachers, best universities." She shook her head as if it'd all been a waste. "But still, they disappoint you."

He blew on his coffee and attempted a sip. "Isn't that just life?"

She didn't find his comment mildly amusing. "Not in this family. We have a lot to give them, but they have to earn it."

The steeliness with which she said the statement made him sure Agnes had repeated it several times. Most likely to her children.

"So, how can I help with this matter?" Henry said, pulling Tessa away from a bumblebee that'd landed underneath the table.

Agnes straightened up and looked him in the eyes. "Can I rely on you?"

He thought it was an odd question to receive from someone he barely knew. "Aye. I suppose so."

She brought her tanned hand to her lips and then cleared her throat. "My son is having issues."

"You've mentioned that. Issues with the police?"

She shook her head. "Not yet, but it could well be heading that way."

Henry couldn't see why Agnes had wanted to talk to him. He was a retired police detective and, yes, he had solved a few crimes recently, but his spheres of influence were limited now, even if he did plan to rejoin the police on a part-time basis. Ideally, he'd be too busy with real cases to deal with spoilt rich kids. "I'm not sure what it is you have in mind, Mrs–"

"Agnes. It'll save you from repeating my inanely long surname."

Henry nodded at her instruction. "I'm not quite sure what I can do for you. I am a retired detective."

"I've hired retired detectives several times."

Henry chuckled. "I'm not for hire, Agnes." He knew a lot of his former colleagues worked as private security and bouncers after they retired, but it was never something he had considered. For him, it was only something the desperate for money did.

She frowned. "I read in the papers that you were solving crimes with the police. Weren't you hired for any of those?"

He shook his head and stifled another chuckle. "Not at all. My involvement in most of them came about through sheer coincidence. And as the police were too busy to investigate them, I took on the lion's share."

Agnes appeared very confused, like she was trying to work out a mathematical formula without having all the necessary variables. "You worked for free?" she asked.

He cleared his throat, as he did when his own motivations were questioned. "Well. I get a police pension."

"But you're owed that, right? So, any further work you do is unpaid."

He couldn't argue with that and tried to change the subject. "Listen, I'm not sure I could help, anyway. I've applied to rejoin the police, and if I do, which is likely, I couldn't really be involved in helping private individuals. There might be a conflict of interest." He didn't know if that was the case for sure, but he didn't like the idea of being entangled with a wealthy family while they went through problems.

"Well, that is a shame. I was hoping you would help me."

"I wish I could, Agnes. But the rules about getting involved in other people's affairs are–"

"This is a very important issue, though, Detective Chief Inspector."

He could see she wasn't going to let it go. She'd set her mind on him helping her, and she wasn't taking no for an answer.

"I'm not doubting its importance. I am just unable to assist," he said. "Can't you ask one of these other detectives you've hired in the past to help?"

"No. Two have completely retired, and the other has already been involved but doesn't want to do anything further."

If he needed another red flag, he'd just seen it. "Well, perhaps the real police could get involved?"

She shook her head. "That won't be necessary. My husband is friendly with some of the higher-ups."

Henry wasn't surprised to hear that.

"And he's spoken to a superintendent. It was him who mentioned your name."

"Superintendent Murphy?"

She nodded innocently. "That's him."

Murphy had suggested his name, Henry thought. Why had he done that? Murphy was one of the senior officers who would approve his application to rejoin. Was it a sign that his application wasn't going anywhere?

"What did Murphy say?"

She shrugged. "My husband spoke to him. Apparently, you were the best man for the job."

He stared down at his coffee and then took a sip. This was all very odd. He didn't like his name being passed to people, and he also didn't like the fact Murphy was involved.

"What is this 'job' you mentioned?" he asked.

She sighed, and for an instant, looked closer to her true age. "My son's in trouble."

"What kind?"

"He's been accused of murder."

Chapter Three

Henry sat back on the metal chair and felt Tessa tug on the lead that was tied to the armrest. She'd strayed off towards the Labrador at the neighbouring table, who'd walked towards her. Their noses almost touched.

Henry pulled her back and shook his head when she glanced up at him.

He returned to meet Agnes's stare. "So, your son's been accused of murder? Has he been questioned by the police or charged with anything?"

"Nothing like that. It's just a malicious rumour."

"Being accused of killing someone is as malicious as rumours get," Henry said.

Agnes raised an eyebrow, which suggested she was already aware of this.

"Where's this accusation coming from?" Henry asked.

"A former friend of my son."

Henry tried to remember how many children the Wentworth-Scotts had. "Which son are we talking about?"

"Thomas. The youngest. I have another son and a daughter."

"How old is he?"

"Thirty-five."

"Alright. And who's accusing him of murder?"

She exhaled like she was summoning the energy to talk about it, as if the whole topic was beneath her, which Henry thought was probably the truth. "He has an old friend called Gabriel," she eventually said.

Henry made a mental note of the name. "Right?"

"Gabriel was with Thomas at a party three years ago."

"Where was the party?"

"My son has a house around here, on the top of Otley Chevin, which belongs to the family. It's a converted barn he moved into a few years ago."

They gifted him a house, Henry thought. Giving a child a property seemed like something only a certain class thought was normal. He sipped his coffee and listened.

"There was a party, and someone died. A young woman – Freya Harrison."

"And this party happened three years ago; so in 2020?" Henry thought back to the time and remembered lockdowns and COVID-19 restrictions. "When did they have this party?"

Agnes cleared her throat as if she was embarrassed. "It was in May, during one of the lockdowns."

"Right," Henry said. "I guess it wasn't just 10 Downing Street that was having 'alleged' parties."

Agnes hunched her shoulders, clearly uncomfortable with the fact.

"So, did this Gabriel accuse your son of murdering Freya at the time?"

Agnes shook her head. "It only happened within the last few months. A business deal between the two fell through, and Gabriel threatened to make the accusations public if my son didn't pay him a hefty amount of money."

"Blackmail?"

She nodded. "It's not unusual for a family like mine to receive such threats. That's why we have a team of solicitors."

"Right. But your lawyers didn't really help much here, did they? So, your son didn't pay off Gabriel, and was accused of being a murderer?"

Agnes nodded. "Gabriel went to the local papers and some national ones, but we managed to keep them quiet." She gave a faint smile that suggested she found hushing tabloids a fun hobby. "But we were unable to stop the rumours on social media, and the word spread."

Henry wafted away a wasp that'd got too close to their table. He was fighting the temptation to ask more questions, as his brain would want to get involved just to know what had happened.

Agnes's eyes gleamed as if she were aware of this, and she took the opportunity to add more information. "Freya was in a relationship with Gabriel, but apparently she slept with Thomas a few times before the party."

Henry watched Agnes as she spoke about her son's sex life, which she seemed comfortable discussing, almost as if the topic was a stallion at stud.

"How did she die?" Henry asked.

"She was found dead in a bath. She'd drowned."

"At a party?"

Agnes nodded. "She was fully clothed. The police said there were no signs of foul play and concluded it was a suicide."

Henry thought that sounded odd. Forcing oneself to drown in a bathtub must've taken an enormous amount of willpower. "Had she been taking drugs?"

Agnes's eyes flickered, and she stared down at her cup. The topic of drugs was a touchy one. "Well. I couldn't say… There wasn't an autopsy done."

Henry nearly spat out his tongue. The waitress came to the table with two plates of salad and placed them down, so he waited before asking further questions. After she had left, he leant over his plate and asked, "How wasn't there an autopsy done?"

Agnes started eating her salad. "The coroner's office deemed it unnecessary."

"On what grounds?"

"It was evidently suicide. The woman had a history of mental health issues, and…" She shrugged. "It just didn't seem to warrant one."

Henry repeated her words in his mind, it just didn't seem to warrant one. A lot about this case was off. The party had happened during a COVID lockdown when all parties were forbidden. A young woman, who appeared to be in a love triangle, was found dead in a bath. And no autopsy was done.

The whole event had also slipped past the attention of the press, but Henry remembered Agnes's smile as she talked about suppressing news stories.

"Well, this is all very irregular," he said.

Agnes didn't respond. She was too busy eating her lunch.

Henry picked up his cutlery and dug into his salad. Tessa was next to his chair, looking up and licking her snout, but he didn't think she'd like anything on his plate.

He pushed around a tomato with his fork and ran through the details he'd learnt. Then he leant back in his chair. "What is it you'd want a detective to do?"

Agnes finished chewing some rocket salad and swallowed. "We're suing this Gabriel for libel, and we'd like someone to investigate this suicide to help our case."

Suicide? Agnes said it with such surety, Henry almost believed her. He couldn't help but feel intrigued by the whole affair, but he didn't want to wade into the personal matters of a powerful family embroiled in controversy. Then he recalled Agnes had already hired an old detective. "You mentioned one of the other retired officers had looked into the matter?"

Her eyes flickered in slight annoyance. "Yes. He felt he couldn't make much headway, and we have a deadline the legal team has imposed on us."

"What's the deadline?"

"We have around five days until we take Gabriel to court, but we'd need the investigation to be concluded in three to allow the team to build up their case."

"You want some mug to find out what happened in three days so you can sue this fella for spreading rumours?" Henry shook his head and returned to eating his salad.

Agnes stiffened up in her chair. "You think the timescale is unrealistic?"

Henry sniggered. "Whatever gave you that idea?"

She stared at him through her thick-rimmed glasses while pouting. "I thought you handled all your cases quickly? Most of them were over in a day or two, I read."

Henry hadn't really thought of it like that, but most of his recent cases had to be solved quickly to ensure the culprits were apprehended. "Well, possibly…"

"That's why I felt you might be the best person for the job."

Henry shook his head again. Not only was the whole case an oddity, but he also didn't like being hired by a rich family that only wanted him to do what they told him. Besides, what if he investigated the case and found the son did kill the girl? What would the Wentworth-Scott clan do to him? Would they ruin him? Would they put in a bad word with Murphy, giving him an excuse to deny his application to rejoin the police?

Henry bit his lower lip and heaved a sigh. Agnes carried on eating her salad, feigning an air of innocence, but Henry suspected the whole thing had been arranged so that he had no choice but to accept.

The family was too powerful, and they already had decided Henry would help them, and if he didn't do as they said or didn't satisfy them, they'd cause problems for him.

He peered down at Tessa on her lead, who was sitting on a stone slab in the sun. Was he anything more to the family than a trusty terrier, hired to sniff out trouble instead of foxes?

Agnes finished her salad, and after she'd stopped chewing, looked at Henry. "So, Detective Chief Inspector? What is your answer to be?" she asked.

Henry's head slumped lower, and he put the cutlery on the table next to his half-eaten salad. "What do you think it is?"

She smiled. "I'm very glad you've agreed to help. My legal team will be in touch shortly with the details, and they will discuss payments with you–"

Henry waved his hand in the air. "No payment. I just want to know the truth about this girl's death."

Agnes tilted her head, confused. "I insist you be paid."

Henry bet she did. That was how she controlled people. "No. It's alright," he said.

She shrugged as if the matter would be resolved later on to her satisfaction. "Jonathon Radcliffe will be in touch within the hour."

She collected her small handbag from the ground and pushed her metal chair back. "It was so good to meet you, and I do hope you can resolve this matter." As she stood up, she gestured to the plates. "Don't worry about the bill, it's all been taken care of." She checked her large, sparkly watch. "Unfortunately, I have another meeting to get to, so, Chief Inspector, it's been a pleasure."

She left the table and hastened towards the courtyard's gate, then disappeared.

Henry slumped back in the metal chair and peered down at Tessa. "Why've I got the feeling I'm being played?" he asked her, but she didn't reply. Instead, she stared up at his plate as if wondering why he hadn't offered her anything.

Chapter Four

The call from Agnes's solicitor came through when Henry arrived back at his cottage. The sun was bearing down on the flagstones in his backyard, and Tessa was lapping up water from a large clay dish that Henry had just filled. She then strutted off into the backyard to find shade under a large potted fern.

Henry's smartphone rang in his pocket, and he was going to answer the call there and then but heard Jean Whitehead in her yard next door. She was talking loudly to someone, and Henry wondered if her grandson, Robbie, was over.

Henry knew Jean had the ears of a bat and took the call inside his kitchen with the back door closed.

The kettle had just boiled, and he poured some water into a cup and added a teabag when his phone started buzzing in his pocket. Henry didn't bother answering, guessing the solicitor would ring back later. And he guessed right, his phone buzzed a second time almost immediately.

Henry plumped down at the circular kitchen table covered in piles of unopened mail and medicine boxes, and eventually answered the call, after letting out a deep sigh.

"Henry Ward, speaking."

"Detective Chief Inspector?" The voice belonged to a man younger than Henry had expected. When he'd heard the name Jonathon Radcliffe, a solicitor who ran the Wentworth-Scott family's legal team, he imagined a man in his fifties or sixties.

"Yes," Henry said. "Well, I'm not officially a detective chief inspector. And you must be Jonathon?"

"Good detective skills already. I'm sure you'll help us no end."

"There weren't any detective skills involved there. No one rings me apart from my neighbour, and I can hear her talking to someone else right now." Henry looked through the window in his back door at his yard outside and sipped his tea. "So, what is it that needs to be done?"

"I'd just like to say, first, that I'm glad to have you assisting us with this investigation."

Henry grunted as if he didn't accept the compliment, despite Jonathon sounding genuine.

"We've had some assistance already. I'm not sure if Mrs Wentworth-Scott told you?"

"Yes. Agnes mentioned another detective had been involved."

"Right." Jonathon stopped for a moment as if assessing what Henry's use of his boss's first name implied. "Well, let's get down to business, shall we?"

"Aye." Henry pulled an envelope from a pile next to him, which looked to be from his electricity company, and snatched at an old pen. "I've got the names of the principles. The son, Thomas; his friend, Gabriel, who's making the allegations against him; and the deceased, Freya Harrison."

"That's correct. Did Mrs Wentworth-Scott mention the time constraint?"

"She did. I've got three days?"

"That's the very maximum we have, I'm afraid. We need two days to compile everything, and then we're in court on Friday."

"So, what you're actually saying is I need to get everything to you by the end of play on Wednesday?"

"That's correct."

It was now mid-afternoon on Monday, so Henry had less than three days to get to the bottom of these murder allegations. Annoyance fizzled in his limbs, and he hissed in frustration. "Right!" He shook his head, trying to calm himself down. It wasn't Jonathon's fault he had agreed to take on this case. Not that he had entirely agreed voluntarily. "And what is it you actually need from me?"

"Ideally, we want you to investigate what happened, speak to the people involved, and verify that the official investigation didn't miss anything."

"Alright. I guess there's a coroner's report?"

"There is, but it's scant on info. The death occurred during a lockdown, and not many people at the party wanted to share evidence, as they didn't want to admit to being present."

Would any of the people at the party want to talk to Henry now? Probably not, he concluded. Besides, he had no authority to make them speak to him. He shook his head again. What had he agreed to get involved in?

Henry pressed his fingers into his forehead as he felt a headache coming on. "These allegations against the son. What are they?"

"Well." Jonathon cleared his throat. "Gabriel claims he heard Thomas in the bathroom with Freya on the night of the party, and that he tried to get inside, but they wouldn't unlock the door. He heard the sound of splashing water, and then Freya was later found dead."

"And did Gabriel mention this to the police at the time?"

"No, he didn't. The allegations came to light when their business venture collapsed two months ago."

The timing suggested it could be a vexatious claim, but Henry wondered if the police had done anything recently. "Have the police re-examined the case?"

"No," Jonathon said, in a tone of voice that suggested he didn't think such a thing was required. "The allegation has no merit."

"Really?"

"Thomas claims he barely saw Freya that night, and he was witnessed being in a different part of the house at the time Gabriel claims he heard him in the bathroom with Freya."

Henry thought that was interesting. "What did Gabriel say he heard inside the bathroom?"

"I'm…" Jonathon uttered. "I don't know."

"Oh, don't worry. I'll find out myself."

"Listen, Detective Chief Inspector. Don't forget you're being paid to clarify what happened in order to help our libel case? Nothing else."

"Well, don't you forget, Jonathon, that, first, I'm retired, so stop using the titles. And second, I'm not being paid. So, I'll be coming to this case with an open mind."

Jonathon was silent for a moment. "You're not being paid?" he asked.

Henry sniggered to himself. Of the things he'd said, that was the one which had stood out. "Aye. I've told Agnes I shan't be paid, but I'll let her sort it out with you."

"Right…" Jonathon didn't sound convinced. Henry heard him scribble something down.

"Listen," Henry said, breaking the silence. "Let me have the coroner's report and anything else you have. I'll need addresses and phone numbers for Thomas and Gabriel."

"Ah. That'll be tricky. Thomas is happy to speak to you, but Gabriel isn't."

Henry wasn't too surprised to hear that. Gabriel probably thought that as Henry was being employed by the Wentworth-Scotts, he wasn't to be trusted. Henry would have to disabuse him of the idea.

If Henry was going to get embroiled in this mess, he'd do so as an independent operator in search of the truth, no matter where it took him.

"I'll try speaking to Gabriel," Henry said.

"That might not be such a good idea," Jonathon replied.

"No, I think it's necessary. And Freya's family and friends, I'll have to speak to them?"

"I'm not sure that's…" he mumbled down the phone.

"If I think it's necessary, then it is."

"Hmm." Jonathon went quiet again, then said, "Listen, Detective Chief Inspector, there seems to have been a misunderstanding. You've been brought on to confirm the coroner's report so the family can be satisfied nothing else happened."

"Aye. And I shall do that by speaking to the people involved." Henry bit his tongue to prevent him from venting, but he thought to hell with it. "Listen, Jonathon, this case is very irregular. A woman dies in a bath during a large party when such gatherings were banned. Someone waits several years until a financial deal breaks down, and then they make these allegations–"

"These allegations are without merit," Jonathon repeated.

"That's your view, and you might be correct. But I don't know. What I'd like is the chance to investigate what happened before I draw any conclusions."

Jonathon went quiet on the other end of the line.

"Of course, if you're sure these allegations are false, then you shouldn't have anything to be worried about in court."

"Fine," Jonathon said. "Let's see what the other individuals involved have to say for themselves. But I very much doubt they'll talk to you."

"Well, let's not assume things straight away."

Henry gave his email address to Jonathon so he could send over the documents he had. Then he ended the call, reclined in the wooden chair and finished his cup of tea.

He knew what Jonathon and the family wanted him to do. Namely, confirm the official story so they could tell themselves and the community their son wasn't involved in murder. But the fact an autopsy hadn't been done, and that the police had treated the death as a suicide and not a homicide, made Henry wonder if the official verdict was accurate.

He remembered those panicky days three years earlier, when the pandemic was running rife through the country, and everyone was forced to stay in their homes. Henry didn't doubt the fact that this could have disrupted an investigation into a suspected suicide.

That led Henry to wonder who had been involved in it. He picked up his mobile, found DI Barnes's number and dialled it.

She picked up after a few rings. "How are you doing?"

"Not bad, thanks. The hip's doing better. I managed a walk on Otley Chevin this morning."

"Good for you," Barnes replied. It sounded like she was in a car, talking to Henry on loudspeaker.

"How's your day going?"

She exhaled in frustration and tiredness. "Not too bad, I suppose."

"Good. Listen, I'm calling about a suicide that happened in 2020."

"Why are you calling me about a three-year-old suicide?"

Henry took his turn to exhale. "I've been asked to investigate something."

"By who?"

"Ever heard of the Wentworth-Scott family?"

Barnes went quiet as she tried to place the name. "I don't think I have," she said, not sounding convinced with herself.

"They're a wealthy family in the area. Anyway, the son's being accused of murdering some lass three years ago."

"During the COVID lockdowns?"

"Yep. The son had a big party, and the lass was linked to him romantically. The official verdict was suicide, but now the son's mate has come out and accused him of murder."

Barnes went quiet. Henry assumed she was processing the information. After a moment, she asked, "What does this family want you to do?"

"Check what happened. Speak to people. Well, speak to their son at least. They want me to verify the coroner's report so they can sue this friend for libel."

"Hang on. Was it a young woman? Found in a house on the moor near Otley?"

Henry sat up in his chair. "Aye."

"She'd drowned in the bath?"

"You do know it, then?"

"I went to the scene, but I wasn't the lead investigator. I was taken off and placed onto something else." She didn't say anything for a moment, and then added, "I'd nearly forgotten about that case."

"Who was the lead investigator?"

"I'll double-check, but I'm pretty sure it was DC Hargreaves."

Chapter Five

This was all getting odder and odder, thought Henry. DC Hargreaves, who couldn't have been on the force for that long, had been in charge of a suicide investigation?

Henry repeated the thought aloud, hoping DI Barnes would correct him. "A detective constable was in charge of a suicide investigation?"

"Yes. I guess it doesn't sound good when you look back on it. Murphy was involved as he knew the family, and then he passed it to Hargreaves."

Henry didn't like the matter-of-fact tone in which Barnes talked about it. "You do know it's very irregular for a DC to lead an investigation?"

"Yes. In normal times. But can you remember what it was like then? I think we had half of the detectives off sick, or they'd been pinged and were self-isolating. We were strapped for officers, and then there was that increase in domestic abuse, which took up most of my time."

Henry could imagine how the situation had come about, but he wasn't sure he wanted to hear any more about it. In his day, everything had been hierarchical, and odd decisions like that would've been questioned. He also knew Hargreaves was close to Murphy, and that Murphy knew the Wentworth-Scott family. And, according to Agnes, Murphy had recommended him for their private investigation.

Henry started to feel queasy.

"Are you alright?" Barnes asked after a few seconds.

"Aye. Just thinking things through."

"From what I remember, Hargreaves handled it well. But I'll need to check the file. Listen, I have to go, but I'll call you when I get back to the station. Might not be until late, though."

"That'd be great. Thanks, Barnes."

She rang off, leaving Henry to stew in his kitchen. His first thought was to bow out from the arrangement he'd struck with Agnes Wentworth-Scott. Tell her his hip was playing up, and he didn't need the aggro.

But she would tell Murphy, who was the key to him getting back in the police.

Was that the game Murphy was playing? Had he only given the Wentworth-Scotts Henry's name so they had Henry by the balls? Murphy could torpedo his application whenever he wanted.

Henry would be forced to confirm the coroner's report on a case that stunk of cronyism – if not corruption. Had Henry just become a pawn in a corrupt little plot to save face and protect a potential murderer?

He shook his head at it all. His headache had come back with a vengeance, and he grabbed one of the boxes of pills next to him, looking for a painkiller. He took two tablets with the dregs of his cold tea and went to the back door.

He stepped outside and breathed in the fresh air. His yard was colourful for late May. Purple and yellow pansies bloomed out of in several pots on the wall under the high fence. And next to them were the pink geraniums he'd planted last year. A scarlet snapdragon waved at him in the light breeze from the corner.

Tessa was lying on her back under the shade of the fern. Her eyes were closed. Henry wished he could follow suit and take a nap himself, but he had a job to do. He had two and a half days to find what the police had missed while investigating Freya Harrison's death.

There was no hope he'd find any forensic evidence, so all he could do was find the truth of what happened to her. Hopefully that'd provide her family some solace, which he suspected they needed.

The best-case scenario would be he uncovered enough proof for the police to reopen the investigation and make sure anyone accountable for her death faced justice.

A high-pitched whine came from Jean's backyard. It sounded like a giant hornet beating its massive wings. Henry looked up at the high fence that separated their two yards and saw a small, black drone hover in the air.

It must be Robbie, Henry thought. He remembered Jean's grandson helping him with a case the previous year. However, it hadn't gone very well for young Robbie; he'd ended up in hospital with a head injury.

The drone flew over the fence and hung in the air above Henry. Its sleek, black body dropped slowly down until it buzzed less than a metre away from his head. Its small camera turned to watch him, and then he heard Robbie's voice, which sounded robotic. "Hi there, Henry."

Henry frowned at the drone, unsure if he should talk to it or find Robbie and speak to him instead. The drone hovered in the air, watching him.

"Hi," Henry eventually shouted.

"How've you been? Gran said you had your hip done."

Henry tapped his left hip, as he normally did when he talked about it. "Aye. It's fine, lad. How's your head?"

"What? Oh, yeah." He laughed. "It's fine. Yeah, I'd nearly forgotten about that mad guy."

Henry glanced at the fence, wondering out if Robbie was standing on the other side so they could have a normal conversation.

"Where are you?" Henry asked.

"Inside. I'm testing this drone. Apparently, it has a two-hundred-metre control range, but I've not tried it yet. I'm going to fly it to the park."

Henry tilted his head as he stared at the drone. "How the hell are you talking to me if you're inside?"

"It's got a speaker. Can you hear me alright?"

Henry nodded, and then said, "It's fine. Where's your grandma?"

"In the kitchen."

"Right. Shall I pop round?" he said, feeling uncomfortable talking to a flying robot.

"Yeah, why not? She thought you'd come over earlier."

Henry nodded and went to his back door. The drone remained in the air and then took off over the back wall.

Henry left Tessa resting under the fern. The yard had high fences, so she couldn't get out.

He knocked on Jean's latte-coloured front door, and she opened it, holding a red and white tartan tea towel. She wore a white top dotted with blue and yellow flowers, and she appeared more tired than usual. Henry suspected it had something to do with keeping her eighteen-year-old grandson occupied.

She smiled when she saw Henry. The breeze rustled her blonde wavy hair. "How's your hip?" she asked.

"Fine, I've been on Otley Chevin this morning."

"Good for you. Didn't you have lunch out today?"

He nodded. He hadn't told her whom he had his lunch with, as he didn't want her to bombard him with questions. "Robbie's staying over, then," Henry said. "I heard his drone."

She glanced at her front door and then shook her head. "He's not flying that bloody machine, is he?"

"He flew it over my fence. He plans to send it into the park."

She huffed. "I bloody told him about that." She folded the tea towel in her hands. "I suppose he is off to uni to do information technology in September, so I'll let him off. But he bloody shouldn't be flying that thing around Addingham. I mean, is it legal?"

He shrugged. "Probably not. But I doubt anyone will say anything."

Jean rolled her eyes. "Are you coming in for a cuppa?"

He shook his head. "I can't."

Jean frowned. "Why not? You don't have any appointments today." Since Henry's operation, Jean had taken on the role of managing his diary, which included ringing up for appointments and driving him to check-ups. Henry hadn't asked her to do this, obviously. She'd volunteered and insisted.

"No. I don't." He waited a moment, wondering how he'd tell her. "But I've been asked to look into something."

She approached him to stand on the doorstep. "Look into what?"

"A possible… murder."

She huffed and then flapped the tea towel in the air, nearly hitting him in the face. "What the hell are you doing? Another case? You're recovering from major surgery."

He stepped backwards, moving out of striking distance. "It's been six weeks. And I'm okay to drive now."

"Aye, you're fit enough to drive to Tesco to do your shopping, but not to run around chasing after killers. You ended up on the hills in a gunfight last time."

He cleared his throat. "Well… I stayed in the car through most of it."

"Yes. Until they started shooting at it. Isn't that what you told me?"

Henry leant against the wall next to him for support.

"I can't believe it." She shook her head and then glanced inside her house. "And I can't come out and help. I've got my grandson here. And no way is he getting involved in this."

He winced as she brought up the idea of Robbie being involved in cases. He would never live that one down. "Listen, it's just a small inquiry. There shouldn't be any shooting or fighting. I'm just looking into a favour for someone."

"For who?" she demanded.

"The Wentworth-Scotts."

"From Otley?" When Henry nodded, Jean folded her arms and raised an eyebrow. "How do you know them?"

"I helped them when I was a DCI, and now they want me to assist them with something."

"I can't believe you're getting involved with them, especially when you're in ill health." She shook her head while wearing an expression of faint disappointment.

"Ill health? I only had my hip replaced."

"You're sixty-four but still think you're forty."

It was Henry's turn to fold his arms and shake his head. "I'm fine," he said.

Jean folded the tartan tea towel again and stewed in her frustration. She tutted to herself. "The Wentworth-Scotts."

She said the name with such distaste, Henry thought she was going to spit on her own doorstep.

"What about them?" he asked.

"They were involved with Peter's businesses."

Peter was Jean's late husband, who passed away before she moved to the village. From what Henry knew of him, he ran several companies in Harrogate, one of which was a large art gallery that was still there.

"Which business?"

"The gallery and the printing company. He's a monster is the husband, Brian. He ran Peter ragged. And she, the wife, is a complete bitch."

Henry felt his cheeks redden. He rarely heard Jean swear, let alone with such intensity. "Why? What did she do?"

"What didn't she do? She was known for stealing husbands and dumping them, causing all sorts of hell for the families. She flirted to get whatever she wanted."

Henry recalled Agnes's striking looks when he'd had lunch with her earlier on. He also remembered her being attractive when he came into contact with her over a decade earlier. She'd never been overtly flirty with him, but he could imagine her using charm to get what she wanted.

"Is that how she ended up with her rich husband?"

Jean shook her head. "She's the Wentworth, and he's the Scott."

"Come again?"

"She's the one from the old family who owns loads of land around here. He was just a dishy solicitor from Harrogate, and, from what I heard, he's not so dishy anymore."

"So, that explains that long surname?"

"She insisted on keeping hers, and he wanted to use his."

"How well did you know them?"

She huffed like the idea of it was a funny thing. "I didn't know them personally until Peter got involved with them." Then, after staring at a flagstone in her front yard, she locked her eyes on Henry. "What is it you're investigating?" she asked.

Henry sighed as he didn't want to tell her but also didn't fancy the aggro of not telling her. She was clearly already in a mood. "Their son's been accused of murder."

"Murder?" Her eyes narrowed. "Well, if you ask me, from what I've heard of them, he probably did it."

Chapter Six

A double-decker bus rolled past Jean's front yard, pumping out fumes. Henry wafted the air in front of him as he watched Jean, who was staring at a pot containing lavender. The purple heads stood tall to reach the sun, but their sweet smell hadn't kicked in yet.

Jean shook her head as if trying to rid herself of the negative thoughts that mention of the Wentworth-Scotts had stirred up.

Henry noticed this. "What was the family's link to your Peter?" he asked.

She stared off into Main Street, not focussing on anything in particular. "They made investments. Well, they pretty much bullied Peter into taking their money. And then, at the end, after Peter had passed away, they were impossibly nasty about everything. Making sure they got what they were owed, plus extra."

"Isn't the art gallery still going?" Henry asked carefully, as he knew Jean didn't like talking about her late husband.

She nodded. "They kept it. Brian, the husband, was always holding events there and thought it was a money-earner."

Jean was clearly getting worked up by the topic, so Henry stopped asking questions about it. "Right. Well, they've got me helping them. And it wasn't exactly my choice."

"Sounds like their modus operandi."

"And their son, Thomas? You think he's suspicious?"

"I've not seen him for nearly ten years, but when I last did, he wasn't a pleasant chap. He seemed to have taken the worst parts of his parents." She hesitated. "The eldest, Charlotte, is nice. She's the only sensible one. Everyone calls her Lottie."

"There's another son, isn't there? Aren't there three children?"

"Aye. Benjamin. He lives in Rome." Her eyes narrowed as she thought about it. "I think he was into shooting or something. He did competitions." She shrugged as if it wasn't worth the effort of remembering. "Anyway, he lives over there. I don't know what he does now. By all accounts, he's just as hopeless as his brother."

Henry processed what Jean had said. "Do you think this Charlotte, the sensible one, would be worth talking to?"

She shrugged. "As best you'll find with that lot."

"Where does she live?"

She shook her head as if in doubt. "I think on the hills above Otley. She married a local farmer, who seemed fairly decent as well. But I'm not sure where she is."

Henry thought it might be worth him talking to this Charlotte. He glanced at his watch and saw the afternoon was hurrying towards 3 p.m. "Well, I'll keep you updated."

He was at her gate when she called out, "Be careful with that lot, Henry. I wouldn't trust them as far as I could throw them."

Henry nodded. He understood what she was getting at. From what he'd learnt about the case so far, it was all very irregular.

He entered his cottage and welcomed the coolness inside his home's thick stone walls. Tessa had come in from the backyard and was sitting in her spot on the sofa opposite the television. Henry tutted at her as she gave him a lazy look. He went into the kitchen and shut the back door.

He returned to the living room, after getting a large glass of water, and took a seat in his armchair. He switched on his iPad, and saw that the email from Jonathon Radcliffe had come through. It had seven documents attached.

Henry sighed as he contemplated the amount of reading he'd have to do, and then opened the coroner's report first. The PDF document was several pages long.

He skimmed the document and, as he'd thought, it lacked detail and precision. The coroner had concluded Freya Harrison met her end by forcing herself to drown in a half-full bathtub.

Henry shook his head at the verdict and scrolled through the pages to see if anyone had actually questioned whether it was possible. A human's instinctive reaction, when their face was underwater, was to push upwards and break the surface. Unless they were unconscious.

Henry stared at his iPad and bit his thumbnail. What would the verdict have been if it was proven Freya had been asleep when she'd drowned? The coroner would have then been compelled to conclude her death as misadventure or accidental.

Henry refocused on the report and wondered why a verdict of suicide had been reached. Surely, it was more likely that, at a party, someone would drown in a bath if they'd been drinking or taking drugs.

He then saw statements from Freya's friends and family that all had the same theme: the deceased had been depressed and upset in the days prior to her death. He noticed Gabriel had made a statement as her boyfriend and claimed she'd been moody and difficult to talk to before the party.

That would all suggest Freya had taken her own life. But Henry thought it didn't add up.

He then considered that a verdict of death by misadventure would have resulted in more questions being asked. Had Freya been taking drugs at the party? Which drugs had she taken and where had she obtained them? Who else was taking them? Was Thomas Wentworth-Scott involved in drugs?

If the deceased had killed herself, there wouldn't be as many questions about drugs. It would be a case of ascertaining Freya's state of mind at the party and the days preceding it, which Henry had in the statements from her friends and family. The fact there had been no post-mortem or blood tests done on the victim suggested there was an attempt to keep things contained.

So, who had decided Freya Harrison had died by suicide? A senior investigator must have decided which line of inquiry to follow, ignoring the possibility that she might have been unconscious when she'd died – or that she'd been murdered, as Gabriel was now claiming.

Henry remembered his phone conversation with Barnes. "Murphy was involved as he knew the family," she had said.

He felt an icy cold lump shift around his gut. Had Murphy pushed the investigation in one direction to spare the Wentworth-Scotts humiliation and to avoid difficult questions?

Henry exhaled and wished he'd never met Agnes for lunch. This whole thing was turning into a nightmare.

He opened the second document and saw it was a statement from Thomas Wentworth-Scott, which had been taken recently. Most likely the solicitors had questioned him, or the other retired detective the family had hired.

Henry read the two pages, which were well-constructed and made Thomas sound articulate. The statement gave a coherent account of him being at the party, which he accepted was 'a bad move considering the rules of social distancing in place at the time'. Thomas said that he had been in the dining hall for most of the party and hadn't spoken to Gabriel or Freya. At around 4 a.m., some partygoers alerted him to the fact Freya was dead in a bathroom upstairs.

The statement was signed and dated several weeks previously. There was a countersignature from Chris Nelson. Henry faintly remembered a detective inspector in Bradford who had the same name and wondered if this was the detective the family had hired before him.

He'd have to have a chat with Chris Nelson to see what he thought of all this.

Henry glanced through the remaining documents until he found a sheet with a name of the key players and their numbers and addresses. Thomas Wentworth-Scott was first, and his address was the same one as Henry had found on the coroner's report. He guessed it was a fancy farmhouse on the hills above Otley. It must be big, he thought, if it had a 'dining hall'.

Gabriel Silverstone lived on the outskirts of Leeds. There was a sentence in brackets next to Gabriel's address, which read: 'avoid contacting'. Henry chuckled at the idea and decided he'd visit him first. He also noted he hadn't received the details of Gabriel's allegations from the solicitor.

Opening the map application on his iPad, Henry planned his route so he could speak to Gabriel in Horsforth, visit the parents of Freya Harrison in Guiseley, and then arrive at Thomas's farmhouse. Hopefully, he could be done with the interviews and be back home before dinner.

The clock on his mantelpiece over the empty wood-burning stove stated the time was nearly 4 p.m. Henry would have to get a move on.

He got up out of his chair while typing Gabriel's number into his phone. He better see if the accuser would speak to him first, as a drive to Horsforth would take an hour.

After dialling the number, a delicate voice answered. "Yes?"

"Is that Gabriel Silverstone?"

"Speaking." The voice was defensive and weary.

"I'm former Detective Chief Inspector Henry Ward."

There was a pause. "Yes?"

"I'd like to know if I can pay you a visit to discuss your allegations against Thomas Wentworth–"

"Oh. Are you their new lackey?" Gabriel asked, interrupting him. "Their new washed-up detective?"

"I can assure you, I'm no one's lackey and neither am I washed-up."

"Whatever. I'm not interested in talking to you."

Henry could appreciate Gabriel's apprehension, but he needed to get a clear idea of the allegations. "Why won't you talk to me? You've made some very serious accusations against Thomas, and I'd like to know what they are."

"Wouldn't everyone, but I told the papers and the local TV, and not a word's been published."

"Complaints against the press lie with the Independent Press Standards Organisation, not former police detectives."

"Huh? Yes. I suppose that's correct."

"Listen, Mr Silverstone. I see my role in this as a way of finding out what happened to Freya Harrison, so that we can all be sure of the truth."

"Truth? You're working for them. You don't want the truth; you want the very opposite."

"I am not receiving payment from the family. They are not my superiors. They have asked me as an independent investigator to look into the matters surrounding Freya Harrison's death."

"Christ. I bet they're happy about that."

"Well," Henry said, losing his stride. "They don't fully understand the arrangement they've reached with me."

Gabriel paused. "What is it you want from me, then?"

"I want only the truth, Mr Silverstone."

Gabriel exhaled down the phone. Henry could almost hear the wheels in his head turning. "Alright. When can you be here, as I have to head out at six?"

"I'll be there in the hour."

Chapter Seven

Henry was in his Skoda Octavia and had the two front windows down as the air conditioner was acting up. He'd fished out some old sunglasses from the glovebox, as the sun was bearing down on West Yorkshire.

He headed down the main road in Horsforth, passing large, detached houses and their gardens. People in shorts and T-shirts walked the pavement, some squinting at the bright sunlight. Henry followed the sat nav as it took him to Gabriel's house.

He had rarely been to Horsforth. He only knew that it was a fairly wealthy town with a ruined abbey, and that some of the players from Leeds United had lived there – back when the team used to win games.

He turned off the main road and into a narrow street lined with perfectly sculptured hedges. He entered a cul-de-sac, and his sat nav declared he'd arrived at his destination.

Gabriel Silverstone's house was set back from the road. His front lawn was expertly cut, but his garden wasn't fenced in like his two neighbours on either side. His house was detached and, despite an attempt to make the property look old, it had clearly been built within the previous decade. Giving it away were the modern window frames and the Yorkshire stone facade that had only a few years' worth of grime on it.

Henry parked up on the pavement and walked past a silver Audi hatchback on the drive. He knocked on the door and, when he didn't get an answer, rang the doorbell.

After a few moments, a man in his late forties opened the door. His head was stooped, and he was thin, with stringy limbs. His earth-brown jumper failed to hide his sunken chest. He had tanned features, and his scraggly greying hair was thinning on top, exposing a scalp that frequently saw the sun.

Gabriel Silverstone gave Henry a toothy smile and held out his hand. "Detective Ward, I presume?" He had an elegant voice. It was breathy and slightly effeminate.

Henry shook his hand. "Afternoon, Mr Silverstone," he said.

Gabriel let him in and took him down a long corridor, past a large living room, and into an open-plan living area.

French doors were wide open, giving a panoramic view of the Japanese-influenced back garden. Blossom trees were arranged around a large water feature. A fountain bubbled over some round stones, emerging out of the cool water.

Henry stood in the living area and admired the view. Just looking at it made him feel relaxed. "Well, that's just lovely, isn't it?"

Gabriel didn't answer and sat at a high table made of black marble near the kitchen.

Henry followed and took a seat opposite him. He spotted more Japanese elements around the living area. A framed ink painting of Mount Fuji hung next to the French door.

"What is it you wish to ask me, Detective?" Gabriel asked, picking up a mug of green tea.

Henry noted he hadn't been offered a drink, then pulled out a reporter's notepad from his jean pocket. "Well, I'd like a clearer understanding of your allegations," he said.

Gabriel took in a breath and glanced at his garden. "You do know it's difficult for me to talk about."

"I can understand," Henry said. "How about we talk about something else first? What is it you do?"

Gabriel stared at the mug in his hand. "I'm an entrepreneur. I run several businesses."

"Such as?"

"I own restaurants in Leeds and part-own a boutique hotel."

"Are they Japanese-themed as well?"

"What?" He gazed at the Japanese memorabilia around the room. "Well, one of the restaurants is a sushi bar. But that's all."

"How long have you known Thomas Wentworth-Scott?"

"Several years. I came into contact with him when I set up the sushi bar, and then he and I planned to open a local brewery."

"Ah. Is this the business venture you two were planning?"

Suspicion clouded Gabriel's expression. "Yes." He squinted at the few notes Henry had scribbled. "Is that what you think? You think the brewery plan collapsed, so I spread rumours about him?"

"Not at all," Henry said. "But is that what you did?"

"Not at all!" Gabriel seemed insulted.

"Good, well let's ignore that for now. How did you meet Freya Harrison?"

Gabriel's fingers dug into the side of his mug. His eyes dropped to the black tabletop as he presumably reflected on his relationship with Freya. "We met a year before she…"

His hand covered his mouth while he coughed.

Henry pushed on, as he sensed Gabriel was stalling. "Right. And where did you meet?"

"At a party."

"Whose?"

Gabriel pulled up his nose as if he wasn't happy being asked questions.

"Mr Silverstone, I need to get a clear idea of this case before I can investigate it thoroughly."

Gabriel hissed through his teeth, and then bit his lower lip as though he was trying not to curse. After a moment, he nodded to himself. "I know. It's just been a very trying few years, and it seems to get worse."

Henry leant forward on the table. "Alright," he said. "Why don't you explain?"

Gabriel sipped his green tea. "Mostly all of my businesses are in hospitality, and with COVID, they all got hammered," he said. "And after all that, we had the staff shortages. Footfall's down, prices are up." He shrugged as if he didn't have to add anything else.

"Okay. And what about Freya?"

Gabriel closed his eyes. "She was wonderful. I met her at one of his parties."

"Thomas Wentworth-Scott's?"

Gabriel opened his eyes and looked slightly startled as though he hadn't meant to give it away, but eventually nodded.

"So, you met her a year before she died?"

Gabriel nodded again, then sipped his tea.

"How was Freya, leading up to the party?" Henry asked.

Gabriel exhaled. "Do we have to talk about that?"

Henry felt like raising his hands up in despair but didn't. "You've accused Thomas of her murder, haven't you?" he said. "Didn't you think you'd have to explain what happened?"

Gabriel showed some frustration. "Yes. Yes," he said. "I did, just not over and over again."

"Mr Silverstone, why don't you humour me?"

Gabriel looked him in the eye, then relented. "She was odd a few days before the party. I thought it was just the lockdown. Her family were close, but her parents were classed as vulnerable, so she couldn't see them. It was her choice more than theirs. Her father's got prostate cancer, and she didn't want him to catch COVID."

"Right. And the party?"

Gabriel stared at the tabletop for a moment. "She was funny at the party as well. Depressed and snappy. I'd almost had enough of her."

"Were you living together at the time?"

He shook his head. "She came here often, even though she wasn't supposed to, but no one seemed to mind."

"And at the party, what happened?"

"We were upstairs near Thomas's bedroom."

"Why were you there?"

Gabriel shifted in his seat. "I suppose it won't shock you to learn we were doing coke at the party."

"Nothing much shocks me, Mr Silverstone."

"It was hard to come by back then, but Thomas managed to get loads. Freya and I were doing lines in his bedroom, away from the others, as otherwise it'd run out quickly."

"Okay?"

"Anyway, she'd been in the room with Thomas before I went in, and I noticed an atmosphere. They'd been arguing about something. He pretended nothing had happened and left, but she was in a foul mood."

"Was this before or after you took the cocaine?"

"Well, we'd done some before."

"What time was this?"

He narrowed his eyes as he tried to remember. "I thought it was before midnight, but I'm not sure."

"Then what happened?"

"I went back down to the party after Freya and I had done a line, and then I saw her talking heatedly with Thomas in the kitchen. I lost track of her after that."

"You lost her?"

"Have you seen Thomas's house? It's a castle."

"I thought it was a farmhouse."

Gabriel scoffed. "A farmhouse for a lord, maybe."

Henry wondered what he'd think of the house when he visited it later that afternoon. He'd noted down Thomas's bedroom, dining hall, and bathroom as places he wanted to check. "So, what happened then?"

"I went looking for her at around 1 a.m. – I know the time as I was trying her phone, and the calls are on my phone records. I couldn't find her, so I walked around the house and its old corridors. Ringing her, and ringing her, and then I heard the sound of her ringtone, coming from behind a closed door."

"The bathroom?" said Henry.

Gabriel nodded. "It's odd. As that wasn't even the bathroom Thomas used. It was one for guests. Anyway, I heard her ringtone behind the door and hushing."

"Hushing?"

"Like a man was telling someone to hush. Then I heard whimpering and, finally, a scream." He closed his eyes and shook his head as he relived the moments in his mind. "I… I thought it was her."

"From her ringtone?"

"That and her voice."

"You didn't see her, though?"

He shook his head. "There was the sound of running water, the pipes in the old house were going, and then I knocked on the door and demanded to be let in."

"What did you think was going on inside?"

Gabriel frowned as if he'd not been asked that question before. "Erm… Well. I don't really know."

"Did you think her life was in danger?"

"Well, I heard a scream… Which I suppose was more of a yelp."

"Did you think they were being intimate?"

Gabriel's tanned cheeks reddened.

"Can you be sure Thomas was in there? That he was the man you heard?" asked Henry.

Gabriel pursed his lips, then lifted his mug. He took a long sip and swallowed slowly. "I don't know for certain."

Henry scribbled a note down. "What happened then?"

"Well, is there any point in telling you? You seem to have made up your mind already, so why bloody bother?!" Gabriel slammed the tabletop, knocking over the mug, which landed on its side, spilling the last dregs of tea.

"Mr Silverstone, I'm just asking you questions to clarify what–"

"Bullshit! You're here to undermine my argument so those fuckers can sue me for every penny I've got."

Henry held up his hands to calm him down. "Listen, Mr Silverstone," he said. "If you can't survive some gentle questioning, how are you going to fare in court on Friday?"

Gabriel chewed his lower lip as he contemplated Henry's point.

"If you tell me everything you know, and I find your case has merit, then the libel suit will disappear, won't it?"

Gabriel looked around the room as if searching for an argument but couldn't find one.

"Now," Henry continued, "I can't see the harm in you telling me what you know and in answering my questions. Unless you're making up these accusations that Thomas murdered Freya."

"I'm not," Gabriel said, sullenly.

"Good. So, what did you do next?"

Chapter Eight

Gabriel picked up his mug and placed it on a marble tabletop by the sink, seemingly lost in his own thoughts.

Henry glanced out at the back garden. A purple butterfly fluttered above one of the clay ornaments in the pond. The fountain gurgled gently nearby.

Gabriel sighed as if coming to a painful conclusion. "Fine," he said. "I'll tell you."

The butterfly zipped off over the fence and into the next garden. Henry watched it go and then refocused his attention on Gabriel. The man appeared to have aged while they'd been talking – the stress of the lawsuit and of what he knew was clearly sitting heavily on him.

"So, Mr Silverstone. What did you see?"

"I didn't see anything, as I've said. I tried pushing the door to get inside the bathroom."

"Why?"

He pulled a displeased expression. "I thought she was screwing Thomas."

"What gave you that idea? Didn't you hear a scream?"

"Sometimes she moaned like that during…"

"Is that why you thought she was sleeping with Thomas?"

"It'd been going on for months." Gabriel's expression soured, and he looked grey and worn out despite his bronzed complexion. "I even think they were fucking before I met."

"So, you tried to get into the bathroom…?"

"I tried the door, but it was locked. I knocked and banged and shouted. But they didn't let me in."

"Right… and?"

"And then, after five minutes, well… I gave up and thought, to hell with them. I walked off down the hall to get a drink and a taxi home."

It was Henry's turn to pull a face. "You suspected your friend and business partner was having relations with your girlfriend inside the bathroom, and when you couldn't get inside, you just walked away?"

"What else was I to do?"

Henry tried to think of an answer but couldn't, apart from barging down the door. But when he looked at Gabriel's feeble frame, he doubted the man could barge down anything.

"So, you left the party?"

"Not immediately. There was a girl there who'd been giving me the eye all night, and I pursued her. Then, at around 4 a.m.–"

"You were still there at 4 a.m.?"

He nodded.

"I thought you wanted to leave?"

"I did, but then this girl, Alison, got my attention. And, what with Freya being unfaithful…" He gestured to Henry as if expecting him to understand his point.

Henry didn't. "So, you hung around this party with Alison, and you didn't see Freya for the rest of the night?"

Gabriel nodded. "Yes. We were chatting, Alison and I." He grinned to himself. "We met a few more times after that, but then it fizzled out. As these things sometimes do."

Henry thought it odd for a man to meet another woman at the party where his girlfriend died, and then continue this new relationship afterwards.

But he didn't ask about that. "Mr Silverstone," he said, "I'm not interested in your love life unless it's connected to this inquiry."

Gabriel became serious again and nodded.

"So, what happened around four in the morning?"

"Well, there was panic at first. Someone had found Freya in the bathtub."

"Do you know who?"

He shook his head. Henry guessed he'd find out in the documents the solicitor had sent over.

Gabriel continued, "Then people rushed out of the dining hall to go upstairs and look."

"How many people were at the party?"

He shrugged. "More than thirty, I should think. It was a small affair."

Henry scoffed and shook his head. A party of thirty people during a lockdown in which social gatherings were banned. He then recalled the solicitor, Jonathon Radcliffe, telling him that many people who'd attended the party were unwilling to go on the record.

Henry suspected lots of them had reputations and careers that could be damaged if their attendance at the party was confirmed. His mind started pondering how he could use that to his advantage.

Gabriel appeared to have no such qualms about being at the party. He returned to his seat at the high table and dipped his fingertip into the spilt tea on its surface, watching Henry.

"Did you see Freya's body in the bathroom?"

Gabriel's finger stopped moving. He placed his hands on his lap and nodded. "It was unpleasant. I asked people what the fuss was about, and they said someone had OD'd."

"Overdosed?" Henry asked.

"It's not possible. She did a few lines of coke now and again, but she'd never overdose on the stuff. And she never took anything else."

Henry noted the sincerity in his voice and nodded his acceptance. "What happened then?"

"Everyone freaked, of course. They were worried about being caught at the party. People drove off and others called taxis."

"Were taxis even available back then?"

"Yes," said Gabriel. "You might have to pay a bit extra for their silence, but it was mostly fine."

Henry suspected the taxi firms near Thomas's farmhouse would have records from that night. "What did you see when you looked at Freya?"

Gabriel shut his eyes. "I don't like…" He shook his head as if he was forcing himself to remember. "It was devastating. She wore her clothes, which was the oddest thing. Why would she keep them on and get in a bath?"

He opened his eyes slowly and gazed at Henry as if expecting a reply but didn't get one.

"I ran to her side and tried to pull her out, but someone told me to leave her alone. The bathwater was ice cold, and Freya was freezing, too," Gabriel continued.

Henry scribbled some notes. "Can you remember who was in there?"

"No," he said. "Everything was a blur."

"When did the police arrive?"

Gabriel gnawed at the inside of his mouth. "Well… there was a debate."

"What about?"

"Lots of people didn't want the police to arrive. I mean, we weren't oblivious to the fact that the party was illegal, and there were drugs everywhere. Plus, Freya had been taking them."

"So, you delayed contacting the emergency services because you were afraid of the police arresting you all?"

"Or fining us. Yes."

"Did anyone confirm Freya had died?" asked Henry. "For all you knew, she might have still been alive, and you all denied her life-saving treatment. Which is a pretty serious criminal offence."

Gabriel smiled as if he thought Henry was overreacting. "There was a GP there who checked her. If there were any chance of us saving her, we would have."

"A doctor was there?"

Gabriel nodded. "I can't say who, but there was one. Yes."

Henry's biro hovered over the page in his notepad. "Best give me a name, or I'll have to get the police involved and cause more problems for you."

"What? Wait? What are you talking about?"

"Give me the name of the doctor who unofficially confirmed Freya's death."

Gabriel winced at Henry while he pouted his lips. "I can't."

"You can either protect this doctor or tell me who they are so I can have a chat with them. If you don't tell me, you can tell one of my colleagues in CID."

Gabriel huffed. Henry suspected he was coming to realise he faced enough problems. "Fine. If you're going to be like that. It was Dr Emma Parrish. She's a GP in Leeds." He seemed annoyed with himself for giving in.

Henry noted down the name and then glanced through his notes. Something was missing. After he'd gone back a few pages, he stared at Gabriel. "When did you decide Thomas Wentworth-Scott had killed Freya?"

Gabriel lowered his eyes, searching the black tabletop but finding nothing.

"I mean, why've you only made the accusation now? Why did you wait three years before saying anything?"

Gabriel wiped his nose with the back of his hand and stared into the living room behind Henry, not focusing on anything.

"Mr Silverstone? If you can answer my question, as this is the part I'm not clear on."

"I can't…" he said, still looking at nothing in particular.

"Well, how do you know Thomas killed her?"

Gabriel's eyes slowly focused, as he stared at Henry with a new-found intensity. "It was at her funeral. It was a small, sad affair. The weather was grey and miserable, and not many people could come, because of COVID. Thomas came.

"Freya's father looked sallow and beaten. He'd expected to die before his daughter, not the other way round. And her mother looked numb. She barely said a word. I think there were ten of us. I was invited as I'd been seeing Freya for a year, but Thomas…? I have no idea why he was there.

"Anyway, at the small reception, which Thomas insisted on having at his…" Gabriel shook his head as if he found the idea distasteful. "Which I thought was awful. I mean, bringing that poor wretched couple to the house where their daughter died? Anyway, at the house, I noticed Thomas acting oddly."

"Oddly?"

"He…" Gabriel's shallow chest expanded as it took in a breath. He looked upwards. "It was like he was happy or free. The inquiry hadn't finished, but he was telling people Freya had killed herself – as a fact. Something I thought was odd, as, yes, she was a bit down in the dumps. But suicidal?"

"You don't believe she killed herself?"

Gabriel grimaced, as if he didn't think the suggestion was serious. "Not at all."

"Then why were you quoted in the coroner's report as saying Freya had been depressed in the days leading up to the party?"

Gabriel rolled his eyes. "That old chestnut? They asked me if I thought she was depressed."

"Who's they?"

"That goth detective."

Henry raised an eyebrow. "Who?"

"The young detective with jet black hair and bright red lipstick."

DC Hargreaves, Henry thought. "So, Detective Hargreaves questioned you?" he said.

"Yes, and she mentioned nothing about murder or overdose, which, to be honest, I thought was the real explanation."

"I thought you said she couldn't have overdosed?"

Gabriel nodded. "Well, I thought she could have passed out in the bath or something. But that was before the funeral. After the burial, when we were at Thomas's farmhouse, I had a flashback of the party. Of standing outside that bathroom door.

"I think, with the stress of everything, and the booze and coke I'd taken that night, that I'd forgotten all about it. But it came back to me, and I remembered hearing Freya's scream, and a man hushing her, and the water pipes running, and splashing.

"I looked at Thomas across the room at Freya's wake. He was talking to her parents, and the realisation came to me that he had killed her. He killed Freya."

Chapter Nine

Henry could almost picture the scene, even though he'd never been in Thomas Wentworth-Scott's farmhouse or met the man himself; Thomas, or what he imagined him to look like, talking to two bereaved parents, smiling and putting on a brave face, while knowing that he'd got away with their daughter's murder.

But there was still something niggling at Henry. An element didn't fit. He glanced at Gabriel, who appeared so tired, Henry thought he was about to shut down and ask him to leave.

The party had happened in May 2020, and three years had passed, and it was only after the brewery business run by Thomas and Gabriel had collapsed that the murder allegation became public.

Henry leant back in his chair, listening to the birds in the back garden and the gurgling of the water feature. He cupped his chin in his hand and rested his elbow on the tabletop.

"This all seems possible…" Henry said, using his free hand to flick through his notes.

Gabriel came alert at the prospect of Henry believing him. "Yes?"

"The only problem is the three-year gap."

The alertness quickly left Gabriel's face, and he slumped back into his chair.

"Why did you wait three years before voicing your concerns?" Henry eyeballed him, hoping his nasty glare would get the truth out.

Gabriel was drained, and he waved his hand in the air. "I can't…" he said. "I don't think I want to talk anymore."

"Mr Silverstone, why did you wait three years before voicing your allegations?"

"Because…!" He snapped but stopped himself from saying anything else.

Henry raised an eyebrow expectedly.

"Because I'd have been ruined. Why do you think?"

"Sorry? You withheld allegations of murder for financial reasons?"

"Ha!" Gabriel's laugh was patronising and spiteful. "Financial reasons? Have you seen me?" He held out his arms wide. "I'm an aging sickly loser. No one likes me. They only put up with me because I have money."

Henry's judgement of Gabriel was changing quickly, and not for the better.

"You think I can get with the girls I like because of my looks? I need cash. I've always needed cash," he said. "I got some from my parents, but nothing like rich-boy Thomas. The rest I've had to earn, and I have. I've made millions. But it's all precarious. It's not… you know."

Henry didn't, so he remained quiet and watched.

"Inherited. It's not fertile land like they have. They invest in businesses and stuff for fun. They don't care if they succeed or fail; not really. It's just a game, because they have the rents from acres of land to fall back on. They'd only be in trouble if there was a catastrophic global event, like a nuclear war. Otherwise, they're set. They're fine. They'll always get richer and richer."

"Mr Silverstone," Henry said, almost sighing, "can you get to the point?"

"The point is, I needed that brewery business to succeed. COVID nearly wiped me out, and I needed the money from it. And it was a money-earner, at first, and then rich-boy Thomas got bored and pulled out."

"So, did you accuse him of Freya's murder out of spite?"

"Spite? No. Well… a little. Maybe. Does that matter? I genuinely think he killed Freya."

"But you withheld that accusation during the coroner's inquiry and didn't tell anyone."

"Would they have believed me?"

Henry was about to answer and say the first thing that came to mind – 'of course they would have' – but stopped himself.

He wasn't sure if the police would have looked into the allegation seriously, especially if the love triangle between Thomas Wentworth-Scott and the boyfriend of the victim had been uncovered. Gabriel would've been seen as exploiting a tragedy by making a vexatious claim against someone he thought was stealing his girlfriend.

Besides, DC Hargreaves was an inexperienced detective leading a large inquiry, and it seems someone higher up had already decided Freya had died by her own hand.

"See!" Gabriel said, taking Henry's silence as his answer.

"So, you kept quiet to stop Thomas from ruining your brewery business, and when he pulled out several years later, you publicly accused him of murdering Freya?"

Gabriel's tired mind took a moment to think through Henry's summary, and then he nodded.

"I can see why they're suing you," said Henry.

"They're suing me because they want the official verdict to remain as it is. They want you, I suspect, to confirm it." He gave Henry a toothy grin.

"It's very brave of you, in that case, to have made the allegations," Henry said.

His grin wavered. "Yes, well… I didn't think of that at the time. I told everyone when I was pissed off and in a rage."

"You didn't think they'd sue you?"

He shook his head. "I should have, but I let my anger get the better of me. My mistake."

Henry didn't say anything and closed his notepad. "Well, Mr Silverstone, I'd best be heading off. I've got more people to talk to."

Gabriel narrowed his eyes as he thought about something. "The court hearing is on Friday. So, you only have a few days to find out what happened."

Henry nodded gloomily and stood up.

Gabriel remained seated at the table. "I hope you find the truth. Because, if you don't, they'll crush me."

Henry pocketed his notepad and biro. He stood tall and took in a breath. "I'll find out the truth as best as I can, Mr Silverstone, but there's one thing that's eluding me right now. If Thomas Wentworth-Scott killed Freya, then why? What was his motive?"

Gabriel shrugged. "I've not a clue. You're the detective, aren't you?"

Henry patted his jeans pockets to make sure he had everything, and then looked at Gabriel. "Aye. Unfortunately, I am," he said.

Henry got back into his Skoda Octavia and opened the two front windows. He'd failed to park the car under some shade, and the afternoon sun had borne down on it, blasting its windscreen and heating the interior.

He pulled out his notepad and flicked through his notes. Glancing up at Gabriel's detached home, he wondered if the man would survive the financial shock of being sued. The house looked expensive, but as Gabriel had said, he didn't have cash to burn and his small empire was precarious.

Henry rested his own greying hair against the hot headrest and pondered Gabriel's accusation against Thomas. It was convincing, but there wasn't much to it apart from Gabriel's 'feeling' that the sounds he'd heard inside the bathroom at the party were Freya screaming in fear and nothing else.

Henry tapped on the near-scolding steering wheel, which had taken the brunt of the sun. He believed Gabriel. Or perhaps he wanted to. It was easy to hate a rich irresponsible playboy like Thomas and assume the worse. But there wasn't any evidence Thomas Wentworth-Scott had been near Freya that night. In fact, Henry recalled there being a witness who confirmed he hadn't.

As for the irregularities surrounding the police's handling of the case, well, Henry could forgive some of it. At the time, the country was experiencing a once-in-a-century crisis. Corners were cut, and detectives without the necessary training had handled cases they shouldn't have. It had been all hands on deck.

But still. Henry couldn't shake the feeling that something terrible had happened to Freya Harrison, and that the Wentworth-Scotts, possibly in cahoots with the police, covered it up.

The issue was, Henry very much doubted he'd be able to prove anything in the remaining few days he had. Sitting in his boiling hot car on a lovely May afternoon, Henry questioned what the hell he was doing.

If he found out what happened to Freya, what good would it do if he couldn't prove it? The Wentworth-Scotts would probably sue him if he spoke about it. They'd take his police pension and house from him, and then he'd be homeless and would probably have to sleep on Jean's sofa. If she'd let him.

Well, she'd let *him* stay, but not Tessa, as her cat hated dogs.

Henry shook away his thoughts of doom. He'd forgotten an important element. Behind every case like this, was a grieving family.

He put the address for Mr and Mrs Harrison into his sat nav, started the engine and wound up the windows so the barely functioning air conditioning could do its best to cool the car.

Henry set off through Horsforth to speak to Freya's parents and learn what they knew about their daughter's death.

Chapter Ten

The Harrisons' house was old, three storeys high, and made from golden Yorkshire stone. It was in the centre of a street lined with similarly sized detached residences. In one of them, a neighbour mowed his lawn while keeping his eyes on Henry.

The grass in the Harrisons' large front garden was freshly cut, and in its flowerbeds grew bright pink foxgloves, as did some red rhododendrons near the ground-floor windows.

Henry walked down the garden path, looking up at the house. A happy energy came from it, but as he got closer, he noticed the interior was dark, and some of the window frames were chipped and damaged. The guttering was old and had collapsed in spots. It was all in need of repair, he thought.

A woman in her sixties answered his knock, wearing a light-grey cardigan over a thin white dress. She had dark shoulder-length hair and stared at Henry with a mixture of fear and confusion.

"Hello, Mrs Harrison?"

She nodded as if uncertain she should speak.

"I'm former DCI Henry Ward."

The anxiety didn't leave Mr Harrison's expression.

"I'm here to discuss the legal case–"

"No. I don't want anything to do with it." She shook her head and narrowed the gap in the door so only her face was visible.

Henry guessed she was too polite to slam it in his face. "Mrs Harrison," he said, "I'm investigating your daughter's death for–"

Mrs Harrison let out a deep, guttural sob and bowed her head; her hands covered her face.

Henry felt incredibly awkward. He looked over the street and spotted that the neighbour opposite had stopped mowing his lawn. He was now glaring at Henry, probably wondering how he had the gall to bother this sad couple.

"I understand it's a very difficult subject," Henry said to Mrs Harrison.

She wiped her eyes with the sleeve of her cardigan, leaving black mascara marks on it. "Please. I want you to leave. I don't want to talk about it."

Henry stood his ground. It was nearly 5 p.m. on Monday afternoon, and he had two days to uncover what happened to this woman's daughter. He could return tomorrow or Wednesday, but his gut told him he'd need those days for following up leads.

He tried again. "Listen, Mrs Harrison. I really understand this is upsetting–"

"You don't… you've no idea." Her voice came out brittle.

The neighbour across the street was now standing at his gate, scowling at Henry.

Henry continued, "Mrs Harrison, I'd really appreciate it if I could just speak to you and your husband–"

She sobbed louder than before and hid herself behind the door.

"Oi!"

Henry turned as the neighbour strutted across the street. Henry guessed the man was in his fifties and was probably a neighbourhood-watch busybody who thought he had to control his everything.

The man ran his hands up his thick arms as if rolling up his sleeves, despite wearing a short-sleeve pink polo shirt.

"Leave her alone!" the man shouted as he approached. "Can't you bloody see she's grieving?"

Henry wondered why Mrs Harrison would still be grieving three years after Freya had died. He then recalled Gabriel mentioning Mr Harrison had prostate cancer and had been ill at Freya's funeral.

He stared into Mrs Harrison's bloodshot eyes and realised he'd put his foot in it.

Shaking his head, Henry struggled to think of the right words. "I'm so sorry about your loss."

The neighbour mustn't have heard him. "Her bloody husband's just passed away, so she doesn't need dickheads like you upsetting her," he said.

Henry raised his hands in surrender. "I'm leaving," he said to the neighbour. To Mrs Harrison, he added, "I apologise. I didn't know."

She peered at him from behind the door and gave the slightest nod of acknowledgement. But in her watery eyes, Henry spotted flickers of hatred.

He got back into his car and watched the neighbour try to console Mrs Harrison, who didn't appear to want him there. Henry couldn't blame her. The man looked like a know-it-all brute. He pointed at the grass in the Harrisons' front garden and appeared to be saying he was going to cut it again.

Henry exhaled and started the engine. The air conditioning kicked in better than before, and Henry keyed Thomas Wentworth-Scott's address into his sat nav. He'd have to visit the man in the centre of all this, as he doubted he'd be able to speak to Freya's remaining parent again.

Henry hoped Mrs Harrison didn't know something that would be crucial for his investigation.

* * *

Henry kept his eyes on the narrow country lane, slowing down as he approached each sharp corner. The last thing he wanted to do was scratch his car or have a head-on collision. The sun glared through the windscreen, and luckily, he was wearing the old pair of sunglasses, otherwise he wouldn't have seen a thing.

He felt wretched after his visit to Mrs Harrison's. The poor woman was a wreck. What a buffoon, he thought, glaring at himself in the rear-view mirror, and seeing his dark shades reflected back. He used to be able to pick up on stuff like that, or he could have at least asked someone else or checked up on her circumstances to see–

A primal instinct ordered him to slam on the brakes, but he didn't know why.

Before he realised what was going on, he'd done an emergency stop, forcing both the clutch and brake pedals as far as they could go.

His wheels shrieked, and he gripped the steering wheel as his car shuddered.

The black Land Rover sped around the corner, going stupidly fast. Its shiny grill almost careened headfirst into Henry's, missing by a few inches.

Henry pulled into the drystone wall and heard something on his left crack.

The Land Rover sped past and even had the audacity to beep its horn at Henry as if *he* was the problem.

Just as quickly as it came, it was gone. Henry knew he was taking deep breaths as if he'd just had a shock. And he had to admit he had.

"Blood and sand!" he hissed.

When it was safe, he pulled the car away from the wall and got out to check the damage. It appeared to be fine, but then he saw some of the plastic on the side mirror had broken.

It wasn't worth paying to get it fixed, he thought. But it was pretty damn annoying, nonetheless. Thankfully, his instincts had kicked in as he hadn't seen that Land Rover coming.

He stared at the blind corner ahead of him. There were signs telling people to slow down, but that driver had sped up instead.

Who would drive like that? he wondered. He hoped it wasn't Thomas Wentworth-Scott, as he needed to speak to him. He suspected this Thomas would be the kind of idiot who drove like that.

Hoping he hadn't missed his chance to speak to him, Henry got back in his car and carried on his journey to Thomas's farmhouse.

* * *

Thomas Wentworth-Scott's house was nothing like the 'farmhouse' Henry had imagined. In his mind, it'd been an old, run-down stone building in the wild moorlands above Otley. He pictured it having a slate roof turned green by moss, and several rotting corrugated-iron barns in a dirty farmyard.

What he found when he travelled down the long gravel drive was a huge two-storey building that appeared to have once been the home and barns of a gentleman farmer. Its facade had been recently power-washed, and the sandstone was bright and fresh. Its clay roof had skylights in over a large barn that had been converted into, what Henry presumed, were luxury living spaces. It really looked like a castle, as Gabriel had said.

Henry pulled up next to a Porsche and an Audi in the drive and observed them. It didn't seem like Thomas was someone who owned a Land Rover.

Stepping out of his car, he felt a gentle breeze blow over him. The house was on the top of the Chevin, on the hills above Otley. Henry craned his neck to look at an airplane above him, which had taken off from the nearby airport. The plane's engines sounded like distant roars, and then the plane banked right and flew over the valley.

Henry heard footsteps in the gravel and saw a big man moving towards him. The man smiled and appeared happy to see him. He wore a red and white chequered shirt underneath a light-brown leather jacket, and dark tight-fitting jeans.

Holding out his large paw for Henry to shake, the man said, "Thomas Wentworth-Scott." He gave Henry a knowing smile when he shook his hand. "I suppose you're the poor sod Mum brought in to help?"

Henry nodded. "Aye." He noticed Thomas's accent didn't sound local, but like his mother's, there were hints of Yorkshire in his vowels.

Thomas checked the Rolex on his right wrist and then said, "Listen, the thing is, I don't have much time. You're a bit late. I've got to meet some people for drinks."

"I've just got here."

"Yes, but… I've been waiting for you since this afternoon on Mum's orders, and that bloody dreary solicitor kept droning on at me to stay." He pulled a face that suggested he didn't enjoy taking orders from subordinates. "I've got loads of stuff to be getting on with."

"Right." Henry shut his car door, and noticed Thomas was looking at his Skoda as if it was an oddity. "The thing is, Mr Wentworth–"

Thomas cut him off. "Thomas or Tommy. Please."

Henry nodded. "The issue is, Thomas, I've just been speaking to your old friend Gabriel."

The bonhomie vibe coming off Thomas evaporated in the breeze. He sneered. "What did that snake want?"

"Nothing. I went to speak to him."

"Wait a minute. Didn't we hire you to prove his claims were nonsense?"

"Kind of." Henry didn't think Thomas was in the mood to hear about the non-payment arrangement he'd made with his mother. "But in order to help prove you're not involved in Freya's murder, I had to speak to the man making the allegations."

Thomas snorted, clearly enraged. "That snake accused me of… all sorts."

Henry noted Thomas couldn't bring himself to say 'murder'. "He's made some allegations that are worth looking into."

"You can't be serious?" Thomas scoffed. "I pulled out of the man's crappy brewery thing; which was a dud, by the way. DOA, everyone said so. I'd been warned about doing deals with that snake and should've listened."

"Well, Thomas. Why don't we discuss these allegations and see what you have to say about them?"

Thomas checked his silver watch again. "Now? But I've got to be making a move."

Henry sighed. "I only have two days to look into this investigation. And as you're the accused, I really think it's important I speak to you now."

Thomas scrunched up his nose like a naughty schoolboy who'd been asked to finish all his homework. He checked his watch again. "Fine. You can have twenty minutes."

"Right. Twenty minutes it is."

As Henry followed Thomas to the front door of his large house, he listed the questions in his mind he wanted to ask this accused murderer.

Chapter Eleven

Henry reckoned Thomas's kitchen was bigger than most studio flats. The marble flooring looked new, as did the white worktops running along the walls and on the large island in the centre of the space.

All the appliances were top of the range and looked to have just come out of their boxes. There was a double oven, and a glossy ceramic hotplate set into the island's worktop. Both appeared to never have been used. Henry could faintly smell fresh paint in the air and glanced at the white walls.

Thomas groaned as he flopped down in a large grey comfy chair at the island. He pulled a large smartphone from his pocket and laid it in front of him so he could keep track of time.

Henry pulled a chair opposite and took a seat. Taking out his notepad and biro, he flicked through the notes he'd taken at Gabriel's. He didn't need to read them, as he remembered the pertinent details. He was just doing it for dramatic effect.

Thomas made a show of checking the time on his phone. "We only have fifteen minutes."

"We have twenty," Henry said, not looking up from his notes.

Thomas was affronted. "If I say we have fifteen, it's fifteen."

"Be quiet." Henry glared at Thomas. It was a risk, but Henry wanted to know how far he could push him before he fought back. Despite the man's size, Henry had sussed he was a big mummy's boy at heart and would crumple under pressure.

"I beg your pardon?" Thomas nearly jumped out of his seat, but Henry held up his hand.

"We have twenty minutes. End of. Now, I have questions for you."

Thomas was still agitated and didn't seem willing to play along. "You've just ordered me around in my own house."

"I'm investigating whether you murdered Freya Harrison in May 2020. So if I choose to boss you around, I will. Now start answering my questions."

Thomas was lost for words. The mention of murder startled him.

"Did you kill Freya Harrison?" Henry asked, eyeballing Thomas.

Thomas gritted his teeth at the direct question, causing his big jaw to stick out.

"Did you?"

Thomas's cleft chin quivered. "Of course I didn't. The coroner said I didn't."

"You're talking about that irregular coroner's report?"

"Irregular?" Thomas asked, attempting a laugh. "There's nothing wrong with it. It was all investigated, and everything was fine."

"So, if I tell you I believe the investigation was irregular; that it might've been pushed in one direction to avoid going in another, would you say I was wrong?"

Thomas thought about it for a second. "Not just wrong, but potentially slanderous," he said in a low voice.

Here we go, Henry thought. Whenever he got anywhere near the truth, the Wentworth-Scotts would wheel out the lawyers.

Henry changed tack. He'd seen Thomas was comfortable with forceful questioning and thought another approach might work better. "Alright, Thomas. Well done."

Thomas flexed his shoulder muscles as if he was preparing for a fight.

Henry leant back in his chair and smiled. "I think you did a good job."

Thomas frowned. "At what?"

"Handling an interrogation."

He exhaled and started laughing. "Oh. You had me there. For a second, I thought Mum had messed up and hired a looney." He chuckled. "Yes, I've done all sorts of training on questioning and that. Mum's lawyers put me through it years ago. You know what they say. Avoid their question and answer the one you want to answer."

Henry nodded along, humouring him. "Very good. Now, I do have a few questions to ask." He looked down at his notes.

"Sure. Fire away. As long as they aren't like your last ones."

Henry forced a smile. "Now, Gabriel mentioned he heard Freya in a bathroom. Would you know which one?"

Thomas shrugged. "Who knows? I have four of them."

Four bathrooms, Henry thought, in one house. "Do you remember which one Freya was found in?"

"Oh right, yes. It was the one near the guest bedrooms upstairs."

"So, could he have heard her in that one?"

"I've no idea what he's on about. I wouldn't pay that snake any notice." He waved his large arms around. "All of this nonsense is because he wanted some attention after I ditched him," he said, shaking his head in frustration.

"You mean after your brewery business ended?"

"Yes, and as I've said, that was a complete waste of time." He crossed his arms over his chest and sulked as he dwelled on it.

"Why was that?" asked Henry.

"Well, the bloody thing lost money from the beginning."

Henry recalled Gabriel saying the opposite. "I thought it made money?"

Thomas huffed. "Is that what he told you? Yeah, he told people it was a great business idea. I mean, everyone was getting into it. He said we needed to get involved. But in reality, it was a joke. He didn't know what he was doing, and neither did I. We'd never run a brewery before. I know about drinking beer, not making it. And the guys he got in to run the thing were idiots."

"Who did he employ?"

"Two fellas he knew from Leeds – one was a food scientist or something – but they didn't know what to do, and the whole business lost money hand over fist."

Henry nodded while he contemplated the two versions, Gabriel's and Thomas's. If the brewery turned out to be involved in the investigation, he might have to get to the truth by inspecting the company's financial records. However, Henry hated poring over accounts, so perhaps he could hand that off to someone.

Henry spotted Thomas check the time on his phone again, so he continued. "Where were you during the party?"

"Me?" He shrugged. "I'm all over the place when I have a party. I never stop. I try to spend equal amounts of time with my guests."

"Why's that?"

He smirked. "Parties are the best way to network. And I invite people I want to speak to. My guest lists are legendary."

"Right," Henry said, not sure what Thomas was talking about. "So, this gathering in 2020, was it a networking event?"

Thomas nodded like the fact was evident. "Of course it was." He placed one hand on the tabletop and counted his outstretched fingers with the other. "I had doctors and local government officials there because I wanted to get the facts about the pandemic. I also had people involved in breweries and beer-making, as we were setting up the brewery at the time. Then I had that snake and his friends come."

"Is that why Freya Harrison was invited?"

Thomas's expression soured as he heard her name. "She wasn't just *his* friend." His eyes clouded over for a moment, and he spoke with low energy. "I knew her through some PR firms in Leeds and Manchester. I have investments in a few agencies, you see."

"Were you ever more than just friends with Freya?"

Thomas bowed his head in deep thought. His eyes then went to his phone screen as a notification popped up. "I knew her before Gabriel did," he said.

"Gabriel seems to think you and Freya were in a relationship–"

Thomas shook his head before Henry had finished his sentence. "Lies. Complete muck-spreading."

Henry suspected it wasn't a lie and Thomas was avoiding the subject. His tone of voice had changed, and his eyes shifted around, making him look guilty.

He had clearly lost the ability to handle tough questions, Henry thought. No wonder his mum's solicitors had needed to train him.

"So, on the night of the party, did you see Freya?"

Thomas pretended to consider the question. "I spent time with everyone at the party, so obviously I spoke to her," he said. "But I didn't spend much time with her. As I said, I was interested in finding out about the pandemic and setting up the brewery, so speaking to Gabriel's then girlfriend wasn't any use to me."

Henry got the impression his answer had been rehearsed. The sentences were too complete and complex, almost like they'd been written by a solicitor and memorized by Thomas.

"Okay, so you didn't see her upstairs?"

Thomas shook his head again before Henry had completed his question.

"What about cocaine?" Henry asked.

"What about it?"

"Gabriel said he was in your bedroom with you and Freya, snorting lines. Is that true?"

"Absolutely not. And anyone who's come to my parties would know I have a rule about my bedroom. No one can enter, except for me. We have…" He counted in his head. "We have five guest rooms that people can use to… you know, do their thing. But mine is strictly off limits. You can ask anyone about that rule. They'll tell you the truth."

Henry scribbled a reminder in his notepad.

"Any more questions? It's just that our twenty minutes are coming to an end."

"Just a few. So, you can categorically confirm you were never in the bathroom with Freya during the party?"

Thomas shook his head, this time waiting for Henry to finish his question before doing so. "I'll even take a lie-detector test to prove it," he said. "I've never been in a bathroom with her in my entire life. It never happened."

Henry watched and got the impression he was telling the truth. "Why do you think Gabriel is making this accusation, then?"

Thomas shrugged. "I don't know. The brewery? The…" He waved his hand in front of him as if it'd help him remember.

"The affair between you and Freya?"

Thomas's eyes bulged. "There was no affair. I never slept with her."

Henry nodded as if he agreed. "Alright."

Thomas grabbed the phone up from the table. "Now, I really must be heading off." He pushed his chair back, scraping the floor tiles.

"One final question. Would I be able to look around the house?"

Thomas was stumped by the question. "Erm… Why?"

"I just want to check the bathroom, the dining hall, and your bedroom."

"My bedroom?"

Henry nodded. "Just to get an idea of the house so I can try to picture what happened that night."

"Well, this place has been renovated since then. I'm not sure you'll find anything."

"Oh? You changed the whole property?" Henry had guessed the kitchen had been redecorated recently, but the whole house?

"I fancied a change."

"I see. Well, can I still have a look around?"

Thomas glanced at his phone, which started vibrating. He stopped the incoming call. "My bedroom? I'm not sure why you want to look in there? I mean, if that snake said he was in there, he's lying," he said.

"I just wish to take a quick look, that's all. It'll help with the investigation." Henry gave his best doctor's smile, which was intended to say 'trust me and don't ask further questions'.

Thomas hesitated, and then his phone vibrated in his hand again. "Alright, fine. Have a look."

"Do I need a key to lock up when I leave?"

Thomas shook his head. "Vince's here."

"Vince?" Henry asked.

Thomas didn't take his eyes off his phone. "Yes, he's living here at the moment. Right, I'd best be off." He headed to the kitchen door and said, "Don't touch stuff in my room."

Henry heard the front door close, then he started his search.

Chapter Twelve

Henry walked down the hallway to the front door. The walls were all painted white and had light-grey skirting boards. Despite clearly being a bachelor's pad, the house was tidy, which suggested Thomas had a cleaner; unless Vince, who apparently lived here, did the housekeeping.

Henry turned a corner and found the dining hall. It was like something out of a period drama. It had a high ceiling and three arched windows through which the sun shone, lighting the long table. Twelve chairs were arranged around it, and its varnished oak was bare. An old open fireplace opposite was spotless, and Henry didn't think it had held a fire in years.

Henry suspected a painting had once hung on the wall behind the head of the table, but nothing was displayed now; the wood-panelled walls were bare.

Looking around the room, he could imagine it was a great place to have a party. He also thought there'd be enough space to hold thirty people. Even more, if they moved the long table out.

He left the dining hall through a second door and found himself in a narrow hallway that opened up into a large space. This must be the converted barn, he thought. It was a huge room, with two three-piece sofas and a massive television on one side, and a snooker table and arcade machines on the other.

Henry inspected the snooker table and saw it was well used. Blue chalk stained the green covering, and the tips of the snooker cues were worn down. A huge photograph was mounted on the wall above the table.

Henry stepped towards it and made out a young man, who looked a bit like Thomas, with the same cleft chin and dark hair. The man was aiming a rifle away from the camera, while wearing a bright red gilet and purple sunglasses.

This must be the other brother, Henry realised. He couldn't remember the name, but then saw it printed on his gilet: Benjamin Wentworth-Scott. A large panel in the background identified the scene as a European Shooting Confederation event in 2019.

Henry stepped back from the photo to notice the five gold trophies in the glass cabinet before him. They'd been awarded to Benjamin for coming in first place in several high-level competitions. Resting underneath the shelf holding the trophies was a rifle on display. It had a brilliant silver barrel and a scarlet stock. A small Union flag emblem was near the trigger. Some boxes of ammunition were piled up next to it, and Henry realised the cabinet wasn't locked.

Looking around the games room, he found a second door and, after walking down an old corridor, came to an old multi-pane window that looked out over the grassy moorlands. Henry peered through the old misshapen glass at the fields outside, spotting what looked like a farm in the distance.

A staircase was behind him, and its wooden steps creaked as he walked up.

The hallway on the second floor also had white walls and a neutral-coloured carpet. Henry saw several doors lining both sides. He should've asked Thomas where his bedroom was, or for a map.

Just as he was about to move on, he heard a door close. Glancing down the corridor, he couldn't work out which one it was. Then, after thinking about it, he wondered if his ears were playing tricks on him.

He opened one of the old-fashioned boarded doors and peered inside but found nothing but a double bed and some furniture. It was a guest room, and counting the five doors, he wondered if they all served the same purpose.

He continued down the corridor slowly, as he imagined Gabriel had done on the night of the party. The corridors in the house were like a maze; eventually, he found a bathroom.

He guessed this was the one Freya had died in, as it was near the guest bedrooms, but he wasn't completely sure. There wasn't a bathtub, only a walk-in shower. A sink stood next to the toilet, and Henry caught his puzzled reflection in its mirror as he turned around, wondering if this was the right place.

He headed back into the corridor and noticed the wall outside it was curved, almost like the old wooden beams inside had warped and nearly protruded out of the plaster. The other walls were all normal, which made him wonder if this wall had been water-damaged.

Spotting a white-and-black clock on the wall opposite the bathroom, he saw time was getting ahead of him and continued towards the front of the house, hoping he would find Thomas's room.

And then he heard talking.

He stopped outside a half-closed door and listened.

A man was talking to someone on the phone. "Yeah. I'll get a couple."

There was silence.

"Yeah, two," replied the man. "How much will that be?"

The man huffed at what he heard. "Three grand for two?!"

The man went quiet again.

"Alright, make it two and a half. Anyway, I'm not paying; knobhead is. So, I'm not fussed either way."

The man shared a laugh with whomever he was talking to.

Henry guessed the 'knobhead' being referred to was Thomas Wentworth-Scott, and that the man talking was Vince.

Vince continued, "Yeah, never you mind what I have hanging over him. That's between him and me. Right, nice one, mate. Talk later."

Henry froze in the corridor as he heard footsteps approach the door.

Vince then closed it and remained within the room.

After a few moments, dance music played loudly inside. It was the electronic stuff that Henry thought sounded like pots and pans being hit with spoons.

Henry let out the breath he'd been holding in, grateful Vince hadn't caught him sneaking around the house.

He crept past Vince's door while the music blasted inside, and then came to the room opposite.

The door hung open. Inside was a double bed, its dark brown sheets unmade. Clothes were strewn on the floor. Against the far wall was an expensive computer linked up to three screens.

Henry stepped inside what he reckoned was Thomas's room and looked around. The walls were bare and painted white. A strong smell of aftershave hung in the air, and Henry noticed a door leading to an en suite in the corner.

He avoided the clothes on the carpet while he walked around, trying to picture Freya, Thomas, and Gabriel being in here on the night of the party. He guessed they'd have been near the unmade bed, as the computer desk only had one seat.

Gabriel had said he'd been snorting cocaine in here with Thomas and Freya; and then later, he heard them in the bathroom further down the hall.

What had brought Freya over there? Henry wondered. It was a fair trek away, he now realised. Plus, there was a perfectly good en suite in Thomas's bedroom.

Henry went to check it. It had a large white bathtub, which looked dated. In fact, the dark emerald tiles on the walls were faded. This room obviously hadn't been redone in the recent renovation. Henry wondered if Thomas's room had either.

The bathroom down the corridor must have had a tub in it at some point, Henry thought. He suspected the Wentworth-Scotts had it ripped out recently.

But how did Freya end up in there?

Just like everything else in this case, nothing made sense.

"Who the fuck are you?"

Henry spun around to find a man in his late twenties with a shaved head, standing in the doorway – glaring at him.

Henry was shocked at first, as Vince had made him jump, but he quickly regained his composure.

The young man wore a bright red and yellow Hawaiian shirt with white trousers. He was quite short but appeared to be in good shape. His left ear was pierced, and a tribal tattoo ran up his neck past the collar.

He eyeballed Henry – his fists clenched like he was readying for a fight.

"Hello," Henry said, with as much authority as he could muster; the kind he'd used to get serial killers to crack under questioning. "I'm former Detective Chief Inspector Ward."

The steeliness in Vince's eyes slipped away, and panic seeped in. "Why are you here?"

"That's between me and Mr Wentworth-Scott and his family." Henry let his words settle in Vince's mind; then he asked, "Who are you?"

Vince swallowed hard. "I'm a mate of Tommy's." He had a rough Leeds accent, and as Henry looked at the tattoo on his pallid skin, he suspected he had spent time at His Majesty's pleasure.

"Ah, right? Vince, is it?"

Vince nodded and then frowned an instant as if realising something. "How long have you been here?"

Henry wasn't sure which approach he should follow, but thought to hell with it, and went with the riskiest one. It had been a long day, after all.

"I've been here long enough to have heard your drug deal," Henry said.

Vince's eyes widened in alarm, then he controlled himself. "I don't know what you're on about."

"Oh, really?" said Henry. "You don't know what I'm talking about? I must be imagining things in my old age. It's just that, when I was walking past your room just now, I'm pretty sure I heard you discussing something."

Vince clenched his jaw muscles.

"But maybe I misheard?" Henry added.

Vince latched onto this. "Aye. You did. I wasn't talking about anything."

"Good."

The tension in Vince's face dissipated as he realised Henry wouldn't do anything about the conversation he'd overheard, but he was still clearly on edge. "What are you doing here?" he asked.

"Were you friends with Thomas three years ago?"

"What's that got to do with you?"

"A possible murder."

Vince's eyes widened. "I don't think I knew him then."

"You don't think? Can't you be sure?"

"What is this?" He lost his temper. "Do I need a lawyer or summat? I'm only walking around my own fucking house."

"*Your* house?"

Vince didn't catch the question. He was too wrapped up in his frustration.

"Listen," Henry said, trying to calm him down. He'd realised he was alone in the house with a potential criminal after all. "I'm working for the family, and they want something investigating."

Vince's frustration didn't die down, but he held his tongue. The mention of 'the family' seemed to hold sway with him.

"Have you ever heard Thomas talk about a woman being found dead in this house?"

Vince shook his head. His mouth was set in a grimace. He seemingly had the 'I'm not a rat' mentality.

Henry decided to end their discussion, but before he did, he asked, "And it's Vince…?"

"You what?"

"What's your last name?"

"Why? You going to go check up on me?"

Henry didn't see the point in lying. "Is there much to check up on?"

Vince clenched his fists. "Fucking pigs. You're all the same."

Henry chuckled at hearing that. If he had a pound for every time…

"I've been in trouble, aye," Vince felt compelled to say. "Is that what you want to know? But I'm clean now. I'm out of trouble."

"Clean? I just heard you organise a considerable drug deal."

"Considerable?" Vince asked. "Whatever. You've no proof I said anything, so why don't you stop snooping around here and sod off?"

Henry didn't see the point of saying anything else and waited for him to go. And he did after a few moments, slinking off back to his room.

Henry made a mental note to ask Barnes about him, because he suspected there was a lot to know.

Chapter Thirteen

It was after 6 p.m. when Henry left Thomas Wentworth-Scott's farmhouse. He didn't see Vince again but heard his music thump through the property.

Henry was driving down the narrow country lanes he'd driven up earlier. The breeze rustled the clumps of dry grass covering the plateau and blasted through his open windows. He was high above Otley on the wild hills, heading to the road that would take him down the Chevin.

The sun was low in the sky, and Henry was back wearing the sunglasses he'd found. A large greasy thumbprint was on the right lens, which annoyed him, as he couldn't scrub it off.

He spotted an old marine blue Land Rover parked ahead on the road. It was positioned next to a drystone wall, but still blocked the entire lane.

Henry slowed down, knowing he wouldn't be able to pass it easily. He stopped just as a blonde woman in her forties walked around from the front.

She smiled at him, waving.

What the bloody hell, Henry thought. He pulled up the handbrake and leant out of his open window.

The woman bent down, sticking her face close to his. Her long hair was tied back, and she wore a dark-green gilet over a yellow top. She looked to have been in the fields all day and had straw and grass in her hair. Her brow was wet, and her skin red from the sun.

"Sorry, do you know anything about Land Rover cars?" she asked, breathlessly.

Henry shook his head. "I know next to nothing about cars, and even less about Land Rovers."

She huffed. "Shame."

"Although, I came across one earlier around here, which nearly ran into me."

She winced. "Ah. Right. A black one?"

Henry nodded. "You know it?"

She coughed as if she were embarrassed.

Henry noticed her Land Rover's bonnet was up and smoke rose from its engine. "It's broken down?"

She nodded. "I can normally get it started." She looked down at her hands, which were slick with engine oil.

"I can give you a lift?"

She waved off his suggestion with a shake of her head. "It's alright, thanks. I don't live far." She bit her lower lip. "It's just the eggs," she said. Another idea struck her, and she squinted in the direction Henry had come. "Have you been at the farmhouse down there?"

"If you can call it a farmhouse," said Henry, realising she was talking about Thomas's house. "Aye, I have."

"Ah." Her blonde eyebrows lifted in recognition. "Are you the old detective?"

Henry couldn't hide his puzzlement. "Erm… Perhaps? Who's asking?"

"Oh, sorry," she said, instinctively offering a dirty hand for him to shake. "I'm the sister."

"Sister?" Henry's brain stepped up a gear to work out whom he was talking to. "Ah. Charlotte, is it?" He shook her hand.

"You've heard about me?" Charlotte Wentworth-Scott looked impressed.

"I heard you live around here."

"Oh, is that all there is to know about me?"

"I'm sure not," Henry said, noticing he'd probably said it with too much charm in his voice.

Charlotte didn't seem to mind. "Please, call me Lottie. How did you get on with my brother?"

"Erm…" Henry's brain went into a higher speed as he thought of an acceptable answer. "He's a character."

She sighed, which expressed thirty years' worth of exasperation with her sibling. "You could say that. Though I have other words to call him."

Henry noticed bright-blue trays piled high on her back seats, and recalled her mentioning eggs. "Erm, is your car full of eggs?"

She glanced at her clapped-out Land Rover. "Yes. Is that a problem?" Her faux-serious face cracked into a smile. "I keep hens in some huts in a field down there." She gestured towards Thomas's farmhouse. "It's all above board, Detective. I assure you. Well, a fox did get in the other week and took five."

"Ah. That's a shame."

"Don't worry. I won't be hiring you to look into that mystery. I already figured out the cause was a faulty electric fence."

"Very good," Henry said, chuckling. "Listen, shall I give you and your eggs a lift somewhere?"

She huffed and turned to her car. "I don't want to put you out, but Simon, my husband, won't be back until late. He set off a bit ago to the Lakes to discuss sheep."

Henry wondered what a discussion about sheep in the Lake District could entail. Then he noted she said her husband had set off recently. "It's not your husband who's got a black Land Rover, by any chance?"

"Yes," she said as if expecting the complaint to follow.

"Are you aware your husband drives like an idiot?"

She gave him a simpering look. "I've heard it said, yes. Why? What has he done?"

"A black Land Rover sped around a blind corner and nearly knocked me off the road."

She winced, and Henry got the impression she was used to apologising for her husband's driving. "He's lived around the area his whole life and knows all the lanes really well, so he thinks he can drive around them quickly."

"Quickly? He wasn't going quickly. He was speeding." Henry then grunted, realising it wasn't her fault her husband drove like a madman. "Anyway, do you want a lift?"

She shrugged as though she was giving into events, and peered at the back seats in Henry's car. "You should have space. There aren't that many boxes."

Henry noticed the stacks of them in the back of her Land Rover and wondered what she considered a large amount to be.

He helped her transfer the trays into the back of his Skoda. She insisted on sitting in the back with them to make sure they didn't topple over.

Henry carefully manoeuvred his Skoda around the broken-down Land Rover, and they headed off down the lane.

After a few moments, Lottie said, "Ah. I didn't even say where I lived. Just follow this lane, and then take the second turning on your right."

Henry felt like her chauffeur as he nodded at her instructions. He took the opportunity to ask, "Have you lived around here for long?"

"Oh, all my life. I got together with Simon when I was sixteen, which drove Mum mad as he was the son of a local farmer. And we got married when we were eighteen, which made her apoplectic. She still hasn't forgiven me." She chuckled as if her mother's fury brought her joy.

"I'm not surprised she was annoyed, considering how he drives," Henry said, half-joking. "And do you have children?" he asked.

"Twins. They're twelve. Two boys. You know, I wouldn't mind if they decided to hang around here all their lives. In fact, I want one of them to take over the farm when the inevitable arrives, but I don't think they will. Tim is into computers and has no interest in the outdoors at all. And Sam, my other one, hates it around here."

Henry noted the disappointment in her voice. "So, you must be aware of what your family has asked me to investigate," he said. "What can you tell me about that death three years ago?" He peered at her in his rear-view mirror as she took in a deep breath.

"Well, I was flabbergasted when I found out," she said. "Especially considering it happened during a lockdown when no one was supposed to leave their homes, and… my idiot brother goes and has a party."

"Can you remember anything of that night?"

The Skoda drove over a pothole, and the subsequent bump caused one of the egg trays to slip. Lottie grabbed it and put it back in place.

"Listen, if it's alright with you, would you mind asking me the questions when we get to the farm? I can make us a cup of tea, and we can have a chat then."

"Yes, sure," Henry said, spotting her apprehensive expression in the mirror.

"It's this one," she said.

Henry turned right, drove over a cattle grid, and then down a gravel driveway.

"Let me get these eggs put away, and then I'll tell you what you need to know."

"Alright. That's a deal."

He parked in a large farmyard surrounded by old limestone buildings. There was a large barn with huge doors, and Henry spotted tractors and farming equipment inside.

He parked up next to another old Land Rover, and Lottie opened the door. "I'll just get these inside," she said.

She took out the trays by herself, rejecting Henry's offer of help, and rushed them into one of the small outbuildings.

A Border collie sat lazily in the sun nearby and got up to investigate Henry when he stepped out of the car.

After two trips, Lottie returned to the Skoda and said, "Let's get that tea."

The kitchen was pretty much as Henry had expected after observing the whitewashed farmhouse from outside. The stone floor and walls looked like they hadn't been changed in a century. There was an old-fashioned cream-coloured Aga range cooker. In the centre of the room was a long dining table covered in magazines, folders, empty egg trays, and seed packets.

Henry took a seat on a wooden bench at the table. A loaf of homemade white bread was on a cutting board in the middle, sitting next to a large bread knife that had an ornately carved handle.

Lottie spotted Henry inspecting it closely. "Ah. Simon carved that. One of his hobbies, when he has time," she said.

She turned on the kettle and, while it was boiling water, took an old biscuit tin from the side and placed it in front of Henry.

"Take one," she said, as she lifted the lid to reveal some homemade ginger biscuits.

Henry took one and bit into it. The sugary taste took him back to his grandmother, who used to make similar biscuits when he visited her house in Bradford fifty years ago.

She plonked a handmade mug of strong tea in front of him and took a seat opposite at the table. Her dark-green gilet was off, and she wore only her yellow top. She wafted air into her face. "Oh. It's been a hot day."

"How do you cope in the summer?" Henry asked, taking another biscuit.

"I struggle, usually. Though, I'm normally more tanned than those who go off on holiday."

"Do you manage to get away yourself?"

She scoffed. "A farmer's wife? Get away on holiday in the summer?" She shook her head like the idea was crazy.

Henry noted there could be another reason she didn't go away, which remained unsaid.

"Alright," he said, sipping his tea. "So, if we may get down to business. What can you tell me about that night?"

Her shoulders sagged. "Can I just sit for a moment first? I'm not normally a telltale."

"It's alright."

She huffed. What she was going to say was difficult for her, and she was building herself up to it. "It's just. Well..."

"What?"

She tapped her own mug of tea with her fingernails as if hoping it'd give her strength to speak. She gave up when she realised it didn't.

"What do you want to tell me, Lottie?" Henry asked.

She scrunched up her lips. "That night... I heard the party."

"You heard it? Isn't his house a good half a mile away?"

She shook her head. "Only if you follow the lane. But in reality, Thomas is only two fields away. Besides, it was the lockdown and a hot night. I heard his bloody music through my open windows."

"Right. What did you do?"

"Well, I was furious. Mum bloody dotes on him, but I had enough of him years ago. He's a complete pain in the arse. As selfish as you like. Anyway, I have a quad bike–"

"You went over there?"

She nodded. "I did."

"Okay?"

She exhaled again. "I got there, and people were standing outside, music was blaring, and that horrid cretin was there."

Henry frowned. "Who's that?"

"The little skinhead who's latched onto my brother. And by the way, Thomas is too stupid to realise he's being used."

"Right," Henry said. He put calling Barnes for information on this Vince on the top of his to-do list. Especially when the little twerp had lied to him about knowing Thomas in 2020.

"So, I told Vince to stop the racket, and he just..." She waved her hand in the air as if he was of no concern. "I found Thomas inside, out of his mind on all sorts, and he told me 'it was fine', and to 'stay and have some fun'." She shook her head, stewing over her brother's stupidity.

"What time was this?"

"Well, it was…" She paused to think. "Must have been after three in the morning."

"And what happened then?"

"I saw that odious Gabriel." Her repulsed expression told Henry all she thought of him. "He even tried to chat me up. Anyway, I got into the house, and someone said that Thomas wanted me."

"Who told you?"

She shrugged. "I don't know. Someone. I went inside, walked around, couldn't find him. So, I went to his room, which was empty… I found drugs and all sorts in there."

She lowered her head into her hand a moment and took a deep breath. She then looked up at Henry as if discovering the courage to carry on.

"And then I saw the weirdest thing in the corridor. Two men were carrying a young woman. Her eyes were closed, and immediately, I thought she was unwell."

"Who were the men?"

"One was that little skinhead."

Henry sucked in a breath.

"The other…" Her eyes fell on the biscuit tin between them. "I couldn't work out who it was."

"Why?"

"I… didn't see his face."

Henry remembered being in the old hallway near the bathroom earlier that day. There was a bend, so it wouldn't be easy to see a man's face, especially if he had his back to her.

But Henry suspected she knew who she'd seen but didn't want to say.

"Where were they?"

"In the corridor, heading to the guest bathroom."

"Did you speak to them?"

"Yes. I told them to get off her, as, seeing the drugs in Tom's room, I assumed the worse."

"What would that be?"

"Well, she'd overdosed or they'd drugged her to… you know."

"Sexually assault her?"

She nodded. "But they said she was fine," she continued. "I argued with them. Thomas came to me and was annoyed I was there. I argued with him, by which time the other two had already walked off with her."

"Do you know who the girl was?"

"Well, I'm pretty sure it was the girl who died. It was Freya Harrison."

Chapter Fourteen

Henry sipped strong tea from his oddly shaped mug. It was still hot, and he wished he'd asked for a glass of cordial. He was feeling the heat inside Lottie's farmhouse kitchen, despite its thick stone walls.

There was a small window that looked out onto the farmyard, which was open. The evening's sun shone through, brightening up the old net curtain that covered it.

Lottie sipped her tea as she stared at the wooden table between them. She scratched a red insect bite on her upper arm, lost in her thoughts.

Eventually, she spoke. "I wish I'd done more. Taken her off them, or…" She shook her head.

"When did you leave the party?"

"I argued with Thomas, called him a… an unpleasant word. He got stroppy and told me to go, and I did. I was too angry to think about the girl. It was only the following day when I learnt someone had died that I remembered…" She exhaled. "I've hated myself since."

Henry took another sip of his tea, and then decided it was making him feel too warm, so he pushed it to one side. "Did you tell the police about this?" he asked.

"I was never asked."

"They never spoke to you?"

She answered with a shake of the head.

"But you could've told them."

"Yes. But I didn't know all the facts."

"You saw suspicious activity, and then the girl was found dead in a bath."

The mask of self-composure that Lottie was wearing slipped, and Henry could see she was beside herself. "I know. I know," she said. "What can I say? I should've said something."

Henry took some pity on her. Hargreaves and the other detectives hadn't bothered to speak to her, and she obviously hadn't had the bottle to volunteer the information to them, fearing repercussions on her brother.

"What do you think happened to her?" he asked.

"The girl?" Her eyes widened as she considered the question. It was as if she'd never given it any thought. "Well, she was found in the bath, wasn't she?"

Henry gave a curt nod.

"They probably…" She winced and couldn't bring herself to say another word. "I do really feel awful about not saying anything."

"You've told me now. At least."

She stared at him. "And what will you do with it?"

"Well, it definitely changes things. If Freya was moved down the hallway…" Henry's voice trailed off as he worked out what it meant.

If Freya had been unconscious and was carried into the guest bathroom by Vince and someone else, how had Gabriel heard Thomas argue with her inside it earlier that night?

Again, the more Henry found out about this case, the less it made sense.

"I don't know, to be honest," he said.

Lottie leant across the table as if she were about to say something secret. "I mean… you are discreet, aren't you?"

"Come again?"

"You're on our side? The family's. We can trust you?" Her eyes searched his, pleadingly.

"Well. Your mother believes she's hired me to confirm the coroner's statement."

"That was all bollocks, clearly."

Henry narrowed his eyes as he looked at her. "Why do you ask if I can be trusted?"

At his question, she leant back and paused. "I…"

"Do you want your family protected, or do you want someone to find out what really happened that night?"

She bit her lower lip.

"I…" she said after a moment. "I think I want to know what happened to her, and just hope to God that he–"

"Your brother?"

She looked at him knowingly. "I mean. If it turned out that he was involved – God forbid – would you make sure he was protected?"

"I don't protect people, Lottie. Not ones who are involved in murder." He leant on the table. "Did you know Freya was an only child?"

Lottie shook her head with an expression that said, 'how would I?'

Henry continued, "Her father was suffering from cancer when she died. He spent the rest of his few years mourning the loss of his daughter, never knowing what really happened to her. All he was given were the 'lies' in the coroner's report."

Lottie was staring at him. Her eyes welled up.

"Her mother, after losing her husband, is now alone and has had some kind of breakdown. That's three lives that have been destroyed by all of this nonsense. Three." Henry frowned. "And you want me to protect the people who did it?"

Lottie didn't move. A tear trickled down her cheek. She wiped it away and stood up. "No, Detective Ward. You're quite right."

She stared out the window, which Henry reckoned faced the direction of her brother's farmhouse. "I just hope he didn't do anything stupid that night."

"Stupid as in murdering someone?"

Lottie didn't answer.

* * *

Henry headed off back to Addingham after driving out of Lottie's farmyard. He made sure to avoid running over the Border collie that sprawled out on the gravel, enjoying the pleasant evening.

The sun was low in the sky, and then disappeared as Henry drove under the tree cover on the Chevin. Splashes of deep orange rays hit his car, slipping between the gaps in the canopy.

It was 7.30 p.m., and Henry needed to head home and have dinner. The leafy salad he'd picked at earlier in the day wasn't enough to fuel him for a case like this. However, thinking through the contents of his fridge, he realised he'd have to stop off in Ilkley and do some shopping – unless he wanted to eat two near-rotten eggs and an out-of-date yogurt, a situation that wasn't unheard of.

He called Barnes while waiting at a temporary traffic light near Burley in Wharfedale. He put the call on speakerphone.

"Can you talk?" he asked, when Barnes answered.

"Would I have picked up if I couldn't?" she asked.

Henry doubted she would have. She normally left his calls unanswered.

"Listen, it's this case I'm doing."

"Oh yeah. I forgot you're a private investigator for the well-to-do these days."

"It's only temporary," Henry said, feeling more than sure of himself. He had nearly had it with these posh types and their secrets and lies and wishes of protection.

"I had a second earlier and looked at the case notes of that suicide for you. Hargreaves was the lead detective," Barnes said.

"Right. And I suspect she had some steering from Murphy."

"Steering? What do you mean?"

Henry grunted. He wasn't sure how much of his suspicion he wanted to share. And if he did decide to enlighten Barnes, he wouldn't do it over the phone. "Doesn't matter."

Barnes wasn't to be fobbed off easily. "What do you mean?"

Henry huffed. The traffic started moving in front of him, and he followed it. "There are many irregularities in this case, and not just how the police handled it."

She sighed wearily. "What have you found out?" she asked, sounding like she didn't really want to know.

"Enough for me to think there are too many irregularities to have happened by chance," Henry said, trying to remain vague.

"What does it mean, exactly? Are we talking fuck-ups or something else?"

"More 'something else', if you ask me." He cleared his throat. "Perhaps we'd better discuss that in person, though."

She exhaled again. "To be fair, I've got so much on at the minute, I'm not sure I can deal with anything else."

"Alright. Well, maybe I should pass on my findings to the Independent Police Complaints Commission?"

"You mean the IOPC? I doubt they'd do much, either," she said. "Anyway, don't you have experience with them? Weren't they the ones that investigated you several years back?"

Henry ruffled at the jibe. "No. I had the PSD." The police's Professional Standards Department was as joyless as their name suggested.

Henry changed the topic. "Here, have you ever come across a lad called Vince?"

"A lad called Vince?" she repeated. "Vince who? Vaughn? Cable?"

"I don't have a surname. But he's a skinhead, must've done some time, going by the look of him. And he's a drug dealer."

"No. I haven't come across a drug dealer called Vince. Well, I can't categorically say I haven't. I don't necessarily remember the names of everyone I come into contact with."

"Oh. That's not how a detective should operate."

Her mood changed. "Is there anything else? I am at my desk and should be doing some real police work."

"Ah. You're at your desk? So could you do a search for this Vince?"

"You want me to search the Police National Computer for someone called Vince? There might be thousands of them."

"Yeah. But you sound like you're looking for something interesting to do."

She huffed down the phone. "Trawling through the mugshots of skinheads isn't my idea of a fun evening. I'd rather go on Tinder."

"What's Tinder?" Henry asked.

"Never you mind."

"So, you won't look?"

"Get me a surname. As per usual."

Henry slowed the car as he came to some more roadworks. "I'll try. Have you asked Hargreaves about this case?"

"No. Why?"

"I think she missed a few things. Well, not a few. A lot. And it might come back and bite her on the arse."

"Are these some of the 'irregularities' you mentioned?"
"Aye."
"I'm not sure detectives like having old farts find stuff they missed."
"I know. I wouldn't like it either, to be fair. But when you really mess up a case through incompetence or design, and people get away with murder, questions must be raised."
"Shit. Is that what you're finding? You think that Hargreaves and… others… withheld evidence?"
"I can't say they did something as specific as that. But what I can say is that they missed lines of inquiry and did a shoddy job. Consequently, a young woman's murder wasn't properly investigated."
"Murder? I thought it was a suicide."
Henry scoffed and shook his head. "After what I've learnt so far, I'm pretty certain Freya Harrison didn't kill herself. And that the people involved in her murder were at that party. I just don't know who they are yet."
"Right. Well, good luck trying to prove all that."
Henry chuckled. "I'll need more than bloody luck. A miracle more like."

Chapter Fifteen

Henry placed the bag-for-life on his white kitchen tiles and opened the back door for Tessa, who was sitting in front of it, barking as if annoyed it wasn't already open. She rushed out as soon as there was enough space and ran into the backyard to sniff the plant pots.
The sun was dying off in the west, and the heat outside was dissipating; but inside, the house was hot and humid.
Henry opened the fridge and felt some relief as the cold air clouded around his face and hands. He put the

shopping away, taking longer than usual, and worked out what he should make for dinner.

Despite buying nearly a week's worth of food, he had little appetite and didn't have the energy or inclination to prepare anything.

He'd been on the go since that morning, when he walked a few miles on Otley Chevin, and then he'd met Mrs Wentworth-Scott for lunch and spent the rest of the day on this blasted case.

Maybe he should have listened to Mrs Whitehead when she scolded him for getting involved? Well, his hips were fine at the moment. It was just him. He felt tired yet overexcited.

He slumped down at the kitchen table and wondered about having one of the Scotch eggs he'd bought with a bit of brown sauce. He should have some greens as well, really. That's what his doctor had said, wasn't it? To watch his weight and eat well. But he didn't fancy making any salad or anything.

Many years earlier, on days like this, he'd be sitting in a beer garden, drinking as many pints as his gut could handle. Which he'd worked out over the years was around ten. That was the maximum. When he was being sensible, he'd stick to three. But when that urge got hold of him, and he lost control of his senses, he could easily reach ten or more.

Unfortunately for Henry, that urge had taken over him for years on end. He couldn't really remember how many. They had just become a chunk of his life. All he could recall of that period were blurry images of sitting in a pub, thinking he was having the time of his life; and his ex-wife Pat's disappointed face as he stumbled back home, pissed out of his tree.

Those years stretched over the police's Professional Standards Department investigation into him, to his almost-forced resignation from the police, and his divorce from Pat. If he hadn't come to his senses, he'd be still drinking like that now. Pouring pint after pint down his throat to fill up that thirst he could never quench.

Despite the shame he felt at remembering those horrid years, he still fancied sitting outside the pub across the road and having a few.

There's nothing better on a hot day than an ice-cold beer, a voice told him.

The knock on the front door stirred him out of his thoughts, and as he staggered to answer it, a part of him was grateful. He knew deep down, he wouldn't be able to fight that urge for long. He'd have given into temptation at some point.

Robbie Whitehead stood on his doorstep. The lad had grown older over the past year. His dark hair had been cut shorter, and Henry hoped it wasn't a consequence of the head injury he sustained the previous summer.

The lad had grown designer stubble that didn't quite cover his face. His pale complexion suggested he still spent too much time inside. Probably staring at screens, Henry thought.

"Robbie, it's nice to see you in the flesh."

The young lad smiled. "Aye. Gran's cooking dinner and said to knock on to see if you wanted to join us."

"Oh." Henry glanced into his living room as if he had other plans besides eating a Scotch egg and trying not to let himself drink.

"She said you're on some case again, is that true?" Robbie asked. The barely controlled excitement in his voice betrayed him, and Henry sussed this was his main reason for coming round.

"Aye. I am. But you're not getting involved. Your gran warned me off this afternoon, after she nearly killed me for accepting the case in the first place."

Robbie smiled as if he already knew that. "She said she'd murder me if I helped. But I don't think she will."

Henry grunted as if he wasn't sure about that. "Right, well. When are you having dinner?"

"In ten minutes. It's salmon quiche. She baked it."

The idea of it made Henry's stomach rumble. "Excellent. I'll just get the dog in, and then I'll come round."

Robbie nodded and headed off through his front gate.

Henry got Tessa back inside, which she was very upset about as she'd been slumped against the large potted fern, keeping cool. He then went around and knocked on Jean's front door. Robbie answered and welcomed him in.

The kitchen table had been prepared for three. A blue tablecloth had been laid, and the dishes were the fancy kind that Jean rarely used.

The patio doors were open, allowing a cool breeze to blow into the warm kitchen.

Jean's backyard was more stylish than Henry's but had the same basic layout. Some fairy lights hung around the top of the high fences. The plant pots were more colourful, and she had two fancy lawn chairs that appeared expensive.

Her grey cat was lying on its back in a corner, eyeing Henry with suspicion.

"Sit here," Robbie said, pointing to a seat at the head of the kitchen table.

Jean took the quiche from the worktop, which had been cooling, and placed it on the table next to a large bowl of green-leaf salad.

"Want a drink?" she asked.

Henry spotted she had a glass of white wine next to her empty plate, and Robbie took a bottle of beer out of the fridge and offered it to him.

The urge from earlier rushed back, and Henry felt his hand reach out for the cold bottle.

Robbie handed it to him, and the cold droplets ran down Henry's fingers as he held it. Then his senses came back to him, and he shook his head.

"Actually, have you got some Coke or lemonade?"

Robbie frowned as Henry handed the bottle back to him but said, "Yeah, sure. We've got Coke Zero."

"That'll do," Henry said.

He caught Jean looking at him as if she was half-remembering something about him.

Henry changed the subject. "So, have you been enjoying the weather?"

Jean took a seat opposite him at the kitchen table and sipped her wine. "I've enjoyed it more than you have. What with you travelling about the place for that lot? Especially in your state."

Henry hoped he hadn't just walked into an hour-long bollocking. "Well, it's been nice to get out a bit."

Jean groaned and then sliced the thick quiche. Chunks of baked salmon lined its surface, and the smell was making Henry feel hungrier.

"What have you been doing?" Henry asked Robbie, who was pouring Henry his Coke.

"The drone went two hundred and fifty metres, which isn't bad. And for most of it, I was inside, just using its camera."

Henry took the glass offered to him and thanked Robbie. "Well, I bet the local birds loved meeting their new robotic overlord."

Robbie sat down and drank from his own bottle of beer. "I don't think they were that upset," he said. "And I think I spotted a hawk near the bypass."

"Aye. We get some of them around here. You want to get that thing up to Otley. Red kites fly around there."

"Yeah. I was thinking about that."

"However, I'm sure they'd destroy your little drone in short order."

"You think?" Robbie asked as if latching onto a new challenge.

Jean passed around the plates with salad and quiche and took a seat. "So, how is it going with that lot?"

"Do you mean the Wentworth-Scotts?" Henry knew who she was referring to but felt like winding her up.

She pouted. "Who do you think?"

"It's going fine." He chewed a mouthful of quiche, which was some of the best quiche he'd had, and then corrected himself. "Well, I wouldn't say it's fine. It's a bit complicated." Not wanting to go further, he stopped there.

"Complicated? Why am I not surprised? Are you saying they did it, then?" she asked.

Henry glanced at Robbie, wondering if the lad should be listening, but he was waiting for his reply.

Henry sipped his Coke, and its bubbles clogged up the back of his throat. "I don't know yet who did it. But I do think the original verdict of suicide was wrong."

Jean shook her head, wobbling her blonde wavy hair. "I bloody knew it. You can't trust that lot. They're always up to something."

"Hmm. I can't say for certain that any of them did it. All I can say is that the lass didn't die by her own hand."

Jean chewed on some rocket leaves. "What is it all about, anyway? I don't think you told me. What lass are you talking about?"

Henry glanced at Robbie and then gave Jean an expression that suggested they should talk about it later.

Jean waved her hand in the air and then picked up her glass of wine. "He's eighteen now, so he can listen."

Henry sighed and ate more quiche. After an awkward silence while he chewed, he said, "There was a young woman, Freya Harrison, who was found dead after a party at Thomas Wentworth-Scott's house."

"How did she die?"

"The coroner's verdict was suicide. She'd drowned in a bath."

"Is that even possible?" Robbie asked, frowning as he tried to imagine it.

"Not unless you've been sedated beforehand, no."

Jean cut up salad on her plate. "So, a young woman drowns in a bathtub at a party, the coroner rules it's suicide, and then the son's accused of her murder several years later? Is that it?"

"Pretty much."

"But you're finding out that it's got nothing to do with suicide, and it looks like things have been hushed up?"

"Aye," Henry said, taking a break from eating to sip some Coke.

Jean shook her head and then dropped her cutlery on her plate with a clang. "It's the bloody Freemasons!"

"Freemasons?" Robbie asked as if he'd heard a word he didn't understand.

Henry intervened. "Jean, we can't just assume things like that."

"Yes, we can. Peter was in it for years before he passed." She sipped her wine, looking peeved that her husband had been involved in such an organisation. "Mr Wentworth-Scott was a member; that's how he and Peter met. I bet a lot of senior police officers are in it, too. Possibly even the bloody coroner himself."

Henry kept his eyes on his plate. He didn't want to think about secret organisations, such as the Freemasons, and their possible interference with a criminal investigation. That way lies madness, he thought, for he'd never get people to go on record to confirm anything, and he'd never be able to find any corroborating evidence.

"Are you talking about cults? Grandad was in a cult?" Robbie asked. He'd taken out his phone and had just done a quick search on the internet. "Are they like the KKK?"

"Jesus!" Henry said. "The Freemasons are nothing like the Ku Klux Klan, Robbie."

"Oh. I see," Jean said, as though she'd just worked something out. "Were *you* a member?"

"Of the Masons?" Henry had to ask, to make sure he was hearing her right. "I've never been a member."

The anger in Jean's eyes subsided slowly. "Are you sure?"

"Very."

Robbie left his phone on the table and quietly ate his dinner. Henry continued to eat but was almost too riled up to. He had been approached to join the Freemasons back in the 1980s. A senior detective had taken a shining to him and, back then, it'd been a sure-fire way to get ahead in the police. If you wanted to climb up the ranks, you had to join.

But then things changed after the Yorkshire Ripper was caught and the police's mishandling of that case came to light. The senior officers' incompetence and arrogance, and the way they covered for each other, made joining a secret society look seedy and self-serving.

Besides, Henry was too much of a contrarian to join a club like that. He was too independent. He needed the freedom to do things how he saw fit, not as dictated to him. Perhaps that was why he eventually fell out of the police. Perhaps he was never meant to stay.

That made him suddenly question if he should rejoin.

"So, if this woman didn't drown in the bath, how did she die?" Robbie asked. He must have spent the past few quiet moments trying to work it out.

Jean was eating her dinner quietly. The rage that had been building in her had apparently died off. She listened to Henry with mild interest.

"Well, I don't know at the moment," Henry said.

"Have you got any leads?" Robbie asked.

"Well, there's the accuser who said he heard an argument between Thomas Wentworth-Scott and the victim at around one in the morning. The sister, Lottie, saw the victim get carried down the corridor around three."

Jean lifted her head. "Oh. You spoke to Charlotte? She's nice, isn't she? The only sane one."

"Aye. What's her story? She told me she married a farmer?"

Jean nodded as she chewed her final bite. "She met him when she was young; just out of school, I think. He was the same age and was looking to take on the farm as his dad wasn't well."

"Does she get on with her family?"

"Charlotte?" Jean asked as if Henry had just told a joke. "Heavens, no! They disowned her."

"Come again?"

"The mother, the bitch that she is… sorry, Robbie."

Robbie's eyes widened at hearing his gran swear.

"She disowned Charlotte. She wanted her to go to university, get an education, and meet someone else, but Charlotte didn't have any of it. The mother said she didn't agree to the marriage, so she took away all the support, all the money, everything. Left Charlotte with nothing. Luckily, the farmer she married turned out alright, and is fairly successful – as farmers go."

Henry recalled the old farmhouse and remembered hearing Lottie laugh at the idea of taking a summer holiday. He thought she'd be too busy, as she said. He hadn't thought she didn't have enough money to go anywhere.

"So, you wouldn't say she had a good relationship with her family?" Henry asked.

"What do you think?" Jean said. "She has to put up living next to her rich idiot brother while she has to scrimp and save."

Henry was lost in his thoughts for a moment. "I suppose you could say she's an unreliable witness?" he asked.

Jean finished her glass of wine and then shrugged. "It depends. She might be telling the truth, but she definitely does have a grudge against her family. And I can't blame her."

Chapter Sixteen

The morning was muggy. Grey clouds blanketed the sky, and as Henry let Tessa out into the backyard, a cool breeze blew, rustling his thin black dressing gown.

He returned to the kitchen, where he'd just started the kettle. As it boiled water, he fished out the cafetière from the cupboard and found some old ground coffee in the fridge.

Thankfully, he hadn't drunk the previous night. He had been tempted, but thought better of it, and he was grateful as he had this blasted case to sort out. It was Tuesday morning, and he had to give his final report to the Wentworth-Scotts' solicitor the following afternoon.

After returning home from Jean's last night – where they'd discussed the case further and then talked about Robbie's future plans, which had involved AI – Henry had started writing up his notes. He'd found a large sheet of A3 paper that he'd taken from somewhere; probably one of the old police stations, he thought.

He didn't have to look at his notes to know the two accounts he'd received from Gabriel and Lottie didn't match. The timings were wrong for a start. Gabriel said he'd heard Thomas and Freya argue or make love in the guest bathroom at 1 a.m., while Lottie said she saw Freya being carried down the corridor by Vince and someone else at 3 a.m. Both could be true, but Henry doubted they were without being able to articulate why.

He also wanted to speak to the GP who had been at the party. She had unofficially pronounced Freya's death to the partygoers but had disappeared before the authorities had arrived. Not the normal behaviour of a doctor, he concluded.

Henry also didn't know who had found Freya's body, and why no one had found her until 4 a.m. Had someone else seen her and not told anyone?

He made some coffee and took his cup to the kitchen table. His notes were in front of him, covered in toast crumbs from his breakfast. He brushed some off and then saw a butter stain on the paper, which had made a see-through smudge.

He cursed and then drew up a list of things to do that day. The first thing would be to speak to the GP. He checked his notepad and found the name Gabriel had given: Dr Emma Parrish. He wanted to know what she had to say for herself and if she had any suspicions about that night.

He also wanted to know why she hadn't officially come forward to explain that she'd pronounced Freya dead at the party. Henry had checked the coroner's report, and there was no mention of the GP's name.

Henry would then look into this Vince. He needed a surname so Barnes could find him on the Police National Computer database. Henry suspected he was involved, especially after what Lottie had told him.

If Lottie could be trusted.

Sitting back in his chair, he sipped his strong black coffee and nearly gagged on its bitterness. But he swallowed it down, needing the energy as he felt exhausted already.

There was a knock on the front door. Henry stared at the clock on his kitchen wall in confusion. It was barely 7 a.m. He got himself out of the chair and walked through his living room to answer it.

Before opening, he realised he was still wearing his dressing gown. To hell with it, he thought. What do people expect a retired man to be wearing so early in the morning?

DC Hargreaves stood on his doorstep. Her jet-black hair had bright purple highlights that matched the colour of her lipstick. She wore a black-and-white polka dot shirt over her considerable bust.

Her sickly-sweet perfume hung around her in an invisible cloud, and Henry coughed.

"Former DCI Henry Ward?"

Her professional tone made Henry suspicious. "Yes, Detective Constable Hargreaves?"

"Can I come in?"

"Erm…" Henry couldn't think of a reason why not, but he didn't want her in his house. Not when he wasn't dressed and didn't know why she was there.

"It's quite important," she said.

"Right. Well… Why don't you…?" He pulled the door open to let her in.

She walked directly into his living room and stood in front of the sofa. Her black leather heels left impressions in the carpet. "I'd like you to take a seat," she said.

She looked him up and down as if only becoming aware that he wasn't dressed. But she didn't seem bothered.

"Right…" Henry closed the door and headed to his armchair.

She seated herself on the sofa opposite. With any luck, her black dress would be covered in Tessa's white and brown hair soon, Henry thought.

She clasped her large pink smartphone in her hands. "Can I ask where you were at 10 p.m. last night?"

Henry guffawed. "Am I being questioned about my whereabouts?"

"Can you answer the questions, please?"

"Can I ask what all this is about?"

She tapped a large silver ring against her smartphone. "I'm asking the questions, if you hadn't noticed."

"Excuse me, Detective Constable, as a former detective chief inspector, I'd like to be questioned by someone a rank above me."

"I can get Detective Superintendent Murphy here if you like."

As a superintendent, Murphy now outranked him. While Henry wondered if it was worth telling Hargreaves to fetch him, she continued, "Or you can just accept that you're no longer in the police and stop pissing me about."

Henry kept his mouth shut. He wasn't going to answer questions, especially not to Hargreaves.

"So, are you going to tell me where you were last night?"

Henry made to get out of his armchair. "Why don't I make a phone call and find out what's happening?"

"Oh. Are you going to call Barnes?"

Henry eyed Hargreaves. "What's that to you?"

"She's busy. We're all busy, unfortunately."

What did that mean? Henry wondered. He sat back in his chair. "What on earth is going on?"

Hargreaves exhaled in frustration. "Were you or were you not near Otley Chevin last night at around 10 p.m.?"

Henry's gut spasmed on hearing Otley Chevin. Did Hargreaves know he was digging into Freya Harrison's death?

"Mr Ward? Can you answer my question?"

"I was here last night," he said, hoping that by giving a little, he might get some information from her.

"Can anyone corroborate that?"

Henry rolled his eyes. "I'm a former DCI. Why would I lie about my whereabouts?"

"I'm asking if anyone can confirm you were here last night?"

Henry thought back to the previous evening. He'd left Jean's just before 10 p.m., so she'd be able to confirm that he'd been with her until then. But afterwards he'd been home alone. Apart from Tessa, but he knew dogs couldn't corroborate alibis.

"Ask my neighbour if you have to. I was at hers for dinner."

"Were you with them around 10 p.m.?"

"I left around then and came back here."

Hargreaves pouted her lips as if she'd just found a problem.

"What do you think I've done? Murdered someone?"

The pink smartphone in Hargreaves' hands vibrated, and she answered the call. "Aye. Right… Yeah, he's here."

She glared at Henry for a moment.

"He's no alibi. No… Are you sure?" She shook her head like she'd heard something she didn't agree with. "Right. Fine. Ta-ra."

Henry didn't have to guess who she was talking to. He could hear Murphy's low voice talking to her from across the room.

She hung up and gripped her smartphone. "There's been a murder," she said, speaking slowly, as though she was explaining a complicated situation to someone hard-of-hearing. "Last night on Otley Chevin. A man at an address was found unresponsive and had multiple knife wounds in his chest and abdomen."

Henry covered his mouth. "Who was it?"

Hargreaves looked at him. "It was a friend of Thomas Wentworth-Scott. Have you heard of him?"

"Thomas or his friend?"

"Either."

"I spoke to Thomas yesterday, and I also spoke to his friend."

Hargreaves' heavily mascaraed eyes widened. "Oh. Can I ask what your discussion was about?"

"That's private."

She tilted her head like she was a nursery assistant dealing with a difficult child. "You are aware that I'm a police detective?"

"I also understand the law, and know that I have the right to remain silent."

She sneered. "Well, Mr Wentworth-Scott's friend, Vince Taylor, was the man who's been found dead. And we'd like to know what you spoke to him about."

Henry thought it through. He had wanted to talk to Vince about the death of Freya Harrison, as Lottie had seen him carry Freya's unconscious body.

But now the lad had been found dead.

Could it have been some criminal link? Henry had heard Vince arrange a drug deal. Had it gone badly?

There were so many questions, his brain could barely manage them all.

"Are you alright, Mr Ward?" Hargreaves asked, looking slightly concerned. "Are you having a senior moment?"

He eyeballed her. "Why are you talking to me about this?"

She seemed taken aback by his hostility, but maintained her composure. "We know you were at the property earlier that day with the owner's wife."

"Wife?" Henry was completely stumped now. "Thomas Wentworth-Scott isn't married."

"No. That's because the deceased wasn't found at Mr Wentworth-Scott's house. He was found next door, at the farm belonging to his brother-in-law."

Henry felt he was about to regurgitate the bitter black coffee. "Vince was found on Charlotte's farm?"

She nodded as though she were teaching Henry a very basic concept that he'd finally understood. "That's right," she said. "Vince Taylor was murdered at the farm of Charlotte and Simon Foster."

Henry couldn't understand what had happened. Had Charlotte or Simon, her husband, murdered Vince? Was it someone else?

He shook his head and then ran a hand over his unshaven cheeks. "What in the name of God has gone on?"

"That's what we're trying to work out, Mr Ward. So, do you mind telling me what you were doing yesterday on Otley Chevin?"

Henry ignored her and stood up. "Hang on. I really do need to make a phone call."

Hargreaves sighed. "If you're calling Barnes, she's not available."

"No. I'm calling someone else." He found his phone on the table and searched for Jonathon Radcliffe's number.

Hopefully, the solicitor could shine some light on what the hell was happening.

Chapter Seventeen

Henry stepped outside into his backyard and closed the door behind him. Tessa was sitting under the shade of the large potted fern. Her legs were sprawled out, with the back ones edging into the morning sun.

He dialled Jonathon Radcliffe's number, and it rang until it reached his voicemail. It wasn't 8 a.m. yet, and Henry could forgive him for not answering this early on a normal day. But on one like this, he thought the solicitor would be up taking calls.

Henry strolled up and down the damp flagstones in his slippers, with the breeze rippling his dressing gown. He thought through what he'd just learnt from Hargreaves, who was still sitting in his living room.

Vince Taylor was dead. He'd been stabbed, and his body was found on Lottie's property.

Now, did 'property' mean in one of her fields or in Lottie's farmhouse?

If Vince had been in one of the fields, it could mean the drug-deal-gone-wrong line of inquiry still had legs.

Vince could have met someone there, the deal went wrong, and someone stabbed him.

However, what could it mean if Vince was found dead in Lottie's farmhouse? Why would he have been there? From the conversation Henry had with her the previous day, it was pretty clear she hated Vince with a passion. Why would she have let him into her home?

Had she stabbed him to death?

Henry instinctively shook his head at the idea. But then again, she had stayed quiet about her family disowning her, leading Henry to believe she was an unreliable witness, at the least.

Something moved beyond his kitchen window, and for a moment Henry thought Hargreaves was snooping around his house. Remembering the notes he'd left on his table, including some that mentioned Hargreaves, he peered through the glass.

But his kitchen was empty.

Deciding to check on Hargreaves, he called through the back door. "I'll just be one minute."

"Yeah, fine. I'm only investigating a murder. Take your bloody time!" she shouted back.

Henry closed the door. Why was Hargreaves questioning him? Was it about him looking into Freya Harrison's death? Was she worried Henry would find proof of her incompetence or of Murphy steering the case?

Could Vince's murder be linked to Freya's death?

His phone buzzed, and he saw Jonathon Radcliffe's number.

"I'm sorry I missed your call. Everything's a bit hectic here." Jonathon sounded ill at ease. Papers rustled around him, and hushed voices argued. "You called about Vince, I presume?"

"Aye. I have a detective in my house asking questions."

"Questions? Why?"

"It's the detective who looked into Freya Harrison's death. I think she's just on a fishing expedition and wants to piss me off."

"Right."

"Which, if you ask me, is a huge bloody waste of police time. But anyway."

"Well, it seems that Vince's death has caused problems for the family."

"Were they close?" Henry asked, almost jokingly.

"Vince was a… close friend of Thomas, but with the upheaval and potential link to Charlotte–"

"Aye. What link is that?"

"Well, Vince was found in her farmyard."

That meant the drug-deal-gone-wrong scenario was dead in the water. Unless Lottie ran a side business selling cocaine. "I see. Are the police questioning her?"

"Yes."

"And will your team be helping her?"

"They won't, no. I'm not sure if you're aware of the situation?"

"That Lottie's mum disowned her decades ago? Yes, I am now. So, I suppose the poor woman's on her own then?"

"It's very traumatic. Her husband found the body. Her children, thankfully, weren't at home. They were with his mother."

"Was Vince found dead on Lottie's farm while she was there?"

"Quite."

"And I suspect there was no one else around?"

"I'm not sure. Only the police would know that at this stage."

Henry wondered what, if anything, the police knew. Probably very little, considering one of their detectives was sitting in his living room like she didn't have a care in the world.

He shook his head and suddenly felt drained and tired. What was this? Would Charlotte kill Vince? Why?

Was there something more to this? Had the family decided to get the attention away from their beloved son and put it on a child they'd disowned?

"This is a bloody mess," Henry said, sighing.

"It is. But luckily for you, as we're hoping to delay the court case, you're no longer required to look into the death of Freya Harrison."

"Excuse me?"

"Yes. We're petitioning the judge to delay the case for the foreseeable. We're fairly certain he'll agree, considering this traumatic episode."

Henry didn't say anything as his mind caught up with events.

"And, as you requested not to be paid, we have acquiesced to your demand and won't be paying you for your time yesterday."

Henry scoffed. "What happened? Did you realise you'd made a mistake by putting a real detective on the case?"

"I'm not sure what you're driving at, Detective Ward."

"In one afternoon, I'd realised the coroner's verdict had no merit. Which would mean your libel case against Gabriel could collapse, allowing him to countersue the family. Any evidence I brought to light would put Thomas and his friends in legal jeopardy. One or all of them could go down for murder–"

"I thank you for your time, Detective Ward," Jonathon said abruptly.

"I have a witness who saw Vince move Freya's unconscious body down a corridor with someone she couldn't identify."

"That raises the question of whether your witness can be trusted." A phone rang next to Jonathon. "Please excuse me, Detective. I really must go–"

He hung up.

Henry shook his head. The posh pretend to be so polite and above board, he thought, when in reality they're a bunch of conniving bastards.

"Oi!" Hargreaves' shout made Henry jump; he nearly dropped his phone.

She was sticking her head out of his back door. "Can you hurry the fuck up? I've got stuff to be getting on with!"

* * *

Hargreaves' perfume had overwhelmed Henry's living room by the time he walked back in. He crossed the carpet and opened the window to let in some fresh air. Along with it came the sounds of cars and buses heading up and down the busy Main Street outside.

He slumped down in his armchair, making sure his dressing gown adequately covered his legs and chest, and then checked the time on the mantelpiece: 7:20 a.m.

Hargreaves cleared her throat to get his attention. "Have you finished pissing me about?"

"Let's see."

She was perched on his sofa as if ready to jump up at any moment. Her smartphone was in her hand; and for some reason Henry wondered if she was recording their conversation.

"What were you doing yesterday at the property of Charlotte and Simon Taylor?" she asked.

"No comment."

Hargreaves nearly spat out her tongue. "What? Are you really going to 'no-comment' me?"

"I'd like to know why you're here, questioning me. And once I know, I'll seek legal representation before saying a word."

Hargreaves pulled a face that he suspected only expressed a fraction of her fury. "You might be a potential witness in a murder investigation."

"I was at the property around six or seven in the evening. I couldn't possibly be a witness if it happened at ten at night."

"As you were at the property earlier that day, you might be the only person to step onto it before Vince Taylor was murdered."

"I'm the only other person you know of."

Her tired sigh conceded his point.

"Listen. You wouldn't be fishing by any chance?"

"You what?"

"You've not come round here to find out what I know about Freya Harrison's death?"

Hargreaves shook her head as if she were lost. "Who are you talking about?"

"Can't you remember all your cases?"

"Cases?" Her eyes narrowed. "Wait. That lass in the bath?"

"The very one. Is that why you're here?"

She scrunched her face up as though she'd never heard anything so incredulous. "What the fuck are you on about? Why would I care about that?"

Henry watched her closely. She was either a very good liar or she was being genuine.

He came clean. "The Wentworth-Scotts asked me to look into Freya's death. Their son has been accused of her murder."

Her pale cheeks flushed. "Murder? But she died in a bath."

"You do know it's hard to drown yourself in a bath while conscious? Your survival instinct kicks in. We don't know if she overdosed and drowned accidentally, as an autopsy was never done."

She bit her bottom lip. "Yeah… Her dad wouldn't allow us to do one. He kicked off. Didn't want her being cut up, he said."

"What can you remember about the investigation?"

She was lost in her thoughts a moment, and then stared down at the carpet, which Henry noted needed to be vacuumed.

She shook herself out of her memories as a thought angered her. "Fuck you! Are you saying I missed something?"

"I'm saying the coroner's verdict was nonsense, and that I have a witness who saw Vince Taylor carry Freya's unconscious body with an unidentified person."

Hargreaves eyes widened in alarm. Then in a flash, she snarled. "Bollocks! I questioned the people at the party. They saw nothing like that. The lass had been depressed and unstable for weeks. She couldn't see her sick father because of COVID."

Henry didn't respond. He just watched.

She thought about it some more, seemingly less confident. But then she shook her head. "No. I did my best on that case. It was suicide."

"What if it wasn't?"

"But it was."

Henry saw he would not convince her. He let a moment pass between them before asking, "Just out of interest, how many people did you question at the party?"

She shrugged like it was a minor detail. "I don't know… Twelve, I think."

"Twelve?" Henry asked, ensuring he heard her correctly.

"Aye."

"I'd heard there were thirty people."

She bit her lower lip again. "Well… I questioned twelve."

"And you never thought to speak to Thomas's sister, who lived next door?"

"Why would I question the neighbours after a suicide?"

"Well, she's the one who saw those men carrying Freya."

Hargreaves scoffed. "Do you know your star witness is currently being questioned for murder?"

"Lottie didn't murder anyone. Are you out of your mind?"

Hargreaves shook her head like she was talking to an imbecile. She was about to carry on arguing but seemingly couldn't see the point.

After getting off the sofa, she patted some of the brown and white dog hair off her black skirt. "I'll be back in touch."

"I bet you will."

She crossed the room to the door, her heels leaving more imprints in the carpet. With her hand on the door handle, she said, "Do you really think that little of me?"

"Come again?"

As she looked out of the open door at his front yard, she asked, "Do you really think I'd mess up a case that badly?"

Henry could see his veiled accusation had knocked her confidence. "I'm not saying you're a bad detective–"

"Of course not! I'm just too thick to know if I'm dealing with a murder or not. Well, with this Vince Taylor, I know what I'm dealing with. And if I see your grubby hands anywhere near the investigation on Otley Chevin, I'll bang you up."

Henry sighed. Why did they always threaten him with arrest? "You do know I'm a former DCI who's applied to rejoin the police? I don't think it'd go down well if you arrested me for helping with an investigation."

There was a flash of something in her eyes – delight or annoyance, Henry couldn't work out which.

"I'll be seeing you," Hargreaves said, as she stepped onto his front step and slammed the door behind her.

Chapter Eighteen

Henry got showered and changed into some clean jeans and a thin, short-sleeved blue and white shirt. He combed what was left of his greying hair while looking in the steamed-up bathroom mirror, and then sucked in his gut, wondering if it was visible in the shirt he was wearing.

Deciding he didn't care either way, he went downstairs to his notes on the kitchen table. After pouring away the vile lukewarm coffee down the sink, he checked Tessa was alright in the backyard. She was on her back in the middle of the yard, in full view of the sun, with her legs sticking out and her eyes closed.

Tessa might be lithe and devoid of energy now, Henry thought, but she'd soon want to go for a walk, and he doubted he'd have time. Maybe young Robbie could take her for one later? The lad could do with some fresh air himself.

Then he thought Robbie was more likely to attach Tessa's lead to that drone of his, and have it walk the dog around the village while he remained on his gran's couch.

Henry turned to his table and picked up the A3 piece of paper to shake off the remaining toast crumbs, and then put it back down. His to-do list from an hour ago looked naive considering how drastically things had changed.

At the top of the list was finding the GP who'd been at the party, but he questioned if that was worth looking into anymore. He wasn't working for the Wentworth-Scotts – not that he'd been before – and Lottie was in the frame for murdering Vince.

Slumping down in a wooden chair at the table, he wondered if Lottie was capable of killing someone but couldn't imagine her doing it.

In self-defence, perhaps.

He thought most people had the capacity to kill, in a life-or-death situation. The primeval instincts learnt when humans fought tigers in rainforests took over. He'd heard it called 'a red haze'. He knew relatively harmless people who'd killed an attacker when their base instincts chose survival over death.

Could that be an explanation?

Henry didn't know. He leant over the table to pick up his pen, and then added a new item on his to-do list: 'go speak to Lottie'.

He tossed the pen across the tabletop, and he recalled Hargreaves' threat to arrest him if he went to Otley Chevin.

Well, he could go where he wanted. This wasn't a police state. Far from it.

He stirred Tessa from her snooze and called her inside. She didn't come at first and had to be persuaded with dog biscuits and a promise of a walk later.

When she was inside, he locked the back door, picked up his notes from the table and folded them up. He then headed out the front door.

The traffic outside on Main Street was calming down from the rush hour earlier. As he passed Jean's front gate, he heard her door open.

"There you are! What's going on?" she called out.

Henry considered pretending he hadn't heard her but knew it would only cause him problems later. He had tried it once years back, and it took her two days to stop going on about it.

He stepped into her front yard so he wouldn't have to shout over her garden wall, and strolled up her path. She stood at her door, wearing a pale-green silk top and white trousers. He suspected she was preparing to go out somewhere.

"Well?" she asked, growing impatient. "What's happened?"

"What do you know?"

"Well…" She looked about Main Street. "I heard that dark-haired woman knocking on your door at seven this morning. And then the local news said someone's died near Otley Chevin. So, evidently, I thought of you."

"Oh. It's on the news already?" Henry didn't know what that could mean. Murders like this were usually kept away from the press for a few hours while the police worked out the basics.

"So?" She folded her arms as she waited for him to speak.

But he didn't have the time to stand here explaining events to Jean. "Look. It's all a bit of a mess."

"Right?" she said, not getting the hint that he didn't want to talk about it.

Henry let a double-decker bus thunder past on the street. "It's the friend of Thomas Wentworth-Scott who's been stabbed," he said.

"Oh dear," she said, with only a hint of concern in her voice.

"And the lad was found in Lottie's farmyard."

Her eyes widened. "Really? But she's the sane one!"

"Aye, as you keep saying." He glanced around the parked cars on the side of the street and located his.

"What's happening then? Do they think she did it?"

"The police are questioning her. I'm about to go over and see what's what."

"Here. I'll come with you," she said.

Henry couldn't think of anything worse than bringing Jean into the situation. Especially when she had a vitriolic hatred of the Wentworth-Scotts. "What about Robbie? Won't you be best staying with him?" Henry asked, hoping it'd persuade her to stay at home.

"He'll be fine. He's still in bed. I've left a note."

Henry stared at her, his mind struggling to understand what was happening. "You've already left one?"

He looked at her outfit and realised she had specifically got ready to come with him. She must have been standing behind her front door, lying in wait.

"I don't think it's a good idea," he said.

She stepped down the front steps and closed the door behind her. "Don't be daft. It'll be fine."

Henry exhaled grumpily. Jean Whitehead had got the better of him – and probably not for the last time.

* * *

White fluffy clouds covered the bright morning sun, casting shadows over the tall grasses that covered the moorlands above Otley. The gentle breeze in the valley had turned into strong gusts of warm air, and Henry wondered how the planes at the nearby airport were coping.

He'd explained the case so far to Jean as he drove along the narrow country lanes towards Lottie's farm. Occasionally, he had to pull up close to the drystone walls to let cars in the opposite direction pass. None of them were police patrol cars. Henry suspected they'd still be on Lottie's property, keeping nosy members of the public away.

He was fully aware he and Jean were the kind of busybody they wanted to keep out, but at least he had the excuse that he was a former detective intending to return to the fold.

That still didn't mean he would be welcomed onto the farm, especially if Hargreaves was there. But Henry had a plan to remedy that.

Thomas's huge 'farmhouse' came into view on the right, and Henry slowed the car. In the distance, he could make out Lottie's smaller farm buildings a few fields away. She had said only two fields separated them, and Henry was about to test her theory.

He parked the car so close to the drystone wall he had to climb out of Jean's door to get out. Jean stood in the middle of the lane, surveying the surrounding fields. The sun broke through the clouds now and then, casting hazy shards of light across them.

He hung the cord of some binoculars around his neck, and Jean noticed them. "Are we birdwatching?" she asked.

"No. We're walking to Lottie's farm."

"Walk?" She squinted into the distance. "But it's miles away, isn't it?"

"Only two fields, apparently. We won't be able to go straight there if it's a crime scene."

Jean huffed. "But what about my shoes?" She pointed at her black-and-white heeled sandals.

Henry shook his head. What she was wearing on her feet had little to do with him, but obviously he didn't say that. "You'll be fine. We've not had any rain for weeks. The fields will be hard as stone."

"What about grass stains?"

Henry ignored her and headed to a metal gate in the wall. He unhooked the old string holding the gate to its post. "You'll be fine."

They walked through the fields, keeping close to the wall. Thankfully, they were free of livestock. Henry avoided fields full of cattle if he could help it. He'd been chased by a herd before.

Going by the round droppings that littered the dry grass, Henry guessed Lottie and her husband had been keeping sheep in here. He could handle sheep, he thought. But not cows.

The ground was hard, and the grass dry and brown. They'd had too much sun for May and not enough rain. He dreaded to think what the summer would hold for them. The previous one had given them heatwaves.

Thankfully, Jean didn't complain about her shoes. She was too busy keeping her eyes on Thomas's house in the distance. "It's big," she said.

"It's bloody huge." But Henry wasn't looking at Thomas's house, instead he trained his eyes on Lottie's farm. He lifted his binoculars and focused on the yard. Two patrol cars, each with fluorescent yellow and blue patches on their sides, were parked outside some outbuildings.

Henry thought he could see Barnes's new black Audi. Her previous car, a BMW, had been damaged beyond repair in a gunfight. However, Henry suspected she'd wanted to change cars, and had used the bullet holes as an excuse.

There were two other cars in the yard, and Henry wondered if one of them belonged to Hargreaves.

A SOCO van was also visible. From what Henry could see in his binoculars, a blue police tape squared off the far corner of the yard. SOCO officers in white overalls were collecting evidence behind it, kneeling on the gravel.

Henry recalled being in the yard the previous day. Lottie had put the trays of eggs inside an outbuilding in that corner; which didn't mean anything, unless she had found Vince stealing her eggs and taught him a lesson.

Shaking his head at his making light of the situation, he focused on the fact that a young lad had died. Even if Vince hadn't been of much use to society, he was still a young man whose life had been ended by someone else.

"What can you see?" Jean asked, coming to his side.

He handed her the binoculars. "The police are still there."

"And we can't go over?"

Henry didn't have an answer. They definitely couldn't walk up and knock on the front door, but they could get closer still. There was another empty field between them and Lottie's farm.

"Come on. Let's find another gate."

They continued up the field, remaining close to the old wall that had collapsed in places.

"What are you planning to do, exactly?" asked Jean, as they stepped over chunks of limestone.

"Speak to Lottie. Somehow."

Jean batted a bluebottle fly away from her face. "What if she's been arrested?"

"Then I'll have to find her a solicitor."

"Why would you have to do that?"

Henry nearly stopped walking as he considered her question. "I don't know, to be honest. I suppose she won't have the money to pay for one. Not that I've got bags of cash myself."

"What's it got to do with you if she's got a solicitor or not?"

"She'll have to depend on legal aid otherwise. And they were crap eleven years ago. I dread to think what they're like now, after fifteen years of cuts. At least I could get her someone half-decent."

He spotted a metal gate in the wall further ahead.

"Fair enough. But I have to ask again: what's that got to do with you?"

Henry stopped walking and turned to her. "Something's going on here."

She gave him a look that suggested she'd already worked that out. "It's all a bit odd, isn't it? Almost like it was planned."

"Planned?"

She nodded. "Charlotte tells you she saw Vince with Freya before she died, and the next day, the police reckon she's killed him."

Henry grunted. He wasn't one for conspiracy theories but he too had been thinking it was a cosy coincidence.

Jean leant closer to him. "It's the Freemasons, isn't it?" she whispered.

"Oh, for God's sake," Henry said, shaking his head.

"It is. Who else could have organised something like this?"

"Are you having me on? Do you really think a group of posh golfers organised a murder?"

She shrugged as if it was a possibility, but then pulled a face that suggested she hadn't fully convinced herself.

With his naked eye, he saw movement in Lottie's farmyard. He lifted his binoculars and watched Barnes get into her new black Audi. She drove over the gravel and then disappeared out of his view.

"Hang on," he said to Jean. He let his binoculars hang by his chest and called Barnes.

She didn't pick up.

After a quick curse, he tried again, and she answered.

"I shouldn't be talking to you," she said, speaking to him on loudspeaker. The sounds of the car driving over gravel were in the background.

"Aye. When isn't that the case?" He didn't hear her laugh. "Do you know what's going on?"

"Going on where?"

"At Charlotte Foster's farm."

"Why would I know anything about that?" she asked, sounding deadly serious.

"Well, I've just watched you drive away from it."

"What the…?! Where the hell are you, Henry?"

"In the field opposite."

"Spying on crime scenes, are we?"

"Is that illegal?"

He could almost hear Barnes's mind go through her knowledge of criminal law. "I don't know, to be fair."

"Are you arresting Charlotte?"

"I can't confirm anything at the moment."

"Barnes, she didn't do it."

"You've not seen the evidence," she said with a sigh.

He felt his gut tighten. That was enough confirmation for him: they were arresting Lottie. "What evidence is there?"

Barnes seemed adamant about not giving away details and remained quiet.

"What evidence?" he asked again.

"You'll have to read it in the papers like everyone else."

"Really? You're going to keep me out of the loop? Is this how we're going to work together in the future?"

The cold silence on Barnes's end of the line made Henry's gut tighten further.

"What's going on?" he asked, no longer caring about Lottie, but about his application to rejoin the police.

"You'd best speak to Murphy."

"Why?"

"Henry. Don't drag me into this. Not after last time."

"Into what?"

"I barely survived Murphy's wrath after what happened on Ilkley Moor, so don't drag me between you two again. It's not fair. Speak to him directly."

She hung up before Henry could say another word.

He stared at his phone for a few moments, wondering what was going on.

Jean took some furtive steps towards him. "Was that the blonde detective?"

"Aye," he said. "It was Barnes."

"What did she say?"

He couldn't quite recall. All he knew was that he had to speak to Murphy about his application to rejoin the police, which Henry now felt was dead in a ditch.

Chapter Nineteen

Henry leant against the drystone wall, gazing towards Lottie's farm. Strong gusts of warm wind rustled his blue and white shirt.

Jean was sitting on the wall beside him, facing the other way, with her head down. She scrolled through the local news on her phone to see if there were any updates.

Henry assumed there weren't any, as Jean hadn't said a word. Unless she still sensed he wasn't in the mood to talk, which he thought was probably the case.

He'd sulked since Barnes had hung up on him. He had no intention of calling Murphy, and giving him the pleasure of dashing his hopes of rejoining the police.

He would wait for Murphy to come to him.

He wondered if his hopes had ever been realistic. Murphy had been against him for years. Henry remembered hearing vague rumours that Murphy had been involved in the investigation that forced him out of the police. But there had never been anything to substantiate them.

He had never cared for Murphy, whom he thought was a fickle careerist. And it wouldn't be a surprise if he didn't let Henry back in the force, especially if he had helped to kick him out.

They had been partners once back in their heydays, and had got on well. But they could never hide the fact that they were very different detectives. Henry focused on police work, finding out the truth, and getting results for the victims of crime, whereas Murphy's sole interest was doing what made him look good – an aim he achieved by brown-nosing those with influence and climbing the greasy pole.

That probably explained how both of them had ended up where they were: Murphy now a superintendent, and Henry standing out in the field, spying on crime scenes. The police force could be a hostile place for those who wanted to solve crimes and put things right.

There was movement on Lottie's farm in the distance.

Henry peered through his binoculars, aiming them over the tall grass in the field in front, and focused on Lottie's farmyard.

The moment had arrived. Lottie was marched out of her house, hands behind her back and cuffed. Strands of her long blonde air blew across her face, and she squinted at the sun like she'd not stepped outside for days.

Two burly uniformed officers guided her towards a patrol car with its rear door open.

Hargreaves followed behind. Her black-and-white polka dot shirt made her easy to spot in the crowd.

Henry huffed, which caught Jean's attention.

"What's happening now?" she asked, getting slowly off the wall to watch the scene.

"Lottie's doing the walk of shame." He passed Jean the binoculars, and then guided her to look in the right direction.

"Nah. I must've missed it," she said. "The cars are driving away." Jean rested the binoculars on the wall before her. "Well, that's it, I suppose. Are you going to get a solicitor for Lottie?"

Henry nodded. He had one in mind. A brutal defence barrister who had bested his side a few times in court, letting people who Henry knew were guilty get away with their crimes.

Perhaps defending someone innocent would prove a better challenge for him, he thought.

"His name's Clive Juniper."

"Juniper?" Jean found the name odd. "Is he any good?"

"Aye. He's very good."

"Likes the gin, I suspect?"

Henry frowned. "I don't know…" He then got her joke and nodded along. "Very funny," he said, with a faint smirk.

"What are you going to do, then?"

Henry glanced at Lottie's farm and then turned to look at Thomas's house in the opposite direction. "I think I'd best have a chat with the man in the centre of all this."

Jean followed his gaze. "Alright," she said. "I suppose that's an idea." She sounded unsure of herself until she added, "I'll have a look around his house while you talk to him. I don't believe he can have four bathrooms."

* * *

Henry drove up the gravel path to Thomas's enormous farmhouse. The sun broke through the clouds and splashed glorious daylight over the imposing two-storey property. Its many windows reflected it back, making them sparkle.

Jean wound down her window so she could stick her head out to size it up as they went past. Henry spotted a police patrol car parked next to Thomas's top-of-the-range Porsche and Audi.

He cursed under his breath.

Obviously, the police were going to be at the victim's home residence. But Henry had hoped they wouldn't be there so quickly.

He parked behind the police vehicle, which Jean looked at nervously.

"Are we allowed to be here?" she asked.

Henry took off his seatbelt. "I'm not sure. Let's find out."

As he walked towards the front entrance. Jean stepped out of the car and followed cautiously behind him, maintaining a few yards between them.

Before Henry could knock on the white wooden door, it swung open, and a uniformed police officer stepped out.

He eyeballed Henry and wore a furious expression. "What are you doing here?"

Henry stopped and nearly skidded in the gravel. "I'm here to see Thomas."

The officer did his best to block the view into the hallway with his large body. His bulky hi-vis stab vest added to his size.

"Who are you?"

"I'm former DCI Henry Ward."

The fury in the officer's expression lowered a few notches as he registered Henry's former position. He then looked over Henry's shoulder at Jean.

"What are you doing here?"

"We've come to offer Thomas our support."

The officer didn't say anything. He was still eyeing them both up.

"I'm working on behalf of Thomas's family on a separate matter and wish to talk to him," Henry said.

The officer nodded slowly as if he was working something out. "Like a private security consultant?"

"Aye. That's it."

The officer was mildly impressed. "I've been trying to get into that. You know, to do it on the side until I retire."

Henry guessed the officer was in his mid-thirties. He'd have a few more years before he could leave the force with his pension.

"Well, I'm happy to have a chat about it at some point if you'd like. I can give you some tips on how to get established."

"Yeah." The officer nodded happily. "Have you got a business card or anything?"

Henry patted his jeans pockets, pretending he normally had some on him. "I don't think I do. But you can always contact me through DI Barnes."

"DI Barnes? Alright. I didn't know she did private work."

"You'd be surprised who does."

The officer seemed to be lost in thought, probably wondering who else on the force worked privately on the side.

Henry took his chance and asked, "Can I speak to Thomas, then?"

The officer turned to the house. "Yeah, I can go get him."

"Have SOCO checked out that lad's room yet?" Henry asked, hoping he hadn't crossed the line and triggered the officer's suspicions.

The officer shook his head in disgust. "Have they heck! They'll be another couple of hours, they said."

"Oh right. They're always running late, aren't they?"

"Who isn't these days?" The officer said. He then gave Jean an odd look that suggested he couldn't figure out who she was or why she was there.

Henry smiled at her. "Alright?"

She nodded nervously. "Fine. Is everything good?"

"Aye, this is Police Constable…"

"Williams, PC Williams," the officer answered.

Jean bowed like she was meeting a foreign dignitary. "Nice to meet you, PC Williams."

The officer was confused for a moment. "Why don't you come in, then. He's in the games room."

"Oh right," Henry said, following PC Williams down the hallway. "Is he alone?"

"Yeah. He wants to get out, but I've told him to stay put."

"Aye. Good thinking," Henry said.

He felt Jean tug his shirt sleeve and stopped to talk to her.

"What are we doing?" she whispered.

"Go have a look around. If anyone asks what you're doing, just tell them you're working for me."

Henry left her in the white-walled hallway near the dining room, looking overwhelmed, but he didn't hang about to help.

Instead, he hurried after PC Williams.

* * *

Thomas Wentworth-Scott was in the converted barn that adjoined the old farmhouse and had been turned into an entertainment room. The snooker table had some balls on its green covering, as though a game had started but was left unfinished.

Thomas was slumped across a leather couch, one of two in the vast room, staring down at his phone. The arcade machines along the far wall flashed and whirred, failing to get the overgrown adolescent's attention.

Thomas looked up from his phone after PC Williams had said his name three times.

"There's someone here," PC Williams said, gesturing to Henry.

Thomas immediately frowned in confusion when he recognised him. "What are you doing here? Mum said she'd–"

"That's everything. Thanks, PC Williams," Henry said, interrupting Thomas.

But the officer had witnessed Thomas's bewilderment and wasn't sure if he should leave.

Henry leant closer to PC Williams. "There are some things I need to iron out with Thomas," he said. "It'd be best if you weren't here; as it could get loud." He gave a knowing wink, suggesting Thomas was due a bollocking.

PC Williams nodded as if he understood the situation: a rich man-child from a family that had a lot to lose was about to have the facts of life explained to him. "I'll leave you to it then."

When he'd left through the door, Henry rounded on Thomas. "Now, shut your trap and listen."

Thomas huffed. "I don't have to listen to a word you say." He held up his smartphone and tapped its screen to start a call.

Henry stepped towards him and struck the phone out of his hand.

Thomas gawked as it slid across the old floorboards, then snarled at Henry. "What the fuck did you do that for?"

"I want a word."

As Thomas got off the sofa, Henry remembered he was considerably bigger than him.

Thomas flexed his shoulder and neck muscles, making him more bull-like, but Henry was having none of it. "Sit down now," he said, "or I'll have you arrested for murder."

Panic flickered across Thomas's chiselled face. "Murder?"

"Sit!"

Thomas lowered himself onto the sofa, staring at Henry like a dog who'd been scolded. The leather creaked under his weight as he sat down. Despite his apparent defeat, his eyes glanced around the room sneakily as if searching for an exit. They alighted on Henry.

"You can't have me arrested. You're not in the police."

"No, but my new pal PC Williams is."

Thomas clenched his jaw muscles at being bested so quickly. Then a new idea struck. "On what grounds? You've no evidence I did anything."

"I'd like to point out you've not denied committing murder."

"I've never murdered anyone," Thomas said, rather perfunctorily.

Henry shook his head in derision. "You're bang in the middle of two homicide investigations." He stuck up two fingers for dramatic effect, and tapped the first one. "Freya Harrison. Died 20th of May 2020. Murdered at your house party."

"Hang on–"

Henry tapped his second finger. "Vince Taylor. Died yesterday. Murdered on a neighbouring farm."

"Wait!" Thomas shoved his large palm in the air. "I didn't kill Freya, and Vince died on my sister's farm. That had nothing to do with me."

"Oh, aye? What's the link between the two, I wonder?" he asked, staring Thomas in the eyes.

Thomas broke eye contact as he couldn't bear it, and his head dropped forwards. "I didn't kill Freya."

"So, you admit she was murdered?"

He shook his head and then seemed to remember something. "No. She drowned in the bath. It was suicide."

"Oh please. If she were conscious, she'd never have drowned in that bath."

"You don't know that!"

"Oh really? Fancy filling up one of your four bathtubs to try it out?"

Thomas was offended.

"Either she was unconscious when she drowned or someone held her head down. That's assuming she was alive when she got in."

Thomas clenched his jaws again and then searched the floor for his phone. "I don't need to listen to this. My sister's just killed my friend."

Henry scoffed. "Please. You really think anyone will believe that?"

He sneered at him. "I do, actually. A knife was found covered in Vince's blood with her fingerprints all over it." He shrugged his huge shoulders as if there was nothing else to say.

Henry lost his stride. That must be the 'evidence' that Barnes had mentioned. So, a knife with Lottie's prints on it had been found near Vince.

"It's very considerate, that," Henry said.

"What?"

"I bet the police didn't have to look hard for it. There lies Vince, stabbed to death, and then the incriminating murder weapon is found right beside him."

Thomas folded his muscly arms across his chest. "It wasn't like that."

"Oh? Were you there?"

"No. Were *you*?"

Henry shook his head and stepped away from Thomas's leather sofa, nearer to the window. He could see Lottie's farm beyond the green and brown fields through the old, warped glass.

"Do you really think you'll get away with this?" Henry asked.

"With what?"

"With being involved in Freya's murder and then covering up your tracks?"

But Thomas wasn't roused. He'd seen that Henry lacked the evidence to back up his claims. He smirked. "I think you should leave, old man, before I ask myself if you've broken into private property to assault me."

"Assault?" Henry asked in disbelief. "Are you kidding me? You big fat baby. Who'd believe someone like me could assault a bloke like you?"

The smirk spread on Thomas's lips. "People believe what they're told. Don't you know that?"

Chapter Twenty

Henry found Jean walking down a curved staircase, stepping quietly on the white-carpeted steps. As she came to the bottom, Henry said, "We're leaving."

In the car, they headed down the drive towards the lane that would take them back to Otley. The clouds had returned to obscure the sun, and the breeze pushed the tall grasses in the fields back and forth.

Jean stared at her phone in silence, having not said much since she had got into the car. Henry had been too wound up from his exchange with Thomas to notice, until the quietness in the car got to him.

"Are you alright?" he asked, glancing at her.

She turned her phone in the opposite direction as if she didn't want him to see its screen.

Henry sensed there was a problem. "What's going on?"

She didn't answer, choosing to stare out the window instead like she'd not heard him.

"Jean. It's not like you to be speechless."

She exhaled. "I shouldn't have gone into his room."

"Whose?"

She considered her answer. "Both. I suppose."

Henry realised what this meant. "You went into Vince's room?"

She bit her lower lip and turned to him, looking desperate. "Is that a criminal offence? Will they send me to prison?"

Henry kept his eyes on the windy lane ahead and did his best not to make the situation worse by having a go at her. "I don't think it's illegal as he died somewhere else, but it's not great. Did you touch anything?"

He glanced at her as she shook her head.

"So, what did you do?"

She exhaled. "I thought it could help."

He gave her a perplexed look, as he didn't have a clue what she was talking about. And then she held up her phone. "I took photos."

"Of Vince's room?" he asked.

She nodded. "Well. All of them…"

Henry couldn't believe what he was hearing. "Bloody hell! What did you think you were doing? You're not an estate agent planning to put the house on the market!"

"I just thought it might be useful. And once I started… But then that police officer came upstairs, and I panicked."

"Did he see you?"

She shook her head. "I hid in a bathroom. Look. I just… was trying to help."

Henry could see she was sincere. "Let's hope they never find those photos."

"Shall I delete them?" she asked, about to press a button on her phone's screen.

"No," Henry said, louder than he wanted. "No. Let's have a look at them first."

They drove back to Addingham in silence. It was nearing 12 p.m., and traffic was light. Henry found a parking spot outside their cottages, and they agreed to go into Jean's first as she had a laptop they could use.

Robbie was lying on the couch in shorts and a black T-shirt when they both entered. He glanced up from the handheld games device he was playing.

"Alright?" he asked, without noticing the dark cloud that followed them in.

Henry grunted, and then Jean said, "You'd best go upstairs, love."

Robbie sensed there was a problem and got up off the couch. "What's up?"

"Nothing. Why don't you play that thing in your room for a bit?"

He didn't move, and instead stared at Henry and Jean in turn. "Have you done something wrong?"

"Robbie!" Jean said, raising her voice.

He rolled his eyes and hauled himself off the sofa before flouncing upstairs.

When Henry thought he was out of earshot, he said, "You know, he might be useful. He knows his tech stuff."

"I can't get him involved. His dad would kill me. I had enough of it when he was in hospital."

Henry recalled the head injury Robbie had sustained the previous year when he had helped with a case. He knew full well not to press the point. "Right, so what do we do?"

Jean went into the kitchen, with Henry following, and removed a gold-coloured laptop from a drawer under the kitchen worktop. She put it on the table, and then messed around with bright white cables until she plugged one into the wall.

The laptop was fancier than anything Henry thought Jean would have. She seemed to have picked up on this. "It's something Robbie got hold of," she said. "He fixed it for one of his dad's friends, who let him keep it."

She typed in a password, and the computer came to life. "So, do I just put the photos on here?" she asked, suddenly unsure of herself.

"You can do. You've done it before, I expect."

"Of course. There are loads of pictures on it. Mostly of grandchildren, cats, wildflowers, but not…" She couldn't bring herself to say, 'a murder victim's bedroom'.

She shook away her concerns and connected a cable to her phone, but then paused. "Should I be uploading these photos? I'm not sure I want them on here. What if the police find them?"

"Well…" Henry didn't have a solution. "We could just look at them on your phone…"

She held her phone in her hand. "I want them off here as well."

"How about…?" Henry started but couldn't finish. Could they upload the photos onto a cloud? But wouldn't they then be on a server somewhere? And how would they get them onto the cloud without giving their names?

"What are you doing?" said Robbie.

Jean jumped and nearly dropped her phone on the tiled floor.

Robbie stood in the doorway, watching them.

"Robbie! Get out, please," Jean said, after gathering her wits.

"What's that?" he asked, pointing at the laptop.

Henry saw the photos Jean had taken pop up on its screen.

She panicked and clicked the trackpad, but it didn't make a difference. "Oh, bloody hell. It must be automatic or something!"

Henry tried to regain control of the situation. "Here, Robbie. We want to save these photos somewhere that isn't connected to us."

He stepped gingerly into the kitchen. "Why? What are they?"

"No, Henry," Jean said. "He's not to get involved."

Henry turned to her. "He's only helping us with an IT issue."

She huffed but gave in when she saw more photos pop up on her screen and couldn't stop them.

Robbie approached the laptop and peered at the images. "It's not anything dodgy, is it?"

"No," Henry replied.

"Then what is it?" He frowned at the screen as he made out the pictures of Thomas's house. "Is it a crime scene?"

"Never you mind what they are," Jean said, standing in front of the screen, blocking Robbie's view.

Henry got Robbie's attention by clicking his fingers. "Robbie, can you put them somewhere that can't be linked to us?"

"Why?" He gave Henry and Jean suspicious looks. "What have you done?"

"Your gran and I have done nothing. We just don't want these photos being traced back to us."

Robbie mulled over this fresh technological problem and quickly had an answer. "You can use a fake cloud account."

"How does that work?" Henry asked.

"Just use a fake email address as you log in and sign up to a cloud service. Then, whenever you want to look at the photos, use a VPN." He shrugged like it was plainly evident.

Henry had followed most of what he'd said, and had heard of VPNs before. Virtual private networks sounded very technical, and he supposed they were, but he knew some colleagues who had retired abroad and used them to access BBC iPlayer, which was only accessible in the UK. "Right. Can you set that up?"

Robbie pulled out the chair closest to the laptop and sat down. He gave Jean a worried glance and then started typing.

She remained standing over his shoulder, watching what he was doing out of concern for her laptop. But after a while, she went to the worktop to switch on the kettle.

Henry and Jean had finished their cups of tea and were discussing lunch plans, when Robbie disrupted them to announce he'd finished.

He showed to them how the cloud service and VPN worked, and explained it was unlikely anything could be traced to them as the VPN was hiding their location.

"Are you sure?" Jean said.

Robbie nodded for the fourth time.

"And you've deleted the pictures from my phone?"

He nodded for the fifth.

She seemed satisfied with that and said to Henry, "Let's have a look at them, then?"

Robbie got out of the chair so she could take it, and Henry stood near the table, peering over Jean's shoulder.

They stared at the first photo. It was an image of a hallway on the second floor of Thomas's house. Henry suspected Jean had taken it near the guest bathroom where Freya Harrison had been found. The white walls and carpets made all the hallways appear the same, but he recognised the curve in the wall near the bathroom door, and the large clock mounted on it.

"Did you go in the bathroom?" he asked.

She nodded and clicked the laptop's trackpad, flicking through several images until the brand-new white bathroom was on the screen.

"It's been done up recently," Jean said. "I wonder why?" she added, with a hint of sarcasm.

Henry concurred. "I think even I'd be squeamish if someone'd died in my bathroom."

"Someone died in there?" Robbie asked, sounding both alarmed and intrigued. He leant closer to get a better look.

As if sensing Robbie was getting too interested, Jean clicked on another photo. "I'll show you the bedrooms I found. I wasn't sure which was whose," she said.

"Vince's was the first one on the left after the bathroom."

She nodded like she knew the one and flicked through more photos until Vince's room came up on the screen.

Henry leant closer to the laptop screen to examine the room in the image. White blinds had been pulled down over the window, casting the room in a greyish gloom. The walls were white like the rest of the house, but there were posters on the walls of DJs and nightclubs.

"Recognise the artist?" Henry asked Robbie, pointing at one.

He shook his head. "I'm into ASMR."

Henry nodded as if he knew what that was.

"His room smelt odd," Jean said. "Smelt of smoke and chemicals. And look, the drawers here were open."

Henry leant over the table to get a closer look.

An oak chest of drawers was positioned under the window, and several of its drawers had been left open – as if they'd been searched.

"Well," Henry said. "That's odd."

Jean zoomed in on the visible contents of the four drawers that were open. Clothing stuck out of most of them. Socks and cigarette papers littered the cream-coloured carpet in front of the chest, which appeared to have fallen out while someone had rifled through them.

"You didn't search these drawers?" Henry asked, just to double-check.

Jean shook her head like the idea was beyond her comprehension. "On no! I didn't touch a thing."

"Well, someone's rifled through them."

"That's what I thought. Look at this," she said, selecting another image of the room, which was centred on the bed. "Look at the drawers in the nightstand here. They've not been touched. So, I reckon someone was looking for something in that chest of drawers."

Henry nodded. He had concluded the same thing.

Emboldened by her own detective skills, Jean said, "And look at the bed."

Henry did so. The double bed had been expertly made. Its grey sheets were crisp and taut over the surface of the mattress. It was almost to hotel-standard, Henry thought. But he couldn't see what Jean was getting at.

"What about it?" he asked.

"Even I can't make beds like that. And a young skinhead is supposed to have slept in it? I doubt he'd have made his bed at all."

Henry had to accept she had a point, assuming Vince wasn't a clean freak. But Henry knew from experience that a minority of former prisoners became obsessed with cleanliness once on the outside. It probably had something to do with the lack of hygiene in most prisons.

"Look at the rest of the room," Jean said, pointing at the nightstand and a desk. Everything was neat. The audio equipment and laptop on the desk appeared to be so clean, they almost shined.

"What about it?"

"I don't think a lad like Vince lived in here."

"He did," Henry said. "I saw him in there."

She raised her index finger. "Just because you saw him in there doesn't mean he lived in it."

Henry went to argue, but then realised she had a point. "So, are you saying Vince didn't live in that room?"

She shook her head. "To me, it was just a place that held his stuff."

"Then, why were his drawers searched?"

She didn't have an answer to that.

"And where did he live if not in that room?"

She bit her lip.

"And who knows, maybe Vince was a clean freak. I believe he spent time inside, and when some prisoners get out, they're sticklers for cleanliness."

Jean didn't quite believe him but didn't argue. Instead, she clicked the trackpad, skipping through more images of Vince's room.

"Hang on," Henry said. "Go back."

Jean did so until Henry instructed her to stop.

"What is it?" she asked, squinting at the screen.

Henry leant closer to the photo of the cream-coloured carpet near the door. "Zoom in on the door handle."

Jean made the image larger so that the door took up her entire screen, then she looked at him as if in need of an explanation.

"Here," Henry said, pointing at the screen. "The door lock."

Jean zoomed closer to it. "What about it?"

"There's a key inside it."

"And?"

"And above it, further up, there's a hasp."

"A what?" Jean asked.

"A hasp. In fact, two of them," Henry said, noticing the surprise in his own voice. "Hasps are used to secure door with padlocks, and Vince had two of them."

"Why would he do that?" Jean asked, even more perplexed than before.

Henry leant closer to the laptop and, touching the metal trackpad, flipped back through the images to one of the windows.

The blinds had been pulled down over the windowpane, but Henry zoomed in and noticed a black mark on the white windowsill.

A handprint.

Well, half of one, he had to admit, as the rest looked to have been smudged away.

"You've lost me," Jean said, getting frustrated.

Henry sat back in his chair and thought it through before speaking. When he was sure of his conclusion, he said, "Vince locked his door with a key and two padlocks. And it looks like someone got through his bedroom window."

He cupped his chin in his hand while he considered it.

Jean didn't have an answer, and returned to the first images of the white-walled hallway outside Vince's room.

"Here, why don't you check the camera?" Robbie said, who'd been standing quietly near the table, trying not get noticed.

"Cameras?" Henry asked. "There aren't any cameras."

"Yeah, there is," Robbie said. He leant over his gran to touch the laptop, zooming in on a large clock on the wall. Its white face and black numbering made it look standard and uninteresting, and Henry vaguely remembered it.

"That's a clock, love," Jean said, almost embarrassed for him.

"It's not," Robbie clicked at his own smartphone, and after a few moments, produced a picture of the same clock on his screen. "They're pricey, but they hide cameras very well."

"It's a covert camera?" Henry asked, taking Robbie's phone off him. He saw the clock could be bought online for two hundred pounds. "You reckon he could have more of these?"

Robbie nodded and took his phone from Henry. "Oh yeah. He'd have an entire network."

Henry considered it. A whole network of cameras around the house, watching everything all the time. Was there a way of getting access to it? He would know what had happened to Vince if he watched the camera footage.

But then he realised that any such footage could have been deleted. "How easy would it be to wipe footage?" he asked Robbie.

Robbie shrugged. "It depends on who controlled it. If it was this Thomas guy, then he could wipe it. But there'd be a trail of its deletion."

"A trail?" Henry asked.

Robbie nodded. "We could see that something had been wiped. We'd have ten o'clock and then it'd jump to midnight. Plus, there's a chance he might not know the cameras are there."

The thought nearly slapped Henry around his chops. What if Thomas didn't know the cameras were there? Was that even possible? If Thomas didn't know, then who had put them in and who controlled them?

Henry didn't like where these thoughts were taking him, as it seemed to suggest someone else knew what was going on inside Thomas Wentworth-Scott's house.

Someone was sitting on the knowledge and doing their best to protect him.

Henry was pretty certain he knew who it was and wondered where Mrs Wentworth-Scott was having lunch that day.

Chapter Twenty-One

Jean made ham and salad sandwiches on brown bread and brought out some cherry scones she'd made the previous day. She kept apologising about not being able to put much of a spread on, despite putting more food on the table than they could comfortably eat.

Henry hadn't voiced his suspicions of Mrs Wentworth-Scott spying on her own son in his house. Instead, he had just nodded at the information Robbie gave him about the covert cameras with faint interest, suggesting it might be useful but more likely wouldn't.

But Henry was pretty certain he'd found something. Mrs Wentworth-Scott had gifted the house to Thomas and probably had it decorated and maintained for him. Henry doubted her son had the stylish eye for detail to decorate anything.

Seeing as Thomas didn't own the house, and it was still the property of his mother, then she could, in theory, have hidden cameras dotted around. Henry knew it was illegal to spy on people, but possibly the matriarch had taken the risk after Freya had been found dead.

That was if the cameras hadn't been installed beforehand.

Then there were the locks on Vince's door, which Henry thought were odd. Why would he have locked himself in his own bedroom like that? A lock and key and two padlocks for a bedroom door? Was he protecting something inside his room, or was he keeping someone out?

And the smudged handprint on the windowsill suggested someone had entered the room from the window. Was that what had happened to Vince? Had he been inside his locked room the previous night, waiting for his drug deal to come through, when someone climbed through the window and attacked him?

Henry tried to picture where Vince's room was in the house's layout. The bedroom faced the driveway, and he recalled there being a bay window on the ground floor directly underneath.

It was possible that someone had climbed onto the tiled canopy of the bay window and used it to access Vince's bedroom. Henry thought even he could manage the climb with his new hip.

Had Thomas climbed in through Vince's window or had someone else? And had the intruder done it before or after Vince's death? Whoever had searched through Vince's chest of drawers was certainly looking for something in particular.

"You alright?" Jean said. She was seated at the table opposite. Her gold laptop and its many wires had been tidied away, and she and Robbie were busy eating their lunch.

Henry noticed his own sandwich on a plate before him was untouched. He shook himself free of his thoughts. "Aye," he said. "Just thinking."

He picked up his sandwich and took a bite.

"Well, give your mind a rest," Jean said.

Henry nodded as if suggesting he would, but he sensed he was working things out now. The opaqueness that had surrounded this case since his lunch the previous day was slowly clearing, and things were making more sense.

"Did you call that solicitor?" Jean asked, before taking another bite of her sandwich.

Henry had forgotten all about Clive Juniper, the defence barrister he thought could help Lottie. "No. I'll call him after lunch."

"Poor Charlotte," Jean said, covering her mouth as she chewed. "Being stuck in a police cell accused of murdering someone. Could you imagine?"

She shook her head as she did.

Henry bit into his sandwich, mulling over the 'evidence' that incriminated Lottie. The knife had been covered in Vince's blood and had Lottie's fingerprints on it. But how was that possible? Henry couldn't imagine Lottie stabbing anyone, let alone Vince.

Henry's phone buzzed in his pocket, and he gave Jean an apologetic look as he took it out. The caller was Jonathon Radcliffe. Henry's stomach sunk, although he decided he should take the call.

He excused himself from the table and stepped into Jean's living room. After answering, he stood on the fluffy bronze-coloured rug in the centre of the small lounge. He stared through the window at Main Street as he answered. "Yes?"

"Mr Ward. Has there been a misunderstanding?" Jonathon struggled to restrain his anger.

"I'm sorry?" Henry asked.

"Did you misunderstand me when I said you are no longer to investigate the death of anyone related to the Wentworth-Scott family?"

"No, Mr Radcliffe. I didn't misunderstand you–"

"Then can you explain why you have spoken to Thomas this morning at his home?"

"Ah. Well, I understand what you told me, but then I remembered I don't need your permission to investigate anything."

Jonathon's anger must have seized his vocal cords, as he couldn't speak for a minute. "Well… Might I suggest you desist from taking any further action on these matters? Or the family will seek legal remedies."

"Such as?"

"Restraining orders, claims of harassment, seeking financial compensation should you decide to slander or libel the family."

"Like you did with Gabriel Silverstone, I suspect?"

"I don't wish to discuss anything further with you, Mr Ward."

Henry took the chance to ask a question while he had a representative of the Wentworth-Scotts on the phone. "Where is the matriarch?"

"Who might you be talking about?"

"The mother. Where is she?"

Jonathon let out a frustrated sigh. "The whereabouts of Mrs Wentworth-Scott are of no concern of yours."

Henry suspected Jonathon didn't know. No matter how posh he sounded, he was still only a lackey. "Right. Well, is that all? Only, I'd best be getting on. These two murders won't solve themselves."

Jonathon nearly lost his temper. "Have you understood what I've just said?"

"Well, Mr Radcliffe, I'm afraid I am getting on in years… Could you make your threat clearer for me?"

Jonathon huffed down the phone, clearly not appreciating the sarcasm. "I'm not threatening you. I'm just making it clear that if you carry on bothering the family, they will sue you."

"Right. So, you're not threatening me, but you are warning me I could face legal action should I legally go about my business? I've got you," Henry said. "Oh, and another thing," he added in an amicable tone. "Who owns Thomas Wentworth-Scott's house? Is it him or his mother?"

Jonathon audibly baulked at the idea of answering the question and hung up.

Henry chuckled to himself. He could find out just as easily on the Land Registry website, but wondered if Jonathon would save him the time.

Thinking over the call, Henry assumed Thomas must have told his parents about his visit that morning.

The Wentworth-Scotts must be scared if they were threatening Henry with legal action so soon. He didn't even have any evidence of anything concrete, but his accusations must have rattled Thomas so much that he went crying to his mother.

Which meant Henry was on the right track.

Before returning to the kitchen, Henry searched the contacts on his phone for Clive Juniper's number. They hadn't spoken to each other for over ten years, when Clive had defended Andy Dwight, a suspected serial rapist, in court. Henry had built an iron-tight case to put this nasty bloke away for decades, but he was let off on a technicality.

Clive had found holes in the prosecution's case and criticized Henry's investigation, which Henry still thought was unwarranted. Ultimately, the jury agreed with Clive's version of the truth, letting Dwight go free.

Henry remembered reading in the papers that Dwight was later arrested for another sexual assault several months later. This time he went down for his crimes, but for a lesser sentence, as he was only convicted for one sexual assault.

While looking at Clive's mobile number, Henry questioned his motives for ringing him. He hated the man; Clive made a good living helping criminals avoid justice, even when all the evidence suggested they were guilty.

But, as Henry always told himself, that was how the British criminal justice system functioned. He felt it was right that people could defend themselves, otherwise the system wouldn't be fair, and it would collapse.

It was just that sometimes the system was fairer on some people, and not on others.

Henry then imagined where Lottie would be at that moment. Probably in a windowless interrogation room, sat opposite Barnes and Hargreaves, having to put up with Hargreaves' sickly-sweet perfume. An overworked and mentally checked-out legal aid lawyer would be sitting beside her, who would have too many cases to keep track of and wouldn't offer anything other than perfunctory advice. And in the middle of the grey plastic table would be a photo of the knife that Lottie had apparently used to murder Vince; an image that the police and prosecution would use to put Lottie behind bars and away from her farm for decades.

Henry swallowed his dignity and called Clive Juniper's mobile number.

"Clive Juniper, QC," came the abrupt voice.

"Now then. It's former DCI Henry Ward."

It took a few moments for Clive to place the name. "Well. Blood and sand. It's you. What do you want with me?" he said, eventually.

Henry sighed at having to ask a sworn enemy for a favour. "Listen, can you talk?"

"I can. Quickly. What is it I can do for you?" Clive sounded suspicious as if Henry was about to detonate a bomb in his life.

"Don't worry, it's nothing bad," Henry said. He heard the sounds of a city around Clive and wondered where he was. "You see, I know someone in need of a good defence barrister."

"Oh, right," Clive said, perking up. "I can help with that. Where is this person?"

"Yorkshire."

Clive let out a grunt. "Oh, up there. I've not worked in God's Own County for nearly ten years."

"Where are you now?"

"In our esteemed shithole capital. I've moved up a few levels, and now I'm running my own firm down here. For my sins."

God, Henry thought. A bunch of barristers like Clive, picking holes in cases to help criminals avoid jail.

But then he realised that if Clive was in London, he couldn't help Lottie.

"Ah, I see," he said, failing to hide his disappointment.

Clive picked up on it. "Why? What's going on up there? You're not in trouble, are you?"

"Crikey. No. It's someone I know. She's been accused of murder."

"And you don't think she did it?"

"Would I be calling you if I did?"

"I suppose not." A bus must have driven past Clive in the street, as Henry heard its engine. Clive talked loudly over it. "Listen. I know someone based in Leeds who could help."

Henry felt hope again. "Oh, right."

"She's bloody good. Like me in the old days. She still needs training, mind; but she's passed the Bar."

The idea of hiring someone cheaper made Henry feel even happier. "Perfect. What's her name?"

"Sophia Juniper."

Clive's daughter, Henry realised. "Okay. I see. Following her father's tracks, is she?"

"It was her choice. I tried to steer her in another direction, but she had none of it."

"And is she experienced?" Henry asked. He'd chosen Clive as he thought Lottie needed someone who could handle the challenge. With the murder weapon incriminating Lottie and being up against the police and a powerful family, the odds were stacked up against her.

"Sophia's handled a lot of cases already. Here, no joke, she'll be better than me soon."

Henry cut through her father's bluffing to see that Sophia wasn't that experienced. But he didn't have much choice. Either he went with Clive's inexperienced daughter, or he spent the rest of the day calling around other barristers to see if they could help Lottie.

And Henry didn't have the time for that. He had two murders to solve.

"Alright, I'm sure she'll do. What's her number?"

Clive sounded overjoyed to have found his daughter some work and told Henry she'd contact him within the hour. Henry wondered if Sophia had been sitting around looking for cases, which was never a good sign.

Anyway, the choice had been made. He'd thanked Clive for his time, and they promised to meet up at some unmentioned time.

At least Henry had found Lottie some legal counsel. Now all he had to do was get to the bottom of what happened to Vince.

Chapter Twenty-Two

Henry went back to Jean's kitchen, where she and Robbie had moved on to eating cherry scones from a plastic tub placed in the middle to the table.

Henry's half-finished ham and salad sandwich remained on his plate, and he sat down and took a mouthful.

Jean brushed scone crumbs off her hands and gave Henry a look, suggesting she wanted to know what he'd been discussing on the phone in her living room.

Henry picked up a cup of tea, which he assumed Jean had made while he'd been on the call, and took a gulp. He'd be damned if he started telling Jean everything he discussed on his phone.

Robbie helped himself to another scone and had a methodical process of slicing it, buttering it up both sides, and slopping strawberry jam all over them.

Henry watched his systematic approach in silence until Jean cleared her throat to get his attention.

Henry slurped his tea again, knowing she was still expecting an explanation, so he gave her one. "Well, Lottie's getting some legal defence."

"Oh, great news," Jean said, beaming at Henry. "That'll help her. Is it that gin guy you mentioned?"

What gin guy? Henry thought. Then he remembered her poor joke. "Oh, right? Clive Juniper? No. His daughter."

Jean pulled a face, expressing her confusion. "Right? Is she any good?"

Henry shrugged. "Apparently. She should be better than any legal aid fella Lottie gets offered. At least she'll be less overworked."

Jean raised her eyebrows in mild disapproval and sipped her tea.

Henry took his phone out of his pocket and opened the web browser. After getting onto the Land Registry website, he typed Thomas's address into the search function. It took a few minutes, and a payment of a few pounds on his credit card, to learn the farmhouse was owned by a company: Wentworth-Scott Estate Ltd.

So, the house was owned by the family within a company structure, Henry concluded. Doing so might offer them more tax advantages. If that was the case, who was the head of the company? Mrs Wentworth-Scott? The husband? Thomas?

Henry turned to Robbie, who'd eaten his scone and was going for another. "Here, you know those covert cameras we found?" he asked.

Robbie nodded and placed the new scone on his plate. "Yep." He started his process of slicing it.

"Would there be any way of getting access to the footage?"

Robbie stopped cutting the scone and considered the question, and then he gave Henry a suspicious look. "You mean, if you're not the administrator?"

Henry nodded.

"The police could access it, in theory."

"If they know about it," Henry added. "But let's keep them out of this for now. Could I access the footage?"

Robbie glanced at Jean, who was quietly sipping her cup of tea, watching. "Well… you could… hack into the servers."

Jean nearly spat her drink over the table. "Henry! No!"

"What?" Henry said.

"No way are you getting him to hack anything. It's bad enough you had him help with those pictures."

"I'm only asking his opinion," Henry assured her. Then he turned to Robbie. "And there's no other way, other than hacking?"

Jean fixed her glare from Henry to her grandson.

Robbie's face flushed as he clearly felt the pressure. "Well, some networks will have software managing them. If you could get the password, you could get inside and see all the footage. But the chances of you getting that password are slim. I doubt they'll just give it to you."

Henry had to agree. It was unlikely he could guess a password, and first he'd have to access the software. It seemed unlikely that he would ever see the covert camera footage, he concluded.

He got up from the kitchen table, taking his phone.

"Where are you going now?" Jean asked.

"I'm making another call."

"Who to?"

"A friend. I hope." Without offering any further explanation, he went back into Jean's living room and rang Barnes.

His call went to her answerphone, and he didn't leave a message.

He then tried her again, but got cut off after two rings.

She must have cancelled the call, he thought. Maybe she was no longer his friend. Or she could be busy speaking to Lottie.

His phone rang in his hand, and he thought it might be Barnes calling him back, but he didn't recognise the number. Then he guessed it was Sophia Juniper.

She sounded very self-assured and slightly out of breath, like she'd been hurrying somewhere. "Is this DCI Ward?"

"Yes," Henry said.

After she'd introduced herself, she asked, "What is it you've got for me?"

"Charlotte Wentworth-Scott, goes by the name of Lottie," Henry said, then realised he had made a mistake. "She'll be Charlotte Foster, actually. Wentworth-Scott is her maiden name."

"Hang on, there were too many names there."

Once Henry had clarified everything, he said, "She's been arrested for murdering a man named Vince Taylor. Vince lived with Lottie's brother up on the moors above Otley."

"Oh right. What do they call it up there? The Chevin?"

"Aye." Henry went into the details of the case, which Sophia noted down, and then he asked the dreaded question. "So, how much are your fees?"

"As this is a private case, I'd say it'll be around two hundred an hour."

Henry was expecting something like that but hearing it out loud made him feel queasy. "How many hours do you think this'll take?"

"Oh. I'm not sure. It depends on the complexity of the case. And this one seems pretty complex. It could run up to hundreds of hours easily, and that's before we get to trial, if it gets that far."

Hundreds of hours, all charged at two hundred pounds. Henry felt beads of sweat form on his forehead. "Right. Fine," he lied.

"Great. Do you know where they're holding her?"

"Probably the station on Elland Road," Henry guessed.

Sophia knew Leeds District police station and said she'd drive over there immediately.

Henry wished her luck and asked her not to go too hard on DI Barnes.

"Oh. Is she a colleague?" Sophia asked.

"We've worked with each other on a few occasions."

"It must feel odd for you, all this," Sophia said almost cheekily, "with you normally being on the other side?"

Henry grunted his answer.

"But don't worry, I'll make sure Mrs Foster has the very best representation and is cleared of these dubious charges."

"Very good. Now, if you could do me a favour and don't tell the detectives I'm paying for you? They already hate me enough."

Sophia giggled. "I never disclose my client's payment information to anyone, DCI Ward."

And with that, she ended the call.

* * *

Jean had cleared away the kitchen table, and Robbie was slumped back in a chair, playing his colourful handheld games device, which made odd whirs and beeps.

She was loading the dishwasher with the plates they'd used for lunch. She watched Henry walk back in and gave him a disgruntled look. "I chucked your sandwich, seeing as you weren't bothered about it," she said.

"I've just not got the appetite at the moment."

That didn't seem to appease her much. "So, who was it you were talking to this time?" she asked, closing the dishwasher door with a bang.

"The defence barrister for Lottie."

"That lawyer's daughter?"

"Aye. She seems like she'll do a good job."

Jean still wasn't convinced. "What are your plans now?" she asked. "Only, I've got a medical appointment this afternoon."

Henry's mind raced through the multiple things he had to do and felt overwhelmed by them all. It was a feeling he used to have when he led major criminal investigations. Over the years, he'd learnt to quieten his mind and think clearly. However, it was a skill he hadn't practiced for a while, mostly because he hadn't had the need.

But he tried it there and then in Jean's kitchen, as she pottered about, wiping down the white kitchen table, waiting for his answer.

He calmed the multiple ideas and voices in his head until he recalled the to-do list he'd made that morning. The first item on it was to speak with the GP who had confirmed Freya's death at the party.

Her name was Dr Emma Parrish, and Gabriel Silverstone had said she worked in Leeds.

"I think I'll go chat with a doctor myself," Henry said, but by this point Jean seemed to have forgotten her question.

"For your hip?" she asked, with a note of concern in her voice.

"No, about these murders."

Chapter Twenty-Three

As Henry drove over to Leeds, he asked himself if it was going to be worth the trip. Getting an appointment with a GP was impossible these days, let alone taking up one's time in the middle of the day without being a registered patient.

He also believed he should deal with Vince's murder first. His gut told him it was linked to Freya's death. Finding out what happened to Vince could answer how Freya came to drown in a bath three years previously.

But Henry couldn't make any headway in Vince's murder with the police all over it. Barnes had shown she wasn't willing to cooperate and share information. Murphy must have his eyes on her, watching her every move. If she wanted to stay in the police at the same rank, she would have to do as she was told.

The barbed words Barnes had said to Henry came to mind: 'You'd best speak to Murphy.'

Call Murphy? The thought made the bile in his gut squelch. Call that backstabbing, brown-nosing wanna-be copper? Henry would rather do a lot more toe-curling things than call that idiot.

His sat nav told him he'd arrived at Dr Parrish's practice, and he pulled into a half-empty car park that faced a single-storey sandstone building. The doctor's practice was on the outskirts of leafy Headingley, close to the centre of Leeds. Henry had come to the world-famous cricket ground here over the years, though he wasn't much of a fan. Oak trees stood around the car park, offering shade from the sun that had returned in full force.

Inside, the reception area looked modern and elegant: shiny metal finishings, and calm grey walls and dark brown furnishings. It looked more like the reception to a stylish office. Then Henry noticed there weren't any NHS posters on the walls. The comfy leather chairs in the waiting area were empty, and the air conditioning made the room feel cool.

Had he walked into a private practice? he wondered. Perhaps they would let him see Dr Parrish after all, if he got his wallet out.

A woman was sitting behind a glass desk with an expensive silver computer in front of her. She was talking quietly and calmly to someone on the headset. Despite standing within a few metres of her, Henry couldn't make out what her soothing voice was saying.

Eventually, she ended the call after a gentle goodbye and smiled at Henry. "Can I help?"

"Aye. I'd like to speak with Dr Parrish."

Apart from a small flicker of the eyes, the woman's smile remained. "Right. Do you have an appointment?"

"I'm not a patient."

Another small flicker of the eyes. "Okay. Is it about a health matter, as we are a medical practice?"

"Kind of," Henry said, smiling. "You can tell her it's about Freya Harrison."

"Freya…?" The woman's smile was eventually replaced with a look of confusion. "Who's that?"

"Dr Parrish will know. If you need to jog her memory, you can mention the party at Thomas Wentworth-Scott's house in 2020."

Well-practiced in taking mental notes, the receptionist nodded, and her smile returned. She welcomed Henry to take a seat while she called Dr Parrish.

Henry relaxed in a leather chair. The magazine selection spread out on the coffee table before him included the latest copies of *Country Life*, *Vanity Fair*, and *Tatler*. All their glossy covers looked untouched. Henry didn't bother picking one up and felt cold as the crisp air travelled through his thin shirt.

The receptionist ended her inaudible call with the doctor and cleared her throat. "She will see you."

Henry wasn't that surprised. He half-expected to find the doctor crouched in the corner of her office having a panic attack. "Right."

He walked down a corridor lined with doors and found Dr Parrish's at the end. He knocked and went in when instructed.

She remained seated behind another silver computer, much like the fancy one in reception. Dr Parrish had long black hair, tied back, and peered at Henry through bright-blue-rimmed glasses. She was younger than Henry had expected, possibly in her early thirties.

She wore professional clothing: a white blouse and some dark grey trousers. The air conditioning in the office was just as severe as in reception, so Henry couldn't blame her for wearing long sleeves.

"Who are you?" she demanded, after sizing him up for a few seconds.

There were two chairs in front of her sleek desk, and he took one without asking. "I'm former DCI Henry Ward."

She placed a blue biro to her lips and bit its well-chewed end.

"I've been asked to look into the mysterious death of Freya Harrison three years ago."

"Mysterious?" she asked, biting down on the pen.

Henry took his small leather notepad out of his jeans pocket. "It's come to my attention, during my investigation, that you 'unofficially' pronounced Freya as dead at the party on 20 May."

The end of the biro crunched in her mouth. She took it out with a shaky hand. "I don't know what you mean."

"Well, I have a witness who says they saw you at the party, and that you pronounced Freya as being dead to the rest of the guests. Is that true?"

Dr Parrish shook her head absent-mindedly as if she was processing too many thoughts at the same time.

"First, she wasn't murdered," she said. "And second…" She seemed to realise her first point would undermine her second and stopped.

"Right? Do you deny being at the party on the 20th of May, 2020?"

"No…"

"Okay. And can you remember seeing Freya's body?"

Dr Parrish winced as she evidently pictured the scene in her mind. "What is it you want? The police investigated all of this. It's all been sorted."

"It certainly hasn't," Henry said, but he didn't want to make light of the coroner's report or suggest Freya's death hadn't been properly investigated. "Thomas's family asked me to look into the matter in a private capacity. Thomas has been accused of murdering Freya. Would you know anything about that?"

Dr Parrish shook her head, almost grimacing.

"What is it?"

She forced a neutral expression. "Nothing. I just don't wish to think about that time."

"Why is that?"

"It was during COVID. Things were crazy. There were lockdowns. We were all mad busy."

"Too busy to attend drug-fuelled parties?"

She sat upright, getting on the defensive. "I didn't take anything like that. Now, there might have been such substances, but I didn't see any."

"Right. And you were aware that the party was against lockdown rules and, therefore, illegal."

She shrugged. "They were having them in Downing Street. What do I care?"

"So, you wouldn't mind me telling your colleagues and patients about it?"

The idea of it stirred her out of her indifference.

Henry continued, "You're a general practitioner. You're supposed to be an upstanding member of the community."

She scoffed. "Do people like that exist anymore? Did they ever?"

Henry moved on to another topic. "When did you see Freya?"

She closed her eyes, clearly moved by having to remember. "It was later on."

"What time?"

"I can't recall…"

"But didn't you confirm the time when you unofficially declared her dead?"

"I didn't pronounce anyone dead."

"So, what did you do?"

She hesitated a moment, clearly debating in her mind if she should say anything. But then she exhaled, which suggested to Henry she wanted to get it off her chest.

"I was in the dining room, dancing away. And it was late, I think. Or early, depending on how you look at it."

Henry shook his head like he wasn't following her. "Can you be specific? What time was this?"

"After three? No, maybe around four. The sun hadn't come up, but the sky had turned that blue-orangey colour."

"Isn't that a bit late for a doctor to be staying up?"

"I was off the following day, and the others there were working from home, so they weren't bothered about sleeping much."

"Right?"

"Anyway, Thomas tapped me on the shoulder, and he looked grey."

"What do you mean?"

"His face was almost white, and he looked ill. I thought he might be overdosing. He dragged me by the wrist out of the dining room and upstairs. I asked what was going on, but he wouldn't tell me. He just pulled me right around that bloody big house and then pushed me into a bathroom."

"Which bathroom?"

"I don't know."

"Was it near the guest rooms?"

"I don't know."

"Was anyone in the bathroom or outside it when you approached it?"

"Yes. That druggie who'd been hanging around with Thomas."

"Did he have a shaved head?"

She nodded. "I didn't like him and had no idea why Thomas was hanging around him."

"So, Vince was outside the bathroom?"

"Vince, yes. That's his name. Yes, he was almost keeping guard outside. Thomas took me inside, and…" She let out a long breath. "There was Freya, lying in the bath."

"What state was she in?"

"State?" She frowned. "Well, she was dead. I could tell as soon as I looked at her. She wasn't breathing. Her eyes were open but weren't fixed on anything."

"Did you touch her?"

She nodded. "I checked for a pulse, but there wasn't one. The bath water was cold, and so was she. She wasn't breathing, and when I opened her mouth, it was clear her airways were closed."

"She'd drowned?"

Dr Parrish nodded.

"Was there any bruising on her?"

"Not that I could see."

"Was there anything odd about her?"

"Despite being found dead in a bath at a party?" she asked, sarcastically. Then she contemplated his question and gave a serious answer. "She was fully clothed."

"What was she wearing?"

"A brown dress. No shoes."

Henry scribbled down some notes. "Was it just Thomas and Vince in the bathroom?" he asked.

"Yes," she said, but then shook her head. "Actually, there was someone in the corner, hanging around the sink. I hadn't seen him before."

A third person, Henry thought. "What did he look like?"

She narrowed her eyes as she tried to remember, then gave up. "I can't recall…"

"Humour me."

She huffed like it was going to be hard work. After squinting into the distance for a few moments, she said, "He was tall. Dark-haired. Quite tanned."

"As tall as Thomas?"

"Almost. An inch shorter. He was thinner, too."

"Did the others say his name?"

"No. They didn't, actually." She frowned and stared into the distance. "Which is odd if you think about it."

"Are you sure you hadn't seen him before?"

She considered his question and then shook her head. "Never."

"And did he have an accent?"

"He sounded like Thomas, come to think of it."

"And what did he say?"

"Not much. I got the impression the other two were upset with him."

"Why?"

She lowered her head. "I got the impression… rightly or wrongly… that he was involved with Freya's death."

"Why do you think that?"

She looked up at him. "I'd rather not say."

Chapter Twenty-Four

Henry nearly fell out of the black leather chair he was sitting in and landed on the doctor's expensive carpet. Why wasn't she going to tell him? he wondered.

He glanced at the notes he'd taken: third man, young, tall, dark hair, sounds like Thomas. Then he remembered what Lottie had told him. She'd seen Freya be carried by Vince and someone else. Someone she couldn't fully make out in the darkness or didn't want to identify.

"No," Henry said, shaking his head. "You have to tell me."

"I don't have to tell you anything, do I?" Dr Parrish said, sitting tall in her chair. "Who are you, anyway? You could be anyone."

"I'm a former DCI–"

"I know who you claim to be, but not who you really are," she said, cutting him off.

She'd appeared to have found a reserve of confidence from somewhere and was putting it to use. "I have an appointment in five minutes if you'd kindly leave," she said.

Henry remained seated. "Are you even aware of what's going on?"

She frowned at his question.

"Have you read the local news today?" he said, elaborating.

"I don't have time for the news."

"The 'druggie' – Vince Taylor – you saw with Freya that night has been found dead. Stabbed multiple times."

This moved Dr Parrish to shake her head in disbelief. "Are you serious?" Without waiting for a reply, she typed on her keyboard and searched for the local news on her large computer.

She covered her mouth when the story came up.

Henry took his chance. "So, you can either tell me what you saw in that bathroom three years ago, or I can tell my former colleagues that you saw something and they can make it official." He waited a moment for her options to sink in, before asking, "Which one do you prefer?"

She didn't answer. Instead, she read the article from top to bottom and then reread it a second time. "But… who killed him?"

"They believe it was Thomas's sister?"

Her mouth gaped. "His sister? I didn't even know he had one."

"Aye. She lives on the farm opposite."

Dr Parrish picked up the biro next to her and chewed its end again. Henry wondered if she'd been a smoker at some point and had transferred the compulsive behaviour to chewing pens. The end of the biro was so damaged, he half-expected it to leak ink all over her lips.

She shook her head as if rejecting the hard choice she had to make. "No. I can't be involved in this. This is murder. It's serious."

"Deadly serious," Henry said, winding her up further.

"I can't…" She shook her head, almost frantically.

Henry had seen this reaction in people before. She feared something, and not just the reputational damage of being involved in two homicides.

"Is someone putting pressure on you?" he asked.

She pulled the pen out of her mouth, and her eyes widened. "Not at all."

Henry saw through the lie as it was a bad one. "Thomas has threatened you, hasn't he? You're not to talk to anyone about this."

Dr Parrish's wide-eyed gaze answered his question.

"What do they have over you?" he asked.

She didn't say. Instead, she took short breaths as if a panic attack was coming on. Her eyes searched the room, looking for something to help her, but nothing could.

She would not give him an answer, he thought. And then he noticed she was still scanning her office; her eyes darted up to the ceiling and then down to the carpeted floor.

What was it about the room? Henry wondered. He glanced at the cool grey walls, and the nice new window with silk blinds that looked out onto the half-empty car park.

She was answering him without saying it aloud. It was the building, he realised.

"Do the Wentworth-Scott family own this practice?" he asked.

She cleared her throat. "I can't say…"

Henry held up his phone. "I can find out from the Land Registry website, so just tell me the truth."

Her head flopped downwards, giving in. "They do. They own the whole site: the doctor's practice, the land, the houses down the street."

"What the hell is a family like that doing owning a doctor's practice?"

"It's not the only one they control. I can't answer for the others, but this one used to be owned by two GPs, the original partners, but they sold everything when they retired."

"So, Thomas's threatened you with what? Dismissal, if you talk?"

She didn't answer, but Henry felt he was near the mark.

"That bloody family," Henry said, almost laughing at the incredulity of it all. "They've got their bloody mitts in everything."

Dr Parrish didn't say anything. She concentrated on picking her nails. "They're… what was it you said? Pillars of society."

Henry chuckled. "I'm not sure about that."

"Well, that's how the world is." She looked at him. "I really do have an appointment now. So, if you wouldn't mind."

Henry went to stand but stopped. "Hang about. They've threatened to sue the living daylights out of me if I say anything about this. So, they've got us both under their thumb. Why don't you tell me what made you think this mystery fella killed Freya?"

The desk phone rang, and Dr Parrish answered it, said a few words, and then hung up. "My patient's here."

"What was it about this fella?" Henry asked, not moving from his seat.

She tapped her nails on the desk, thinking something, and then she glared at Henry like he was a nuisance. "Fine. God, I can tell you're an old copper." Her shoulders slumped as she exhaled. "There was something about that guy. He was standing in the corner near the bathroom sink, just watching. I don't even think he was wearing a top, he was half-dressed. And the other two, Thomas and Vince, they seemed scared of him."

"Why?"

"I don't know. It was just a feeling. They stayed away from him. It was like… I don't know."

"Like what?"

"Like… he was dangerous. A caged animal that had gotten loose. And they didn't want to be in the same room as him. They were worried about him coming near me."

"Why?"

"I don't... I... That's mostly why I thought he'd hurt Freya. I didn't see any bruises on her, but it was just the way he looked at me. Like I was prey."

Prey, thought Henry. What the hell was he dealing with here?

The knock at the door shook both of them.

Dr Parrish rose from her desk, switching into professional mode. "That's my patient."

Henry obliged and stood up. "Thank you for being generous with your time, Doctor."

As she went to the door, she said, "Do me a favour, don't come here again."

"I don't make promises I can't keep."

Dr Parrish rolled her eyes and then put on a smile to greet her patient. She opened the door, letting Henry slip out first before her elderly patient came in.

Henry's car had luckily been shaded by an oak tree. He got inside and flipped through the notes he'd taken.

So, there was a third man involved, he thought. A mystery man who Dr Parrish thought was dangerous.

So dangerous that Thomas and Vince were afraid of him.

And he must be some kind of sicko, Henry concluded, if he made Dr Parrish feel like she was 'prey'.

Prey. What an odd way to put it.

What could that all mean? Then Henry remembered the locks on Vince's door. The two hasps and the lock and key. They all seemed to be more than necessary for an interior door.

Was Vince so scared of this third man that he made sure his bedroom was completely secure?

But where was this third man? Did he live in that massive farmhouse with Thomas? Was he another stray that Thomas had picked up? Or did he live elsewhere?

Henry didn't know. He didn't have an answer to any of this. Only the Wentworth-Scotts did.

He checked the time on the dashboard after he started the Skoda's engine. It was after 3 p.m., and Lottie would have spent her first few hours in a police cell.

Checking his phone for messages, he didn't see any from Sophia. He wondered if the junior barrister had managed to meet up with Lottie yet or whether she had bitten off more than she could chew.

He also had a message from Jean asking him if he was coming over for dinner that night. He didn't reply as he couldn't answer there and then. He had no idea where he'd be that evening.

The continuous buzz of ideas and plans plagued his mind again, and he felt a walk in the wilderness would clear them. It would also give him the opportunity to put his new hip to good use.

Unfortunately for Tessa, she was back in the cottage, sulking, as she couldn't get out into the backyard. She'd miss out on this walk too, as Henry didn't fancy driving back to Addingham to collect her.

Looking at his sat nav he realised that he wasn't far from Otley Chevin. Perhaps a walk around the fields up there would help him get some perspective.

And he could also see if it was possible to get closer to Lottie's farmyard.

After setting the destination on his sat nav, he drove out of Headingley. But a road sign at a junction gave directions for Horsforth, and Henry realised that Gabriel Silverstone's house was only a few miles away.

There were some things that he needed to clear up with Gabriel, Henry remembered, heading in the direction of Horsforth and upsetting the sat nav.

Gabriel claimed he had heard some shouts or moans coming from the guest bathroom at around 1 a.m. on the night Freya died. But that didn't match with what Lottie had said, as she'd seen Vince and this third man carry Freya down the corridor at 3 a.m.

Henry needed to get that squared, as one of them was lying or had got their times wrong.

Or both were correct, and the mystery behind Freya's death was more confusing than it first appeared.

Chapter Twenty-Five

Henry pulled up outside Gabriel's house in the cul-de-sac he had visited the previous day. The sun was hidden behind some grey, ominous clouds that threatened showers later. Maybe a walk on the moorlands wouldn't be such a good idea.

He got out of his car and headed up Gabriel's drive. The fresh green front lawn had been mowed since his last visit. Thinking about the elegant Japanese garden at the rear of the house, Henry wondered if Gabriel had expert green fingers or hired someone who did.

Gabriel came to the door wearing a smart white shirt and black trousers. His thinning grey hair had been combed. Some hair product had been liberally applied, making it greasy. Henry guessed he was about to go somewhere official.

Gabriel gave him a look that suggested he'd forgotten who he was. When the recognition came, he was displeased. "It's you."

"Hello, Mr Silverstone. Can I have a word?"

Gabriel briefly scanned the neighbouring detached houses as if worried he was being watched. "Come in," he said, almost pulling him into his house.

He brought Henry into his kitchen. The glass doors that opened up to the Japanese garden were closed, and the air inside was stuffy.

Gabriel stood near one of his worktops with his neck stooped and arms crossed over his thin chest. "What is it you want?"

Henry noted that all the lights over the marble kitchen worktops were off as if Gabriel was indeed about to go somewhere.

"I wanted to confirm something with you," Henry said.

"What would that be?" Gabriel asked, leaning his backside against the edge of the counter as though he needed the support.

"I was thinking over something you said about the party."

Gabriel blinked. "Right. Is that an issue anymore? As I understand it, the family has dropped the case against me, so…"

"They've delayed it, if I understand correctly."

Gabriel shook his head. "No. I'm to meet their solicitor now and sign a deal with them."

"What deal?"

"If I recant my accusations against Thomas and apologise, the family will drop all legal proceedings."

"And that's what you're doing? You're going to say Thomas isn't a murderer?"

Gabriel looked him in the eye for an instant but couldn't maintain eye contact. "Well… You know, I don't have any evidence that he did kill Freya, and my case seems flimsy to say the least. I mean… you've looked into it and haven't found anything?"

"I've only been at it a day and a half," Henry said.

"But what could a few more days bring? And now, with this other death–"

"Aye, the death of poor Vince. What do you think about that?"

Gabriel shrugged. "I don't think anything about it. I didn't know the man."

"You've never met him before?"

Alarm flickered in Gabriel's eyes, and he shook his head. "No. Should I have?"

"You tell me, Mr Silverstone. I've heard accounts from several people that Vince Taylor was at the party on the 20th of May. I wasn't there, unfortunately, so I can't confirm if he was. But you were."

"Well, if he was there, I didn't see him."

"Weren't you taking drugs at the party?"

Gabriel attempted to straighten his stooped neck. "What if I did?"

"Who supplied them to you?"

When Gabriel didn't answer, Henry continued, "I suspect Thomas didn't obtain them himself. It was more likely Vince who'd got hold of them."

Gabriel sniffed loudly, like he'd got something lodged in his nostril. He excused himself, took several sheets of kitchen roll from the counter and blew his nose loudly. "Apologies. It's my allergies."

Henry nodded as though he accepted the explanation but was really wondering if Gabriel was still using drugs. He didn't ask about it, however. "You know," he said, "it's hard to believe you didn't see or know much about Vince when you must have bought drugs from him."

"You'll have to believe me – as it's the truth." He tapped his kitchen worktop with his hand, trying to cover for the fact it was shaking. "Is there anything else? Only I need to go sign this document."

"Aye, just one thing. You said that you heard screams or moans coming from the guest bathroom. Can you remember what time that was?"

He frowned like he wasn't expecting such a specific question. "Listen. I don't feel it's worth dragging up all of that now. The immediate legal jeopardy is over, and–"

"Immediate legal jeopardy? Wasn't Freya your former girlfriend?"

"Yes, she was, but–"

"So, you're more concerned about getting sued than finding out how she died?"

Gabriel scrunched up his lips like he was disgusted at the thought of it. "No, no. It's not like that. But you're right. It could easily look that way."

"I'm not too fussed about how it looks, Mr Silverstone. I'd just like some clarification as to what happened."

"Why, though? It's all been sorted…" He caught himself saying the words and shook his head. "You're right, it hasn't. I still want to know what happened to her."

"So, will you answer my question? What time did you hear those noises coming from that guest bathroom?"

He exhaled, which made his stoop worse. "Well… It was 1 a.m. I have phone records of the time. I was looking for Freya as I couldn't find her, and then I walked upstairs and heard her ringtone coming from the bathroom."

"What do you mean by phone records? Would you have official ones from your network provider?"

He frowned. "Well… No. I have screenshots of my phone's screen. They show I tried to call Freya several times."

"Right, but no other official records?" Henry asked, knowing full well phone companies rarely kept records of unsuccessful calls.

Gabriel noted the tone of his question. "What are you getting at? Do you think I'm lying?" He pulled his phone from his black trouser pocket and tapped its screen. "Here, I can bloody show you."

Henry held up his hands as if he was surrendering. "It's alright, Mr Silverstone. I believe you. I just need to make sure everything can be verified."

This seemed to placate Gabriel, and he continued to lean against the worktop, placing his phone back in his pocket.

"So, you heard Freya and someone else in a bathroom," Henry said, and then he recalled that

Thomas's farmhouse had four of them. "Which one was it?"

"What do you mean?"

"Can you describe where it was in the house?"

"Well…" He was stumped. "I can't quite say. That place is like a maze."

"Was it on the second floor?"

"Yes."

"Was it near Thomas's room?" asked Henry.

Gabriel shook his head. "No. It was further down the corridor."

"Close to the guest rooms?"

He nodded. "Not too far. But I quite can't remember. It's all a blur, you see. I'd been drinking; I was high…"

"The wall outside the bathroom. Did it have a curve in it?"

Gabriel seemed ready to give up thinking about it, but then considered Henry's question. "A curve? Yes," he said. "There was one on the wall, as I sat against it when I couldn't get inside."

"Explain to me again what happened when you were at the bathroom door."

He checked his expensive watch. "Look, is this necessary?"

"It could be. Yes."

Huffing, Gabriel spoke in a monotone voice as though he'd now repeated these sentences several times. "I heard screams or moans, possibly both, coming from inside the bathroom. I heard someone hushing somebody, and the water pipes were running. There was splashing water. Then I heard her scream. I tried to push the door, but it was locked."

"Okay," Henry said, narrowing his eyes as if he were trying to picture it. "You were standing outside the locked bathroom door, and you heard your current girlfriend inside whose life you feared was in danger. Yet you failed to break down the door?"

Gabriel was offended. "What are you saying? That I didn't try hard enough to get in? I hit the door with my fists. I barged at it, knackering my shoulder, and I stood outside for a good ten minutes, shouting and bawling. What more do you want me to have done?"

"You could have smashed through the door or got help from other people at the party. From what you're saying, you thought your girlfriend was in danger. That some sicko was trying to drown her, and you're the only person right there and then who could have helped. And from what you're telling me, you didn't."

The words stung Gabriel. He closed his eyes as if he couldn't bear looking at Henry. "I… I thought…"

"And the fact you didn't burst through the door or get help leads me to think that something else went on. Isn't that right, Mr Silverstone?"

Gabriel scrunched his eyes tight. "I…"

"What I think you heard wasn't Freya being hurt or in danger, but her being romantic with someone else. I mean, you said the same thing yesterday, that at first you thought she was with Thomas in the bathroom, cheating on you. And these other elements: the water pipes running and the scream, that's all bollocks, isn't it? If you excuse my French."

"No–"

"You added in those details when you wanted to damage Thomas for pulling out of your brewery business. I mean, are you even sure it was Freya you heard inside that bathroom?"

"Yes," Gabriel said, opening his eyes, which were red with emotion. "It was her. I heard her phone, and also her… voice. It was her."

"With Thomas?"

Gabriel snarled as he relived the moment in his mind. "It was him."

"How can you be so sure?"

Gabriel lowered his head. "I walked up the corridor, having tried ringing her several times, and I saw that curve in the wall, and I heard her ringtone from inside the bathroom. I walked up to the door, and then heard her say 'Tommy'." He scrunched up his lips in revulsion. "They were busy… doing it."

"So, all this stuff about hearing Thomas hurt Freya and the sounds of water sloshing aren't true?"

It took him a moment, but eventually, Gabriel shook his head. "They weren't."

Henry continued, "The reality is you heard your girlfriend cheating on you with Thomas inside that bathroom, and then, when your brewery business collapsed three years later, you got revenge by accusing him of Freya's murder?"

Gabriel seemed to hate himself as he nodded, admitting what Henry had said was true.

"So, the Wentworth-Scotts were right to sue you?"

Gabriel scoffed loudly. "Oh. They wish."

"Why's that?"

"I know Thomas was involved in her death somehow. There's still everything I said about the funeral and the wake; with it being held at Thomas's house and how he behaved – like he knew he'd got away with something. And then that botched and pathetic police investigation that claimed that…" He let out a sob and covered his mouth as if he'd just belched. Shaking his head, he forced himself to regain composure. "He did something to Freya or knows someone who did," he said.

"How can you be so sure? As you've said yourself, you haven't got any evidence. All you heard was Freya and Thomas having intercourse in the bathroom, and then you have these opinions about Thomas's behaviour at the funeral." Henry shrugged. "That doesn't add up to him being a killer."

Gabriel stared at Henry as if seeing him differently. "You're on their side, aren't you? You made me think I could trust you, but then it turns out you're their little lackey. You think Thomas had nothing to do with Freya's death?"

Henry couldn't help but laugh. "Oh! I'm nobody's bloody lackey, and never have been. And I know Thomas is involved somehow, but do I think he killed Freya?" He shook his head, answering his own question.

"Well, who did?" said Gabriel.

It took Henry a moment to answer. "I'm not quite sure, yet. But I think I'm getting close."

Chapter Twenty-Six

Henry saw himself out of Gabriel's house, leaving the man looking even more crooked and wretched.

Luckily, Gabriel was about to sign a deal that would end the legal action against him. Henry knew that the man didn't have a leg to stand on and would have got slaughtered in court on Friday if the case had gone ahead.

Gabriel couldn't prove Thomas was involved in Freya's murder any more than Henry could. He had fabricated the noisy water pipes and the scream so he could get revenge on the man who had destroyed his business and stolen his girlfriend.

Fairly pathetic, Henry thought. But as motivations for doing something stupid things went, he had heard worse.

The fact Vince's murder had disrupted the court case was a positive for Gabriel, Henry concluded.

His phone rang as he walked down the drive and past the expertly cut front lawn. He recognised Sophia's number and answered, hoping the junior barrister had an update for him.

"DCI Ward?" Sofia asked, sounding uncertain.

"Yes?"

"Listen, could you come down to Leeds District police station?"

"What? Now?" Henry asked.

"Yes. If you can?"

"Well…" Henry said, wondering if Barnes and Hargreaves would let him visit Lottie. Normally, visitors weren't welcome when a detainee was being questioned, especially for murder. "Am I allowed?"

"Yes, you are. I've insisted they let you, Lottie asked to see you. She seems to think you can help."

Henry huffed down the phone as he opened his car door. "Well, I am trying to help as best I can out here."

"She has something to tell you."

"Can't she pass it on to you and save me the trip?" Henry asked, hoping he'd be spared having to deal with Barnes right now. Their last conversation hadn't gone smoothly, and he'd been keeping himself busy so he could put off calling Murphy. He knew if he spoke to Barnes, she'd insist he'd call the old brown-nosing careerist, and Henry would rather die in a ditch.

Sofia answered his question. "I've asked her to tell me. Believe me, it'd be easier. But she won't. She insists on speaking to you."

"And the two detectives, they're alright with me coming in?"

"Not at all. But I've threatened them both with all sorts, and I've managed to brow-beat them into agreeing."

Henry huffed in astonishment. Sofia had managed to browbeat Barnes and Hargreaves! Maybe her father's extravagant praise wasn't misplaced.

Henry knew he had to speak to Lottie and didn't have a choice. "Alright. I'll be there in…" He checked his watch. Leeds District police station was a fifteen-minute drive away, and that was if he didn't get stuck in rush-hour traffic. "I'll be there as soon as I can."

"Alright. She's waiting for you."

As Henry drove through the busy streets to the police station, his mind ran through the things Lottie could say to him. An admission, a revelation, some family secret? Henry didn't have a clue which.

At least he had eliminated the element that had confused the timeline. As he saw it, Gabriel had heard Freya and Thomas making love in the guest bathroom at around 1 a.m. Then at 3 a.m., when Lottie turned up at the party, she saw Vince and the third man carry Freya down the corridor.

Dr Parrish was pulled off the dancefloor in the dining room at around 4 a.m., went into the bathroom with Thomas, Vince, and this third person, and confirmed that Freya had drowned.

The timeline now made sense. Which meant Freya's death must have occurred between Lottie seeing her and Dr Parrish pronouncing her dead. Unless Freya had died before Lottie saw her, and she hadn't seen her unconscious body but a corpse.

Henry suspected this third man was involved in the murder. He didn't think Thomas could have killed Freya, not if he was in a relationship with her. But then again, they could have had a violent fall-out. However, Henry disregarded the idea. As much as he thought Thomas was a spoilt idiot, he didn't think he was the type to drown his lover in a bath.

No, he thought, this all seemed to involve this third man – whoever he was.

And clearly Vince was involved, as the lad had been stabbed to death on Lottie's property.

How did that come about?

Perhaps Lottie would shine a light on that.

* * *

Henry had never entered Leeds District police station before, despite spending a lot of his detective career in the city. Leeds had nine police stations that Henry had known fairly well, and some of them were long gone. The newish PFI building in front of him had been built just as he retired from the force, and it still looked new from the outside.

Its light-grey concrete walls and tinted windows made it resemble the other office blocks on the busy street. Only the Union Jack and West Yorkshire Police flags fluttering in the breeze gave it away as a police station.

It was on the outskirts of Leeds city centre, near the city's football club that had the same relationship with fortune as a typical gambling addict. Sometimes up, but mostly down.

After Henry introduced himself to the officer at the front desk, he was told to go down a corridor to where a constable would meet him.

He walked down the modern corridor past uniformed officers and detectives in their cheap suits. This is where he could be working, Henry thought. Poking his head through an open doorway, he saw rows of desks lined with computers.

This is where he could have worked, he corrected himself, if Murphy hadn't torpedoed his application to rejoin the police.

He turned a corner, hoping he wouldn't have to run into his old nemesis, the 'esteemed' superintendent, and instead bumped into the uniformed officer he'd seen at Thomas's farmhouse: PC Williams.

PC Williams still looked bulky without his black stab vest, and he stood with his hands on his hips, wearing a disgruntled expression. "Ah. It's you they were going on about," he said as Henry approached.

"You're the one who's meeting me?"

PC Williams nodded and spun around, escorting Henry down a corridor to a reinforced metal door. "I'm taking you to the holding cells."

"Not to keep me in, I hope," Henry joked.

PC Williams didn't express any humour.

They entered a new corridor that no longer appeared like an office building. It was more like a futuristic prison, Henry thought, with white plastic walls and wide corridors. But no matter how modern it looked, it still had the same smells as the custody suites Henry had known: metal, ink, piss, and shame.

"I'm glad you managed to get away from that farmhouse," Henry said, trying to jumpstart a conversation with PC Williams.

But he wasn't having any of it. "They didn't need me up there any longer," he grunted.

He led Henry towards a large white counter behind which a desk sergeant was sitting, watching several large screens. "I've got him," PC Williams said to the sergeant, pointing his thumb in Henry's direction.

The sergeant didn't bother to look up, and PC Williams brought Henry down another corridor, where he found Lottie talking quietly to a young, short blonde woman.

The two women stood outside an entrance to a small interrogation room in which Henry suspected they were going to talk.

"You can go in," PC Williams said, pointing at the door.

They did as instructed and entered the room. There was a white plastic table with four chairs around it. The room was stuffy, with the faint smell of human bodies, and the grey, windowless walls were marked with black smudges, which Henry guessed had come from chairs being thrown at them.

Lottie took a seat on one side of the table. She gave Henry a weak attempt at a smile.

Sophia, who was wearing a stylish dark-blue jacket over a white blouse, joined Henry on the other side. Her elegant perfume would hopefully replace the room's stench.

She gave Henry a firm handshake. "Nice to meet you, DCI Ward."

PC Williams, standing near the door, felt compelled to interject, "He's not a DCI. He's a liar."

Sophia glared at him, asking, "What the hell are you talking about...?"

"It's alright," Henry said, sensing he had to get involved. "Don't mind him."

"Aye. Don't mind me," PC Williams said, shaking his head as if he had more to say but was trying to keep it bottled up. But then he couldn't. "You know," he said, "this 'DCI' here said DI Barnes was into private security, and it's bollocks. Just like everything else that comes out of his mouth."

Henry felt like wincing but kept a straight face as Sophia and Lottie looked at him for answers. Instead, Henry just shrugged like he didn't know what PC Williams was on about.

PC Williams huffed and remained wedged in the doorway, blocking them in the interrogation room.

Sophia placed a leather handbag on the table and then gestured to PC Williams. "There has to be an officer present. That was the one condition the two detectives gave."

"Ah, I should've thought as much," Henry said. He glanced at PC Williams, who was still sulking, and guessed he had been told off for letting Henry speak to Thomas earlier. He must also have spoken to Barnes about private security work and learnt that she would never dream of doing any.

"Well," Henry said, hoping to move on from the subject. "What is it you wanted to talk about, Lottie?"

Lottie was wearing a drab grey hoodie and some matching tracksuit bottoms. The police had probably considered her a suicide risk, he concluded, and made her change clothes.

Black bags hung under her eyes. Her long blonde hair wasn't tied back but hung down; long strands of it covered her face.

Defeated was the word Henry would use to describe her.

"Lottie?" Henry asked again. She appeared to have forgotten he was there. "What is it?"

She shook her head as if waking up from a daydream and made eye contact. "We spoke yesterday."

Henry frowned. "Aye, in the afternoon."

"After you'd been to see Thomas."

"Yes…"

"And yesterday…" She looked over at PC Williams standing at the door and stopped.

He was watching them.

Sophia noticed he was putting Lottie off from talking. "Can you turn around, please?"

PC Williams grimaced and then turned his bulky frame to face the corridor, away from them.

He would still listen to every word they'd say, Henry thought, but at least he wasn't leering at them.

He glanced at Lottie, who looked to have recovered some strength.

"Yesterday, I told you what happened at the party," she said, picking at her fingernail.

"Aye," Henry replied. He made eye contact with Sophia, who nodded, confirming she knew about this.

Lottie continued, "Well… I tell you what I saw in the afternoon and, that night, he turns up dead in my farmyard."

"Yes," Henry said.

Lottie blew air out of her lips, which flicked the blonde hair covering her face. "Well? Is this your fault?" she asked.

"How could it be my fault?" said Henry, turning to Sophia, who kept her eyes on the table as if she didn't want to be involved in the discussion.

Lottie had tilted her head and gave Henry a pleading look. "You worked for them. You came into my home, helped me with the eggs, and then you left… And that night, all hell breaks loose. I'm questioned all bloody night, and then…" She shook her head as though she was seeing her suspicions confirmed. "You planted it, didn't you?"

"Sorry?" Henry scoffed.

"You planted that knife there so they could get rid of me."

"So *who* could get rid of you?"

"My family."

"And why would your family want to get rid of you, Lottie?"

"Because I know who killed her. Who killed that girl."

Henry felt a bolt of adrenaline in his chest. This was it. Lottie had seen the third man and knew who he was. "Right. And who did it?"

"Well, don't you know?" She tilted her head again, making her look even more deranged. "It was my husband."

Chapter Twenty-Seven

Henry stared at Lottie, feeling like he'd misheard her. He turned to Sophia, who seemed just as puzzled as he was. PC Williams, standing in the open doorway, must have also heard. But with his back to them, Henry couldn't make out his expression.

Lottie sniffed and rubbed her nose with her finger, appearing to be unconcerned about accusing her own husband of murder.

"You…?" Henry asked, but then stopped. He still was gathering his thoughts. Could her husband, the mad-driving, mysterious farmer whom Henry hadn't met, be the third man?

"You're saying that your husband killed Freya?" he eventually asked.

Hearing the words aloud must have triggered something in Lottie's exhausted mind, because she broke into tears. She nodded, wiping her cheeks and eyes. "Yes."

"Why are you accusing your husband of murder?"

"He was at the party."

Henry recalled Lottie telling him she had seen Vince and another man carry Freya. "Are you saying you saw Vince and your husband moving Freya on the night of the party?"

She wore a pained expression but nodded all the same.

Henry turned to Sophia, almost looking to her for help, but she just narrowed her eyes and watched Lottie.

Henry asked another question. "Can you explain what happened at the party?"

"I…" She exhaled, blowing the strands of blonde hair that had fallen over her face. "I woke up after midnight, and Simon wasn't in bed. I checked on the boys, who were sleeping, and then I walked around the house, but he wasn't there. I called his phone, as I was worried."

"Had he ever gone missing in the middle of the night before?"

"In lambing season, he's rarely in bed," she said. "But he and Thomas… are friends." She seemed to find the last part of the sentence difficult to say.

She then saw it necessary to clarify. "Well, not friends exactly. He gets bored, does Simon. He…" She shook her head. "I don't know… I think, deep down, he wishes he'd left the area when he was younger, so that he wasn't lumbered with his father's farm. And he feels like…"

"Feels what?"

"That he shouldn't have married me, perhaps. We were young, and I was being rebellious and wanted to piss off my parents…" She waved her hand as if suggesting it wasn't important. "Anyway, that night. I rang him, he said he was with Thomas, and I was pissed off as I don't like him going over there. So I went over."

"On the quad bike?" Henry said, having got out his notebook and reviewed his notes. "You went to the party and argued with your brother?"

She shook her head but then corrected herself and nodded. "First, I argued with Simon. I wanted him home, away from those people. It was COVID, and we shouldn't have been social mixing. He had to get up early to work on the farm. But he didn't care. He said I owed him a break. I got upset, because sometimes I feel like by having my happiness, the farm and the kids, I've taken away his."

She lost herself in regret and self-pity and wept for a few moments.

Henry glanced at Sophia, who was taking notes and watching.

When he felt Lottie had calmed down enough, he asked, "So, you argued with Simon and then Thomas? When did you see him with Freya's body?"

She huffed. "Gabriel was hanging around me, and I wanted to get away from him."

"He was flirting with you?"

"Who wasn't he flirting with? And I wanted to get Simon home quickly, so the kids weren't on their own too long."

"Right."

"And then… I went upstairs and found them carrying Freya. They were arguing while they were doing it. Vince was swearing at Simon. I saw them and asked what the hell they were doing, and both panicked, but then they got angry with me."

Henry remembered what Dr Parrish had said about the third man, that he made her feel like 'prey'. He asked carefully, "Lottie, is your husband the kind of person who could attack someone?"

"No," she said, shaking her head. "He's a good man, does his best, always thinks of others."

"Then what was he doing carrying an unconscious woman?"

"He… drinks. And when he's drunk… it's like he's someone else. Some uncontrollable zombie. He just has this glazed expression, and he's controlled by his impulses."

"Have you ever had issues with him?" he asked delicately.

"Never. I can manage him. But others…"

"What do you mean 'others'?"

"He can be overly flirty with other women when he's like that."

Sophia interjected. "By 'overly flirty', do you mean predatory?"

Lottie considered her question and then shook her head. "Nothing like that. He's just a handful when he's drunk, and he rarely drinks because of it, as he knows what he can be like."

"Does he take drugs?"

She shrugged. "Who knows what he does when he's out of his head? Possibly."

Henry put that as a 'yes'. "Right, so you saw Simon and Vince carrying Freya. Did you know what had happened to her?"

She shook her head. Her tears came back as she thought about it. "I don't… I presume they were drinking or taking drugs, and something happened."

Henry leant his elbows on the plastic table. "Did she look to be alive?"

Lottie seemed shocked by the question. "I… I think so. She made a noise and mumbled a few times."

"While they were carrying her?"

She nodded. "Simon had her feet and Vince her shoulders. I dragged Simon off her at one point, and he dropped her, and her legs landed on the floor, and she stirred herself awake. I told him to leave her, and then Thomas came."

"What did Thomas do?"

She huffed. "The fool pushed me down the corridor, so we had a row – as we usually do."

"What about?"

"Thomas thinks I only married Simon to spite the family and that I don't really love him. He thinks Simon's a super chap and said that us staying married is putting pressure on Simon to stay, when all he wants is to leave the area. He also said I'm depriving my boys of the family's wealth when it was they who kicked me out. And it's all upsetting my parents, who only wanted the best for me. Blah, blah, blah."

"And what did you say to him?"

"I told him..." She took in a deep breath. "I told him he was a spoilt, idiotic fuck-up and then we descended into shouting."

"By which time your husband and Vince had left with Freya?"

She nodded, clearly regretting that fact. "I asked where they had taken her, and I searched for her, but that house is like a maze."

"Aye, so I've seen."

"I didn't hang around after that, as I had to get back to the kids. So, I left, hoping that Freya would be okay, but..."

She couldn't finish her sentence.

"And your husband, how did he react the next day when everyone knew Freya had died?"

"He was cut up about it, but he can never remember what happens when he's legless. So, he wasn't really sure what had gone on. Just that something had gone on."

Henry leant back in his plastic chair and cupped his chin. He considered all that she'd said. That her husband was the third man, had alcohol issues, and couldn't recall anything when drunk.

He and Vince had carried Freya down the corridor, presumably to the guest bathroom, where she had eventually drowned. But how had that come about? Lottie seemed to think Freya was still alive when she saw her in the corridor.

"Are you saying your husband was involved in Freya's death or that he was the one who killed her?"

"I… I don't know. Vince claimed it was him."

"Vince?" Henry asked, sitting forward. "When did you speak to him?"

"Last night."

Henry noticed PC Williams turn his head slightly to hear better.

Sophia glanced at Lottie. "Just be careful what you say, alright," she said.

"Don't worry," Lottie said, her eyes brighter than before. "I didn't kill him. Someone else did."

"Who?" Henry asked.

She shrugged. "I don't know. But I spoke to him last night."

"What happened?"

"He came to my door at around nine."

Sophia held up her hand, trying to stop her client. "Lottie, don't speak unless–"

"It's fine," she said. "I opened the front door, and he was standing there. He had a go at me for speaking to you." She looked at Henry.

"How did he know I had spoken to you?"

She smiled, looking at him like he was naive. "He can see my farm from his window. He must've seen you pick me up on the lane and drive over to mine."

Henry could see how that was possible. Henry had wound up Vince at Thomas's farmhouse just before he bumped into her.

And then he remembered the window in Vince's bedroom, the handprint he'd seen on it, and the multiple locks on his door. "Did he seem nervous?"

"Vince?" Lottie asked, like it was a silly question. "Of course he was nervous."

"Why?"

"He thought I was going to tell the police what he and my husband had done to Freya."

"And what did they do to her?"

She looked down at the white table and rubbed her thumb over a long scratch in the plastic. "Vince said they were taking cocaine and smoking pot with Freya in Thomas's bedroom. Apparently, Thomas had slept with her earlier that night, and…" She pulled a disgusted face, suggesting she didn't want to think about what happened next.

"Go on," Henry said.

"He… Simon… got more and more out of his head, and he thought he could sleep with Freya as well, and then he…"

"What?"

"According to Vince, he hit her when she rejected his advances."

"What with?"

"Some ornament, and then he panicked, and he and Vince carried her down the corridor, where they put her in the bath. According to Vince, Simon thought a cold bath would wake her up. And when she came to, Simon held her head under the water…"

She covered her mouth, unable to recount any further from what she had heard from Vince.

Henry noted down the details and then reread what he had written. "Your husband tried to sleep with Freya, she rejected him, so he lost his nerve and hit her with a blunt instrument."

Lottie nodded, looking so pale Henry worried she might vomit on the floor. "According to Vince. That's what he told me last night. But I wasn't there. I don't know the truth."

"Then they took her to the bathroom, put her in a cold bath… and your husband…" Henry didn't repeat her story, but considered it. If this was true, and Simon Foster was the one who had murdered Freya, then they needed to speak to him immediately.

He glanced over at PC Williams and was about to instruct him to send officers to locate Simon Foster before remembering he had no authority here.

Sophia stopped scribbling notes, scrutinised them, and then turned to Lottie. "You never spoke to your husband about this?" she asked.

Lottie shook her head. "All I knew until last night was that Simon, while drunk, had carried a drunken girl down a corridor."

"But didn't the girl he was carrying wind up dead?" Sophia asked.

Lottie didn't answer, and Henry watched her reaction. She was obviously cut up about not doing more but was putting a brave face on it. He suspected Lottie would never forgive herself for not speaking up sooner.

"And then you didn't tell the police about any of this?" Sophia continued as if she couldn't understand Lottie's logic.

Lottie looked at Henry for help. "As I said to you yesterday, the police didn't ask me, and I didn't want to get Simon in trouble. Plus, I didn't want to start a war with the family, because accusing Vince was the same as accusing Thomas. I mean, look how they treated that slimy Gabriel when he made that accusation."

Henry stirred himself out of his thoughts to ask, "All you have really, that links your husband to Freya's murder, is you seeing him carrying Freya down a corridor, and Vince's accusation that he saw your husband drown her."

Lottie nodded.

Henry bit the end of this thumbnail and returned to his thoughts. Vince was a liar, as proven the previous day when he told Henry he hadn't been at the party. Simon Foster was a lousy driver and a leery drunk, but that didn't make him a murderer. Him carrying an unconscious woman was one thing, and very serious, and he had questions to answer about that. But was he really a murderer?

"Let's go back to Vince last night," Henry said, after a few moments' silence. "What did he say?"

Lottie shook her head as if waking up from a stupor. "He said I shouldn't talk to the police as Simon was the one who killed Freya and that it'd all come out if I talked."

"And what time was this?"

She shrugged. "About 9 p.m., I think."

"Your husband wasn't back?"

She shook her head. "He was still in the Lakes. He got back about 10 p.m., and he was the one who found Vince's body."

"In the farmyard?"

She nodded. "He freaked out and panicked and came inside shouting. He scared the boys to death, and his mum came and picked them up."

"Where is your husband now?"

"He's at his mum's with the boys."

Henry asked for the address so he could go straight there after he left the police station. Lottie said her mother-in-law had moved into a small cottage near her farm when Simon's father passed away.

Henry thanked her for the address, and then pulled a face that suggested something wasn't right. "Don't take offence, but you didn't kill Vince, did you?"

She scoffed like the idea was insane. "Don't start talking like those other detectives. They've given me a headache."

"Well, they do have that knife, which is covered in your fingerprints."

"As they keep telling me."

"Have you seen the knife before?"

She nodded. "So have you. It was in the kitchen when you were there. You remember the bread knife? It's the one with the handle Simon carved."

"A bread knife?" Henry asked, sounding confused. Such knives were typically designed for slicing loaves, not body tissue.

He recalled seeing the knife's ornate handle on her dining table. He then grabbed his forehead, wondering if the headache Lottie had just spoken of was contagious.

The stuffy air inside the interrogation room was getting to him. He stood up, sliding the chair back, and said, "I'll go fetch us tea or coffee. Do you want anything?"

Lottie shook her head, but then said, "Actually, water."

Henry nodded and looked to Sophia, who declined. "Don't be long," she said. "We only have fifteen minutes left."

"Aye," Henry said, heading to the door. "I'll be as quick as I can."

Chapter Twenty-Eight

Henry tapped PC Williams on the shoulder. The policeman had heard him approach and begrudgingly stepped out of the doorway. When Henry asked where the nearest coffee machine was, he grunted and pointed past another interrogation room to the end of the white corridor.

The air wasn't much better outside the interrogation room, and Henry felt his chest complaining about it. And that telltale tickle in his throat had appeared, suggesting his asthma was on the verge of playing up.

He followed PC Williams' directions to the coffee machine, half-expecting the constable to have lied to him, but when he turned the corner, he found the machine, and DI Barnes pressing its buttons.

"Now then, look who it is," Henry said as he walked towards her.

She wore a dark-blue shirt and navy trousers. Her blonde hair was cut short, and she'd put some bright-red lipstick on. Upon hearing his voice, she stiffened and turned away from him. "I can't talk."

"I know." He walked closer to her. "Do you really think Lottie killed that lad with a bloody bread knife?" he said conspiratorially.

Barnes didn't reply and kept her back to him. She took her paper cup of steaming coffee from the machine. Taking a few steps, she remained nearby instead of walking away.

She made a show of sipping her drink, blowing the vapour off the top first. "Of course I don't think she killed him," she said, answering his question.

Henry kept his voice low. "Then why the bloody hell is she still in custody?"

Barnes watched some detectives in deep discussion walk down the corridor. When they'd disappeared around the corner, she said, "Because we have a weapon with the victim's blood on. And her fingerprints are all over it."

"So? She couldn't have killed Vince with a bread knife, unless she asked the lad to hold still while she carved his throat open."

She sipped her coffee. "Murphy doesn't want us to look into any other possibilities at the moment."

Ah, that was it, Henry thought. The police had come across a weapon that could be linked to the murder, and all efforts were being focused on that. Everything else was to be ignored, allowing any other evidence or traces to go cold.

If it was later proven that the bread knife wasn't the murder weapon, which Henry thought forensics would figure out quickly once they looked at Vince's body, Lottie would be released without charge.

Until then, she was to remain in custody as their main suspect.

Henry shook his head at the idiocy of it. "So, she stays banged up when everyone knows she didn't do it, all while the real culprit covers their tracks."

Barnes didn't say anything. She flicked her fringe from her eyes and glanced at him. Offering only a shrug, she blew more steam off her coffee.

"So, what do you really think went on?" Henry asked.

"I don't know…" Barnes glanced around to make sure only Henry was nearby. "But I'd be looking into Thomas Wentworth-Scott if I could."

"Why?"

"We searched the victim's bedroom, and there were a lot of interior locks on his door."

Henry smiled. She'd picked up on the same thing he had. "Aye, I was thinking along similar lines when I saw them."

She glared at him. "When the hell did you gain access to his room?"

Henry realised his blunder by admitting he'd been inside Vince's room. He raised his hands in self-defence. "I'm not going to say. But aye, I did see them. And that handprint on the windowsill."

Barnes's eyes narrowed as she sipped her paper cup. Henry guessed she was either angry about Henry not telling her how he gained entry into Vince's room or with herself for not spotting the handprint by the window.

Henry suspected both irritated her equally.

He continued, speaking quietly, "Someone got inside Vince's room, probably via his window. He spoke to Lottie at her farm at about 9 p.m., and then he walked or drove back to Thomas's, locked his bedroom door and stayed inside."

Barnes nodded along, with her red lips pouted. "He was afraid of someone."

"Aye," Henry said, "but who?"

Barnes didn't have an answer to that.

"What state was his body in?"

She gave him a guarded look, suggesting she wouldn't say anything, but then relented and scanned the empty corridor. "He was stabbed four times in the abdomen. Two hits to the lungs and another to his liver, or so Dr Anderson said."

"And the toxicology report?"

She shook her head. "Not yet. But if you ask me, he was probably stoned as we found a large supply in one of the drawers in his bedroom."

"Any signs he'd been dragged or beaten up before he was stabbed?"

"Possibly. He was in a state. Someone had dropped rocks or stones on him before they stabbed him. It was a frantic and vicious attack."

Henry shook his head in incomprehension. They had arrested Lottie when it clearly wasn't her. A bread knife's point wasn't sharp enough to pierce the abdominal wall and hit the internal organs; and Henry couldn't imagine Lottie dropping rocks on a living animal, not to mention a human.

While he was lost in thought, Barnes asked, "Is there someone we've missed who has a motive to kill Freya and Vince?"

She eyed a uniformed officer who walked past while waiting for Henry's answer.

Henry wondered who would have a reason to murder both Freya and Vince. Before fully thinking it through, he said, "Well, there's Gabriel Silverstone."

"Who?" Barnes asked, suddenly very interested.

"The bloke who accused Thomas of killing Freya. He was Freya's boyfriend and heard her and Thomas getting acquainted on the night of the murder. Revenge is usually a good motive. And then he benefited from Vince dying, as it meant the lawsuit into him was dropped."

"Lawsuit?"

"Aye. The family were suing him over the allegations he made about Thomas killing Freya. Gabriel didn't have a leg to stand on, as he had no evidence that Thomas had killed Freya, so he was going to lose. And lose big, most likely."

Barnes was about to take another sip of her drink and then halted. "Wait… Is this Gabriel a bit of a creep?"

Henry nodded. "Lottie called him 'slimy', why?"

"Her husband, Simon Foster, said something to that effect when I questioned him last night. He said, 'I bet it's that bloody creep'."

"He didn't say who the creep was?"

She shook her head. "No, I asked him, but he wouldn't answer. I assumed he meant Thomas. However, it could be this Gabriel."

It was interesting Simon Foster had mentioned Gabriel, Henry thought. Especially when Lottie believed her husband was involved in Freya's killing. "What did you think of Lottie's husband?"

Barnes shrugged as if Simon Foster was of no importance. "He seemed alright. Why?"

"Do you think he could be a murderer?"

She glared at him. "What have you heard?"

"Nothing," he lied. "Well, nothing that seems believable."

She stepped closer to him, her eyes locked on his. "Tell me."

Henry bit his lower lip as he considered telling her or not. But as she prowled towards him, he knew he had little choice. "Vince Taylor claimed Simon murdered Freya."

Barnes looked perplexed by the revelation. "A druggie claimed the good-looking farmer with two twins is a murderer?"

"I didn't know this Simon was good-looking," Henry said, knowing full well it'd wind her up.

But she didn't take the bait and instead drained her cup. "What do you think?"

"I think someone needs to speak to Simon Foster pretty quickly to see what he has to say."

She glanced around the corridor, worried she was being watched. "I can't."

"Well, *I* can."

She clenched her jaw shut, tightening her muscles. "Fine. Do it. Find out what he says. Keep me in the loop." She pointed her finger at his face. "And don't fuck it up."

Henry shook his head. "I won't. And while I'm there, get SOCO into Vince's bedroom and get them to check that handprint on the windowsill."

Barnes nodded, her cheeks reddening, which Henry guessed meant she was unhappy about missing that piece of evidence.

Henry pointed at the drinks machine. "Does this do water?"

She stared at him, completely confused. "No. Weak tea and bad coffee. Why?"

"Would you get Lottie a glass of water?"

Barnes stared at him like he'd gone half-mad.

"She asked for one ten minutes ago, and she'll be waiting. Oh, and tell her I've gone off somewhere. She'll be able to guess where."

Barnes wasn't happy taking his orders, and her frustration with him seemed to trigger a memory. Her eyes widened in annoyance at the recollection.

She stepped closer to him menacingly. "Thanks a bunch for finding that snotty-nosed barrister. She's done nothing but piss me off all day."

Henry chuckled and stepped away from her. "Wait till you hear who paid for her."

"What?" she asked, but he'd already started walking down the corridor when she realised what he was talking about.

As he left through the door, he could hear her swearing under her breath.

* * *

Hazy clouds with hints of golds and red hung over the tops of Otley Chevin. The sun's rays spread over the tall grasses in the fields. Henry travelled along the country lane that rounded through them, driving faster than normal. He was heading to the cottage where Simon Foster and his children were staying.

Henry thought through Lottie's story as he drove. She had seen Simon and Vince carry Freya down the corridor on the night of the party. And then, according to Vince, Simon had hit Freya over the head with an ornament and drowned her in a bath.

Henry didn't give Vince's account much weight. He was a criminal and a liar, and seeing as he was no longer alive, whatever he'd said couldn't be corroborated.

Even so, what if Vince wasn't lying and Simon *had* killed Freya? Could that mean Simon had seen Vince in his farmyard, killed him in a rage, and then pretended to find his body later?

If that were the case, why would he let his wife take the blame for it? And where did that bread knife come from? That had clearly been planted, Henry felt.

He arrived at the address Lottie had given him and saw a small old cottage just off the side of the lane. A white gate blocked its drive and a walled rear garden backed onto an empty field.

Henry parked next to the wall, ensuring his car was as close to it as possible to allow other cars access. He noticed roadwork signs further down the lane in the distance, but could not figure out what they said. He wondered what kind of work would be done up here in the middle of nowhere.

As he approached the cottage, he noticed one of the netted curtains on the ground floor twitch.

Once he'd opened the gate and was walking up the drive, he found the black Land Rover that had nearly driven him off the road the previous day.

So, Simon Foster was indeed the mad driver.

A door opening caught his attention, and a tall man in his early forties stepped out of the cottage's stooped entrance. He had short black hair and wore a blue fleece over his wiry frame. His jeans were scuffed and marked with oil and dirt, and a thick black beard covered his chin.

He stared warily at Henry as he remained on the doorstep. "Can I help?" he asked, in a deep and threatening tone.

Henry stepped away from the black Land Rover he'd been inspecting. He felt the urge to have a go at Simon for his bad driving but knew it wouldn't get him anywhere. He needed to find out what Simon knew and who this 'creep' was.

Henry put on a disarming smile. "Hello, I'm former DCI Henry Ward." He stepped forward, offering his hand, but Simon didn't move to shake it. He remained standing near the cottage under the shade of the early evening sun, his hands resting on his hips.

Henry withdrew his offered hand. "I'm here regarding the murders of Vince Taylor and Freya Harrison."

"I've already spoken to the police."

"Aye, but I'm here in a private capacity."

"Then you've got no business being here," he said with a grunt. He pointed at the white gate. "You can get off my property."

Henry wasn't moving. "I've just spent some time talking to your wife."

Simon was surprised. "Lottie?"

He nodded. "She's been telling me all sorts, so I wanted to speak to you…"

Simon gritted his teeth. "I don't know what she told you, but it isn't true."

"Listen, Mr Foster. Some very serious allegations have been made against you."

He looked startled. "Me?"

Henry nodded. "Aye. So why don't we get to the bottom of it?"

"What have you heard?"

Henry's mind worked through his options. He could either summarise Lottie's statement there and then, or use it as a carrot to get more information.

Henry chose the latter.

Raising his hand in the air as if giving a stop sign, Henry said, "First of all, I have a question for you. You told DI Barnes that you thought a creep had murdered Vince. Who were you talking about?"

Simon grimaced as his words came back to haunt him. "Do you mean that blonde detective?"

After Henry nodded, Simon said, "I don't know what I meant."

"You agree to saying 'creep', but don't know why you said it?"

Simon's tanned cheeks burned red. "I mean… I don't think…"

This Simon wasn't the sharpest tool in the box, Henry realised. He wondered what Lottie saw in him. She was a bright, intelligent woman who had given up her family's approval and wealth to be with this man. And Henry thought he was mediocre. He had the looks of a farming catalogue model and not much else.

"These allegations against you are pretty severe," Henry said. He watched Simon's face crease up. "Tell me who this creep is, and I might be able to help you," he added.

Simon stared down at the stone driveway as if ready to give in. "I… thought it might be someone… but I don't know for certain."

"Who?"

"Well. That slimy creep. That psycho."

"Gabriel?" Henry asked, scrutinising Simon's expression.

"No," Simon said, shaking his head. The look he gave Henry suggested he wasn't sure who Gabriel was. "No. Thomas's brother."

Henry was so aghast, he had to repeat it. "His brother?"

Simon chewed his upper lip. "Yeah, that psycho brother of his. Benjamin."

Chapter Twenty-Nine

A faint breeze blew over Henry's remaining grey hair and through his thin blue shirt. He felt the need to lean against Simon's black Land Rover parked behind him but resisted the temptation. He didn't want to appear weak in front of him.

Simon had stepped closer and squinted at the low sun. "Aye. Benjamin came back from Rome during COVID. He'd got into trouble there." He didn't explain what the trouble was, but Henry guessed it was something scandalous that had been hushed up.

"Where is he now?"

"He lives between Thomas's farmhouse and his parents'; or he crashes at his friends. Well, people he sponges off, really. He's like a tick."

"Does he work?"

Simon shook his head and smiled as if the idea was funny.

"Wasn't he into shooting or something?"

"He still is. I heard him shooting the other day. Lord knows what he shoots at."

Henry didn't like the sound of that. "Is he an addict?"

Simon nodded. "A rich one, aye."

"At the party on the night Freya died, was he there?"

Simon's eyes widened, making him appear like a rabbit caught in his own Land Rover's headlights.

Henry repeated his question, as he seemed to be lost in a trance. "Simon, the night Freya died, was Benjamin there?"

Simon nodded, clearly traumatised by what he was remembering.

Going off Simon's dazed expression, Henry asked, "And what did you see?"

He lowered his head. "I… I was involved."

"In what?"

"How she died."

Simon turned to the cottage behind him, inside of which were his mother and two boys. Henry glanced at the windows, but none of the net curtains moved.

That didn't mean they weren't listening.

"You don't have to go into detail, Simon. Just tell me the basics."

He looked sadly back at Henry and then stepped closer to him, trying to get away from the house behind him. "I hit her."

"You hit Freya?"

He nodded, but then shook his head as if he wasn't sure. His eyes welled up. He wiped them and then cleared his throat. "I can't… I don't know. Vince told me I did, and all I can really remember is carrying her down that corridor and Lottie being there."

"What about the bath?"

Simon nodded as if he was about to come to that. "I remember that. And the cold water. We put her in, thinking it'd wake her up."

"And what then?"

"We left her in there. I can't think why. To get more drinks, I suppose."

"You left her alone?"

He nodded and gulped on the lump in his throat. "When we were walking back… we heard shouting and water splashing. We rushed inside and there was Benjamin, half-naked, holding her head under the water."

Henry listened and tried to picture the scene. "He was half-naked, you said?"

"Well, topless. I guess he was holding her head down like…" He demonstrated the gesture by pressing both hands downward.

Henry recalled Dr Parrish saying that when she entered the bathroom, the 'sicko' standing by the sink wasn't wearing a top.

"He didn't see us at first, and Vince took a photo of him."

"With his phone?"

Simon nodded. "His old one. He kept it so he could hold it over Benjamin if he needed to."

That would explain why someone would search Vince's drawers after his murder, Henry thought. They would've been looking for his old phone with the incriminating evidence. With any luck, Vince would have uploaded it to a cloud system that the police could access.

If Dr Parrish could confirm it was Benjamin she saw in the bathroom, and if the police could locate Vince's photograph of the murder, they would have enough to charge him with Freya's murder. Should Simon also testify against him, it would only help the prosecution's case.

It all seemed to make sense. The Wentworth-Scott family were protecting Thomas against the murder accusation because they knew it was their other son who had murdered Freya.

That was if the family knew Benjamin had killed her. "Did Thomas know it was Benjamin?" asked Henry.

"Yes."

"Who told him?"

"He saw it all himself. He came to the bathroom and saw Benjamin inside, and he tried to get rid of him, but he wouldn't leave. I went looking for help but ended up just… standing outside, catching my breath. I think I was sick." He wiped his nose again as more tears dripped from his red eyes. "I've never done anything like that before. I'm not a bad person."

"Save it," Henry said. "Why didn't you come forward earlier?"

"They'd blame it on me. Vince said I hit that lass, and the family hates me because I married Lottie."

"Why do you even hang around with Thomas if the family hates you?"

He shrugged. "We've been friends for years. We both grew up around here. He's more annoyed at Lottie than me for what happened…" Simon exhaled as if he didn't want to move onto a more complicated subject.

"Did you find Vince's body last night?" Henry asked.

"Aye. I found him in our yard. Cut up, beaten up…"

Henry remembered Barnes saying rocks had been dropped on Vince. Had Benjamin been torturing him to get the old phone that had the incriminating photo?

"Does anyone else know about the photograph?"

"I don't know. Possibly."

Henry then recalled standing in Thomas's corridor outside Vince's room the previous day and overhearing his phone call. Vince had said, "Never you mind what I have hanging over him. That's between him and me."

Had Vince told Benjamin about the photo, and was he using it to get cash out of him?

"Could Vince have been blackmailing Benjamin?" Henry asked Simon.

Simon shook his head as if he didn't have a clue. "All I know is that Thomas was getting tired of Vince and wanted to clean up his act. He was cutting down on coke and stuff, which meant Vince had less money to buy it."

"Did he work?"

"Vince?" Simon scoffed at the idea of it. "Never. He scrounged around to get enough gear together, then he'd cut it with washing powder and sell it to kids for profit."

That meant Vince's livelihood depended on Thomas's patronage, and once that dried up, Vince had blackmailed

Benjamin, using the incriminating evidence to get cash out of him. A plan that had massively backfired. "When did Thomas stop giving Vince money?"

"Recently, I think. A week or so. You'll have to ask Thomas."

Henry had heard enough to be sure that Benjamin had killed Freya and Vince. Benjamin must have been spooked when Henry had got involved in the case and poked around too much. That was probably the trigger for him wanting to find the image that implicated him in Freya's murder and silence Vince for good.

"Does Benjamin know you and Thomas are aware he killed Freya?" Henry asked.

Simon squinted in the sun as he thought about it, and his answer came quickly. "Yeah. He must do."

"And do his parents know?"

Simon exhaled and shrugged. "I wouldn't have a clue."

Henry suspected they did. He recalled the camera Robbie had found in the picture and thought about the private CCTV network around Thomas's farmhouse. He suspected the network had been there before Freya died, which would mean Mrs Wentworth-Scott was fully aware of what had gone on.

She had also been cagey about handing over details when he met her for lunch. The family only wanted him to confirm the coroner's report and nothing else. Presumably because if Henry dug any further than the police had done, he'd work out the truth.

And where was Benjamin now? Henry wondered. Either he was long gone, having returned to the Continent, or he was hanging around and wanted to silence Simon and potentially his own brother, Thomas.

That all depended on how crazy he was.

Henry's phone buzzed, and he pulled it out of his pocket. It was Barnes. Why was she ringing him? he wondered.

"Are you on the Chevin?" she asked.

"Aye?"

"Get away from there. An emergency call handler has just had Thomas Wentworth-Scott on the line."

Henry scanned the fields around him for Thomas's farmhouse and saw it in the distance, around a mile away. "Right?"

"We have an active shooter situation up there. Gunshots have been fired. Someone's shooting at his house."

Henry held the phone away from his ear and heard nothing but the breeze blowing the tall grass and the surrounding vegetation.

Then he heard it.

A light pop that was unmistakably a gunshot.

Henry pressed his phone to his ear. "Are armed response on their way?"

"Apparently," Barnes said. She sounded like she was running down a corridor. Henry thought he heard Hargreaves say something in the background. "Listen, Henry, get out of there while they deal with it."

Henry recalled seeing that scarlet and silver rifle on display in Thomas's entertainment room, and the large photo of his brother taking part in a European shooting competition. "Here, it's Benjamin Wentworth-Scott. Tell armed response they're dealing with an expert shooter."

"You what?"

"He's won shooting competitions. And unfortunately for them, I've seen his gold trophies."

"I'll tell them. Just get out of there."

"Aye, we will do." Henry spun around to look at Simon.

Barnes hung up, and Henry pocketed his phone.

Simon glowered at him, knowing that something was going on.

Henry didn't know what to say. An active shooter situation, but the shooter was an expert marksman who'd participated in competitions. And he was on a rampage, wanting to silence the people who could put him away for two murders.

Henry felt ice inch down his spine. "We need you, your kids, and your mum in that black Land Rover now."

"Why?" Simon asked, shaking his head in confusion.

"Benjamin's armed, and he's shooting at Thomas's farm. And seeing as we're only a mile away, he might decide to come for you instead."

Simon's tanned face went white with fear. "That bloody psycho's armed."

"Aye. He is. So, hurry the bloody hell up!"

* * *

It took Simon five minutes to coax his family into his black Land Rover. His mum, a grey-haired woman wearing a grey sweatsuit, helped the two twelve-year-old boys into the back of the car. Despite being twins, they looked completely different. One was tall, blonde, and had Lottie's proud chin, while the other was dark-haired and sullen.

Henry had remained near the wall, watching Thomas's farmhouse through his binoculars. He had seen nothing, and no further shots had rung out. Which was a good sign, Henry thought, or it meant Benjamin was sneaking towards them, keeping low behind the old crumbling walls that bordered the fields.

Once Simon had slammed all the car doors shut, he approached Henry. "Where is he?"

"I don't know. He could be with Thomas or he could be on his way to us."

Simon squinted at the hazy fields. The breeze rustled his black beard. "I've got guns on the farm. I could grab one and take him out."

"Do you think you'd be a match for him? He's an expert. Your job is to get your mum and kids out of danger."

Simon nodded. It was his only task right now. "What will you do?"

"I'll be driving behind you." Henry turned to the narrow lane that ran past the cottage. He pointed in the opposite direction of Thomas's farmhouse. "Head that way. It'll take you to the north end of Otley."

Simon smirked. "I know where it'll take me. But the water company needed to fix some pipes down there. The Wentworth-Scotts were complaining about water leakages. That road's blocked."

Henry swore. Bloody typical, he thought.

"The only way is to drive past Thomas's place, and hope Benjamin doesn't shoot at us," said Simon.

Henry didn't like that idea. The black Land Rover and Henry's Skoda would make easy targets, especially for a trained marksman. Henry glanced at his watch and saw ten minutes had passed since Barnes had called him. If the armed response unit showed up, Henry and the family could hunker down in the cottage and wait for the police to deal with Benjamin.

Henry called Barnes, and when she answered, he asked, "How long will they be?"

"Are you still on the moors? Get away from there!"

"We're stuck here. The only route out is past the shooter."

She swore down the phone and then covered it while she talked to someone. Then she then came back. "Armed response unit's ETA is fifteen minutes," she said.

Fifteen minutes until the cavalry arrived. Henry wasn't happy with that. "Right," he said, then hung up and looked at Simon. Pointing to his mum's cottage, he asked, "You wouldn't happen to have guns in there?"

Simon shook his head as if the idea was stupid, and then his eyes lit up. "Hang on. My dad's old gun cabinet is here." He rushed off inside the cottage without another word.

Henry got lost in his thoughts as he ran through the options. Staying here to have a gunfight with a trained sniper wouldn't be an option. Not when they had to protect two children and a woman in her seventies.

Even if they barricaded themselves in the cottage, Benjamin could shoot out every window. And what if one of the kids panicked and got in the line of fire?

However, their only other option was to drive down the lane, which would put them in the open. Glancing at the Land Rover's scratched metal panelling, he didn't think it could withstand rifle fire. Its bullets would cut through and hit someone inside.

Henry noticed the blond boy was staring at him through the car window. He was stressed and nervy as if he knew something was wrong, but not exactly what. Henry forced a smile and waved at him, but the kid did nothing but whisper at his dark-haired brother.

Crikey, Henry thought, how the hell did he end up in a situation like this? Then the idea struck him that he was just being paranoid. Perhaps Benjamin had fled after opening fire on Thomas's farmhouse and was no longer in the area?

Henry tried to cling on to that idea as he lifted his binoculars and scanned the nearby stone walls in the field ahead. Something flashed in the sun. It took Henry a moment to realise what it was. A metal rifle barrel glinted, and it took Henry a second to realise the weapon was being aimed at him.

He jumped down as the shot blew chunks of limestone out of the cottage's facade a few paces behind him.

The explosion echoed a few seconds later.

Henry heard the kids scream in the back of the Land Rover. He knelt in the driveway, trying to gather his wits about him, and watched Simon burst out of the cottage, holding a hunting rifle.

He had a determined expression as he crouched down next to Henry.

"Let me kill the bastard," he said, aiming the rifle over the wall.

Henry looked at the black Land Rover on the drive, with the worried kids inside. He grabbed Simon's arm. "No, lad. You get those kids out of here."

Simon's rage didn't subside until Henry said more slowly, "Simon. Get your mum and kids away from here."

"Where? We can't drive past him. He'll shoot at us."

Henry put his hand on the old hunting rifle Simon was holding. "I'll give you cover."

"But, like you said, he's a trained shooter."

"Aye, I know what I said. But if I keep him pinned down, he might leave you be."

Simon seemed torn between staying to fight and getting his kids and mother away from danger. He eventually relented and handed Henry the rifle. "You know how to use it?"

Henry nodded, but remembered he hadn't held a gun in fifteen years, when he'd gone clay pigeon shooting with some other DCIs in the Dales. He'd also done a few hours' shooting practice back in his police training. Despite being a good shot, he didn't fancy his chances with a shooter who had reached a European competition.

Simon patted Henry on the shoulder. "Right," he said. He then ran to his Land Rover, keeping his head low.

With any luck, Simon would drive like a madman and get the kids and his mum out of there as quickly as possible. Leaving Henry with the psychotic sniper.

He huffed. What the bloody hell had he got himself into this time?

Chapter Thirty

Simon's black Land Rover reversed down the drive, and Henry stayed closed to the wall to keep out of its way. The white gate was still closed, so Henry went to open it while making himself visible to the sniper in the field opposite.

A blast blew a hole in the roof of the Land Rover, and after a few seconds, the sound of the shot travelled in the breeze. Henry glimpsed the panicked faces of the two twins as Simon reversed out of the drive and into the lane. The vehicle waited in the lane for Henry's signal.

Right, Henry thought. Time to get down to business. He leant his hunting rifle on the wall and pressed his chin against its stock to stare down the scope. The weapon stunk of dust and oil, and the scope's focus was terrible, nowhere near as good as his binoculars.

He panned the weapon up and down the neighbouring field as the Land Rover idled in the lane, its engine chugging away.

Henry couldn't see anything but lumps of grass and then the limestone walls. He heard another impact on metal and broken glass. He heard another shriek a second shot hit the Land Rover, but Henry didn't look. Instead, he remained focused on the scope. The gunshot rang out to his left, and Henry followed its source to find and a man with dark hair pointing a rifle at the Land Rover.

Henry fired.

His rifle's handle bucked back and struck his shoulder, nearly sending him flying backwards. But he righted himself, peered down the scope, and spotted Benjamin aiming his rifle at him.

Henry hoped his old weapon had more ammunition and fired again before Benjamin could shoot.

Henry's gun recoiled, smacking his chest this time, but he was expecting it. He heard Simon speed off down the lane, driving as fast as he could.

Watching Benjamin turn his gun to shoot at Simon's Land Rover, Henry aimed and pulled the trigger, causing Benjamin to duck behind a wall.

This time, the butt of his rifle smacked his shoulder so hard, Henry couldn't feel his right arm anymore.

He did not know what his bullets were hitting. He felt the scope wasn't right, and that the wind was blowing the bullets off target. But the idea was to distract Benjamin, not kill him.

The black Land Rover rocketed down the lane and disappeared around a corner, and Henry felt some relief. The kids were safe. Then the realisation dawned on him, as Benjamin levelled his rifle in his direction.

He was alone with an armed psychopath.

Henry pulled the trigger again as he aimed at Benjamin, but the rifle didn't fire. It was out of ammo.

He took cover behind the wall and searched the flagstones to see if Simon had brought any more. There weren't any; only the three spent cases of the rounds he'd fired. Checking the rifle, he presumed the magazine on the underside of the weapon only contained three rounds and was empty.

He placed the rifle on the ground and checked his watch. He had about five minutes until the armed response unit turned up – if they were on time, which was a rare occurrence.

A cloud of dust and debris rained down on his head as a bullet hit the wall above him. Then he heard the gunshot. Looking at the near-ancient drystone wall, which was about a foot thick, Henry felt he should be safe enough. Unless Benjamin repeatedly fired at the same spot and weakened the stone, or a chunk of shrapnel came off and struck him.

He'd have to get inside; the front door of the cottage was wide open. Henry could take cover until the armed response unit arrived. He might also find more ammo.

Realising that was his best bet, he crawled along the drive, keeping the hunting rifle in one hand. Another round struck the cottage's facade, showering more dust on him.

Henry kept going until he was inside the cottage. He kept low, even when out of view, and pressed his back against the wall in the corridor.

A television played somewhere, and Henry heard the canned applause of a game show. Keeping on his knees, he shuffled down the corridor and into the living room.

There was an old battered grey sofa set inside, and a large TV in the corner that played to no one. Small ornaments of cartoon milkmaids lined the mantelpiece above the open fire, and net curtains covered the window.

Henry glanced around for the gun cabinet Simon had mentioned but couldn't find it. Then he noticed an oak dresser on the wall opposite the window. More milkmaid ornaments were positioned on its shelves, and Henry noticed its drawers were open as if they'd just been searched.

Realising Simon must have searched them for ammo, he hurried over and then stood up so he could peer inside. His hand rooted around, trying to find ammo, but he had no idea what he was looking for. Would they be in card boxes or in a magazine?

Glass shattered behind him.

The net curtains blew inwards.

Henry felt the largest, fastest wasp zip past his ear and explode a milkmaid on the shelf. The dresser rocked back and forth from the impact.

Henry dropped to the ground and felt his ear burn. The bullet must have got too close. He tapped his earlobe and felt it was wet with blood.

Well, he thought to himself, as he dropped onto his front and stared out the smashed window, he was a sitting duck now. All Benjamin had to do was walk up to the window and shoot him in the head. And since Henry was the only one who'd figured out what had happened to Freya and Vince, the Wentworth-Scotts would get away with what they'd done.

Once Henry was gone, they could continue as if nothing had happened. They would blame Lottie for killing Vince and continue telling the story that Freya had drowned herself in a bath.

Insanity, Henry thought. No. He would not give up now.

He heard the footsteps at the front door of the cottage and listened as they moved down the corridor.

Benjamin must be inside.

Hauling himself off the floor, he shuffled across the room and positioned himself to the side of the door frame with the hunting rifle in his hand.

Benjamin Wentworth-Scott slowly entered. He was as tall as Thomas, but thinner and less muscular. Stepping almost silently into the room, he held out his silver and red rifle before him. His purple sunglasses scanned the living room.

When Benjamin was a few paces ahead of him, Henry pounced, slamming the butt of his own weapon into Benjamin's head.

Benjamin fired a round as he fell down. The blast blew a hole in the carpet, and Henry came down on top of him, landing on his bony back.

Henry got off him quickly and slammed the butt of his own rifle between Benjamin's shoulder blades. The silver and red weapon Benjamin had used was a few paces away, out of harm's way.

Benjamin moaned in pain. Henry pretended his weapon was armed and pressed the muzzle against the back of his head, pushing it through his dark hair to touch his scalp.

"Benjamin, I presume," Henry said, after catching his breath.

Benjamin didn't say anything, he just hissed through his teeth.

"If I could arrest you, I would. But unfortunately, I can't. So instead, we shall wait until an active officer turns up. But I can read you your rights, if you want to hear them?"

Benjamin swore in reply.

"If I could, I'd arrest you for murdering Freya Harrison on the night of the 20th of May 2020. And then arrest you for murdering Vince Taylor last night." Henry tried to think if there was anything else. "Oh, aye. I'd probably also arrest you for perverting the course of justice, although in all fairness, I don't think you were alone in that."

Henry took a few deep breaths. He could hear sirens in the distance. It was nearly over, he thought, thanking the Lord.

"There's just one thing I haven't figured out," Henry said, relaxing his grip on the rifle, knowing he would have to drop it as soon as the armed response unit came in. "The bread knife. I don't get how that ended up at the scene."

Benjamin scoffed and turned his face away from the carpet. "I took it from Lottie's." His accent sounded like his brother's.

"When were you at Lottie's?" Henry asked, realising it must have been before Vince had been killed.

"After that skaghead turned up at hers last night, she called me in a panic. She thought–"

"Hang on. Lottie called you?" Henry asked, unable to work out what this meant.

"Yep."

"Why?"

"She was worried about what Vince was going to do with the evidence he had."

"What evidence?" Henry asked, suspecting he meant the photos on Vince's phone.

"Wouldn't you like to know," he said, and then coughed loudly and winced in pain. "Why did you hit my back?"

"Why did you start shooting? What was all that in aid of?" Henry asked, ignoring his question.

Benjamin wheezed heavily as he thought about it. "I don't know… I suppose it seemed like a good idea. Silence them both with minimal effort. I'd have left Lottie… I was annoyed at them for speaking to you."

"Thomas and Simon?"

He didn't answer.

"Why did you take Lottie's bread knife?"

He almost laughed. "I liked the idea of getting Lottie in trouble. But mostly it was to muddy the waters and keep you lot confused."

"I wasn't confused, and I was the one who brought you down."

"And for that… old man… I give you some credit. Bravo. You got me. Hurrah!"

"ARMED POLICE!" came the cry at the front door.

"In here!" Henry replied. He let go of the rifle and lifted his hands in the air as the armed officers stormed into the living room and shouted at him.

He stepped away from Benjamin, and the armed police pointed their weapons at him and cuffed him.

Henry felt a certain amount of satisfaction at seeing the handcuffs lock around those wrists.

Chapter Thirty-One

Henry stood in the cottage's driveway, staring ahead at the fields in the distance. The sun was falling over the horizon in the west, and the evening was cooler than the day had been. A plane set off from the airport in the distance, taking its passengers on their holidays, away from their stresses and strains.

Henry felt like he could do with joining them.

His new hip was aching from all the kneeling and shuffling he'd done, and his ear had only just stopped bleeding. Now it stung like it'd been attacked by a giant wasp. But at least he was alive. He had gone head-to-head with an expert gunman and won, not only thanks to the gunman's arrogance, but his own dumb luck.

Benjamin had been placed in the back of a van and driven off to be processed. Barnes and Hargreaves were on the scene, ordering the constables around and managing the SOCO officers who had just arrived. They'd been at Thomas's farmhouse. Apparently, it was fairly shot up, but Thomas had barricaded himself in one of his bathrooms and kept out of harm's way. Unsurprisingly, he wasn't pressing charges against his brother, and claimed it was a hunting accident that had gone wrong.

If Benjamin hadn't hunted his sister's family and tried to kill Henry, that narrative might have stuck.

The armed response unit had left a while ago, but not after they'd admired Benjamin's red and silver rifle. One of them broke procedure by handling it, looking down its sight as if he were in a gun shop about to buy it. Henry hadn't said anything about the massive lapse in evidence collecting, but Barnes had scolded him when she saw what he was doing.

Henry rested his backside against the drystone wall he'd taken cover behind earlier. He felt a slight affinity with it, seeing as it'd saved his life several times. Some of the bullet holes had nearly cut straight through the grey limestone, so he was glad he'd had the sense to get inside.

He'd given a long statement to Hargreaves, detailing how he came to be there and what had happened. She had frowned and tutted through it all. Henry was glad to know Simon and his family were safe at the police station, but Hargreaves wouldn't confirm if they'd seen Lottie.

Henry had also been informed that he wasn't allowed to leave the scene until Murphy had turned up, and apparently, he was on his way over from police headquarters in Wakefield.

Henry had been avoiding his old-partner-turned-nemesis for the past day, but after the experience he just had, he couldn't see the harm in having an argument now.

A near-death experience made most matters seem trivial.

Barnes exited the cottage and walked over to him. She looked drained of energy. Her skin was paler than normal, and she wrapped her arms around her thin frame as if she were cold, despite it being a warm May evening.

"Alright?" she asked, coming to rest against the wall beside Henry.

"Aye. Still in a daze, to be honest."

"I'm not surprised. It's a bit of a mess, isn't it? Thankfully, I think you untangled the worst of it."

"I think so," Henry said. "I never thought it could be the brother who lived abroad. I didn't know he was back on the scene, but as I always say, follow the evidence and it'll take you to the truth."

Barnes grunted an agreement. "SOCO checked over Vince's bedroom and found Benjamin's handprint on the windowsill. They found his prints on the external window and around his drawers. Lucky for us, he didn't wear gloves."

"I think Benjamin was counting on the fact that you'd focus on his sister and that bread knife, which you did."

Barnes nodded. "We were just following the evidence. And orders."

"So, what will happen to Lottie?"

"She'll be released now that we have another suspect. I doubt there'll be any further action against her."

Henry nodded. "Good. I can stop paying for that bloody barrister."

"Oh yeah, about that…" Barnes thumped his shoulder, causing Henry to wince. "If you pay a snotty-nosed posh brat to piss me off again, I'll give you more than a thump."

Henry rubbed his arm. While he was not too old for joking around, the punch was harder than he would have liked. "Right, I'll bear that in mind."

"Just whose side do you think you're on?"

"Well, that's it. I don't know, do I? I've asked to rejoin, and have been left hanging in the breeze."

Barnes didn't say anything else as they had trodden into forbidden territory. She glanced at the lane outside the property as a car approached, and Henry followed her gaze. It was a black Mercedes, which Henry could see was being driven by a uniformed officer.

"Ah. It looks like Murphy's here," Henry said, standing off the wall.

Barnes did the same and turned to him. "You'd best speak to him. But just remember, it's nothing personal."

She nodded respectfully and then walked back into the cottage as if she couldn't wait to be away from the situation.

Henry took a deep breath, held in his gut, lifted his chin in the air, and strode over to Murphy's Mercedes.

The uniformed officer stepped out of the driver's seat and opened the back door for Henry. "In here, sir," he said.

Henry nodded and got into the back.

Murphy was reclining on the black leather upholstery, reading a document from a tablet in his hand. He wore a white shirt and navy suit trousers and stank of aftershave. A navy suit jacket hung on the coat hook by his door. His steel-rimmed reading glasses rested on the end of his bulky nose as he read the report. The tablet's blue light reflected off the lenses.

Once he'd scrolled to the end of the report, he turned his bulldog-like face to stare wearily at Henry. "The worst thing about this job is all the bloody reading."

He tossed the tablet to the side, and it landed on the leather seat between them.

Henry shut his door so they could speak in private.

"It's funny," Murphy said, looking Henry up and down, "some document was sent to me not so long ago, which I read with some surprise."

"Oh right. What was that?" Henry asked, playing along.

"It was the report of an investigation into the irregularities surrounding your retirement. Do you remember all that scandal before you left eleven years ago?"

Henry felt his cheeks redden. He hadn't realised this was the game Murphy wanted to play. "Talking of bullshit reports, I came across a coroner's report yesterday that reeked very badly of the stuff. I thought about digging a hole in my backyard and using it to fertilise my tomatoes."

Murphy exhaled loudly through his nostrils. "Well, I hope you made that hole big enough, because you ought to bury your career with it."

Henry shook his head. "I suppose my request to rejoin the police has been denied?"

Murphy smirked. "Your request wasn't denied. It was rejected immediately. We didn't even receive it. The email bounced. It hit the spam folder on first send. And do you know why? We don't hire bent coppers."

Henry shook his head and pulled the door handle to open his door. "Well, sod off then."

"I beg your pardon."

Henry was so wound up, he let go of the door handle and faced Murphy. "You heard me. I've had enough of it. Me, a bent copper? You're having a laugh. While you–"

"Me?"

"Your grubby mitts were all over this Wentworth-Scott mess."

Murphy's flabby cheeks flushed red. "I don't know what you mean…"

"Bollocks! You know exactly what I mean. Who put an unqualified detective as a lead investigator on a suspicious death?" Henry jabbed his finger in Murphy's direction. "Who pushed the investigation towards suicide when there was no evidence of it, and ignored all other lines of inquiry?" Henry jabbed his finger again. "Who forbade detectives looking into anything but this bread knife nonsense with the Vince Taylor murder?" He jabbed his finger again.

Murphy chewed his fat lip for a moment, and then said, "Are you alleging a senior police officer sought to intervene in two live murder inquiries?"

"Well, did you?"

Murphy's eyes widened, and Henry couldn't work out if it was from anger or fear. "I am a superintendent. I'm making decisions from dawn to midnight; left, right, and bloody centre. So, aye, I sometimes make the wrong call. Who wouldn't? But did we find the right man in the end? Yes, we did."

"No, Murphy. *I* found him. You found diddly-squat, just as you were expecting. You didn't want a proper investigation into this."

"Oh, give over. You know that's nonsense."

"Do I?" Henry narrowed his eyes. "I know you're pally with the Wentworth-Scotts. I know you're in all the right groups and clubs."

"So what if I play golf with the father? Does that make me a corrupt criminal mastermind?"

Henry stared at Murphy, noticing that the man was perspiring slightly around his forehead despite the air conditioning inside the car. "As we both know, just because I can't prove it doesn't mean it didn't happen."

Murphy shook his head. "You need to stop watching those police dramas. That's what you need to do. Watch more cricket. Get a game on, put your feet up, and enjoy your retirement."

Henry shook his head. "Actually, you know what? I have another idea. If I were in the police, you'd be my superior and I'd have to follow orders. But what you didn't realise, you spiteful sod, is that if I'm on the outside, I can be a lot more dangerous to you."

Murphy went to speak, but no words came out. Instead, his mouth gaped a moment. "Dangerous to me?"

"Aye. I'll be on the outside, tinkering away, making sure you never put another foot wrong. And if you do, I'll be onto you." Henry took a breath and felt some resolution in his decision. He opened the door.

Murphy sounded worried. "Henry, don't do this. You'd just be wasting your time. But if that's how you want to spend your final years, so be it. Though you forget, Henry, I'm a senior police officer. I can mess up your life more than you can mess up mine."

Henry turned and gave his most sardonic smile. "Let's see about that."

He stepped out of the car and slammed the door behind him.

* * *

Henry leant on Jean's kitchen table. She had cooked chicken curry for dinner and served it with pilau rice and naan bread. He had showered and changed clothes since he returned from Otley Chevin, but the stink of gunpowder remained on his hands.

He'd recounted what had happened to Jean and Robbie, as they had both seen images on the local news.

He explained how the photos Jean had taken of Vince's bedroom had proven vital, and how Benjamin, the brother who lived abroad, was the missing key.

Upon hearing that, Jean had said, "I didn't say he was still living in Rome. That's just what I'd heard."

Robbie was gobsmacked when Henry explained he'd been shooting at a sniper. "Did his gun flash like they do in the video games?" he'd asked.

Henry shook his head, unsure what he was on about. "I could see his rifle's barrel, as it was silver, but that was it."

They'd finished the main course by the time Henry got to the conclusion and were digging into their dessert of strawberries and cream when there was a knock on Jean's front door.

Jean frowned at Henry as if it was his fault their dessert had been interrupted. "Who's that calling at this time?" she asked.

Henry swallowed his mouthful of strawberries. "I don't know. It's not my house."

She got up from the table and headed to the door. Henry turned to Robbie. "Were you expecting anyone?"

Robbie scooped a spoonful of cream into his mouth and shook his head.

"Henry, it's for you," Jean called from the other room.

Getting up from the table, he walked out of the kitchen and into the living room, where Jean was standing by the front door.

She stepped out of the way so Henry could see who the caller was.

It was Lottie.

She was wearing her own clothes again, and her blonde hair was down, hanging around her shoulders. She attempted a smile when she saw Henry. "Sorry to interrupt."

"No. Not at all," Henry said, closing the door behind him so Jean couldn't eavesdrop as easily. It was past dusk, and the street lights on Main Street were lit. The air was cool and damp.

"I tried your cottage and then remembered that DI Barnes said you might be next door," said Lottie.

Henry nodded. "It's fine. I'm glad they let you out without a problem."

"Yeah, they've dropped all charges." She pointed down the Main Street at a row of parked cars, and Henry spotted the black Land Rover at the end.

It beeped, and Henry thought he could see Simon wave from the front seat.

"Is everyone alright?"

Lottie nodded. "Aye. Thanks. They told me what you did. Incredible."

Henry waved at the Land Rover. "It seemed like the best thing to do at the time. Well, the only thing."

"And thanks for the barrister. I sent her home, and she said she'd send you the bill, but there's no need. I can find a way to pay it."

Henry tried to quell the annoyance. He remembered telling Sophia not to mention the payment to anyone. "Oh. She told you I was going to pay?"

"Yeah, but I forced it out of her. Though, you're not paying. Really. We'll think of something. I'm sure it's not going to be much."

Henry shook his head like he wasn't even going to consider it. Sophia must have billed for the whole day at two hundred an hour. "Nope. I said I'd pay, and I will. I'm just glad you got out."

"Yeah. I can't believe I spent twenty-four hours as a murder suspect. It's not how I thought my day would go."

"Well, that's because you didn't do it."

She smiled. "I guess. Well, good night, Henry."

Before she made it to the gate, Henry asked, "By the way, I spoke to your brother earlier."

She turned to him. "Thomas?"

"No. Benjamin. He said he came to yours last night and talked to you. Apparently, you rang him asking for help?"

Her eyes betrayed some guilt. "Is that what he said? Well, it's not true."

"Then how else did he get that bread knife from yours?"

She didn't have an answer for that.

"What did you tell him?"

She straightened her neck a little and lifted her proud chin in the air. "What are you accusing me of?"

"I'm not sure… Did you know about the compromising photographs Vince took of Benjamin?"

She shook her head innocently, but Henry wasn't buying it.

"Did Vince tell you about them?" he asked, glancing over at the black Land Rover.

Again, she didn't answer. Instead, she looked at him as if he was mildly amusing.

Then it struck Henry. "Wait, Benjamin didn't know about those photos until last night? Until you…"

She stepped towards him.

"Did you goad your brother into killing Vince?" Henry asked. "Did Vince threaten to tell me about Simon, so you called your brother and tipped him off about those photos, knowing full well what he'd do?"

She simpered at him as a cat might do when eyeing up a baby bird. "I might have fallen out with my parents, but I'm close to my brothers, even if I do want to kill them sometimes."

He noticed the unsettling glint in her eyes.

She continued speaking quietly, her voice somewhat changed. "And my little brothers would do anything for me. Anything I asked. Something I think you can understand, Mr Ward."

She gave him a quick malevolent smile and then headed to the gate. "Thanks again for the lawyer. She really was top-class."

Henry returned inside and found Jean standing by the door, clearly having listened. She appeared puzzled. "What did she say at the end?"

Henry didn't know how to put it. "I think, just like Benjamin Wentworth-Scott, I've been played."

The End

If you enjoyed this book, please let others know by leaving a quick review on Amazon. Also, if you spot anything untoward in the paperback, get in touch. We strive for the best quality and appreciate reader feedback.

editor@thebookfolks.com

www.thebookfolks.com

Also in this series

MURDER ON A YORKSHIRE MOOR (Book 1)

Ex-detective Henry Ward is settling awkwardly into retirement in a quiet corner of Yorkshire when during a walk on the moor he stumbles upon the body of a young man. Suspecting foul play and somewhat relishing the return to a bit of detective work, he resolves to find out who killed him. But will the local force appreciate him sticking his nose in?

BUTCHER ON THE MOOR (Book 2)

Ex-DCI Henry Ward is woken in the middle of the night when a distressed woman calls him, demanding he arrest her son. After reluctantly heading over to her house, he makes a gruesome discovery before being attacked. With the police stretched, they reluctantly lean on Ward's local knowledge to track down a man with blood on his hands.

MISSING ON ILKLEY MOOR (Book 3)

Retired cop Henry Ward is taking a walk on the Yorkshire moors when he comes across a child's woolly hat. He quickly connects it with the apparent abduction of an eight-year-old girl from a local town. But when the child's mother acts like she doesn't care, he realises something is seriously wrong and takes it upon himself to investigate.

COLD CASE ON THE MOOR (Book 5)

An unusual spell of hot weather reveals a dark secret on the Yorkshire moors. A woman's body is found in a dried-up reservoir. When the police work out her identity, it brings the past flooding back for ex-detective Henry Ward. He was in charge of the investigation into her disappearance many years ago. Now he is more determined than ever to find her killer.

FREE with Kindle Unlimited and available in paperback!

Other titles of interest

MURDER ON A COUNTRY LANE
by Jon Harris

After the shock of discovering a murder victim, young barmaid Julia isn't too perturbed because local garden centre owner Audrey White was a horrible so-and-so. But when her fingerprints are found all over a death threat, Julia becomes the police's prime suspect. Equipped with an unfetching ankle tag she must solve the crime to prove her innocence.

FREE with Kindle Unlimited and available in paperback!

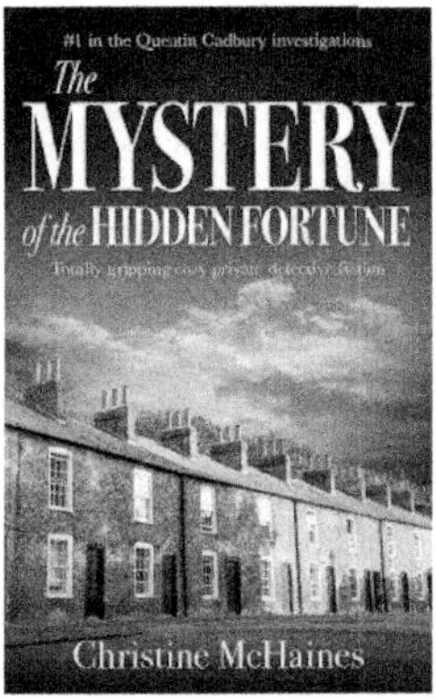

THE MYSTERY OF THE HIDDEN FORTUNE
by Christine McHaines

Quentin Cadbury, a useless twenty-something, is left to look after his late aunt's London house when his parents head to Australia. But burglars seem determined to break in, and not even the stray cat he befriends can help him. As the thieves are after something pretty valuable, and illegal, he must grow up pretty fast to get out of a sticky situation.

FREE with Kindle Unlimited and available in paperback!

THE BOOK FOLKS

Sign up to our mailing list to find out about new releases and special offers!

www.thebookfolks.com

Printed in Great Britain
by Amazon

41754738R00138